CALL OF NIGHT

BOOK FOUR IN THE THORNE HILL SERIES

EMILY GOODWIN

Call of Night
Book Two in the Thorne Hill Series
Copyright 2019
Emily Goodwin
Cover photography by Braadyn Penrod
Cover art by Covers by Christian
Editing by Contagious Edits

❀ Created with Vellum

To my very own Mr. Prickle Paws

My heart hammers in my chest. It's racing, beating so fast it should hurt, but everything moves in slow motion. Blood sloshes through my veins and every single nerve in my body prickles with anxiety.

How do you plead?

I blink, swallow the lump of vomit that's rising in my throat and look at the witches standing before me. Ruth from the Grand Coven is at the podium at our altar, and the council members behind her don't look too sure of themselves. Even Ruby Darrows, who's hated me since the day she met me, is looking at Ruth in question.

Ruth crosses her arms as she waits for me to answer her question, only it's not a question. It's a confession. One I'm actually completely guilty of.

I did show Lucas where the door to the Covenstead was.

I do let him drink my blood.

The first crime is punishable by death, but the second isn't. Though I suppose if you combine the two… My eyes slam shut, and I part my lips, but my mouth is suddenly too dry to form words. Somewhere in the back of my mind, the rational part of my brain is screaming at me. This isn't right. This isn't how things are done.

No one is brought in and immediately questioned like this. I have a right to a fair trial, and it's not like Lucas has threatened any witches. The Grand Coven is taking this threat more seriously than they did the hunter—which turned out to be a demon. And in that case, many witches did die.

Speaking of the Grand Coven... I look behind Ruth. She's the only one here. How did she get here so fast? Tabatha only called on the Grand Coven a few hours ago. There's no way she was able to get here that quickly, unless she was already here.

But why?

My mouth falls open again and I suck in air. Witch law is similar to human law, and I don't have to say anything without first consulting my own defensive council. There was no warning, no serving of paperwork.

"Well, Ms. Martin?" Ruth leans over the podium.

I clamp my mouth shut again and try to think straight. So many thoughts race through my head with the most prevalent one being *I'm so fucked*. I'm too rattled to protest, to state my rights and remind the others in the council that partaking in a trial like this is against our laws as well. Our numbers are dwindling, and sentencing another witch to death is not something to just throw about like this. It's debated amongst the entire Grand Coven as well as a panel of non-biased coven leaders from across the country.

Ruby's brows pinch together, and she shifts her weight in her chair. She's always hated me, but would she actually go so far as encourage my death? I have a feeling I'm going to find out before dawn.

Suddenly, the double doors at the back of the gathering hall fly open.

"What is the meaning of this?" Tabatha storms in, brown eyes flashing with anger.

"High Priestess," Ruth says, a small smile pulling up the

corners of her lips. "Very timely of you to make it. I summoned you nearly an hour ago. Are you aware one of your witches has exposed the door to the Covenstead to a vampire, putting us all at risk? The same witch has allowed vampires to drink her blood. Willingly."

"You have no proof of the crimes you accuse her of. And even if so, this is not the way things are done." Tabatha stops next to me and puts her hand on my shoulder. "Those are heavy crimes with fatal sentencing. You know the proper channels necessary to go through to accuse a witch of treason on that level."

"As a member of the Grand Coven, I feel it is of utmost importance to have these crimes investigated as soon as possible. Is your Academy's history department lacking or have you simply forgotten about the War of Light and Dark? Vampires are our enemies. If one got in…" She clicks her tongue and shakes her head.

"He'd be burned alive before he made it through the warding," Tabatha says, voice strong. "And you know it. Our Covenstead is protected."

"From one vampire, yes, but let's not be foolish. A mass attack would break through, and there's no telling what they'd do to us. Protecting the coven is always my first priority, as it should be yours." Ruth sweeps her hand out at the council members behind her. Their eyes flit from Ruth to Tabatha, and I know they are all struggling with where to put their loyalty. Tabatha is our High Priestess. She knows us on a personal level. She's helped each and every one of us at some point or another.

Ruth is more or less a stranger. She doesn't know our names or what type of familiar the kids hope to get when they come of age. But she's a member of the Grand Coven and has more authority than anyone else in this room.

I open my mouth to tell her off, to remind her that she did a shitty-ass job of protecting us when we sent in reports of a witch hunter after the first witch had been found murdered in the woods. Tabatha presses her fingers into my shoulder, and I take it as a cue to keep my mouth shut.

"I have always protected my coven," Tabatha fires back with venom in her voice. "I hold each and every member of this coven dearly, and they all know it. And of course vampires are a threat! One we all take seriously, and one that is not something we currently have to worry about. There is no reason to suspect any vampire of attempting a breach through the door. The witches of Thorne Hill haven't had any issues with vampires for well over a hundred years, and we plan to keep it that way."

"Showing a vampire the location of the door doesn't sound like a good way to keep things peaceful. I can only imagine the temptation that vampire must feel, knowing there are many of us in here."

I grit my teeth, fighting the urge to stand up and defend myself and Lucas. He's never had issues with witches, and while I can't say he's innocent—because he's far from it—he's not a monster. He loves me more than I deserve and risked his own afterlife to help witches he didn't even know pass through the door.

"If you are to accuse her of these crimes, you need proof and a fair trial," Tabatha repeats. "This is not the way we do things, and there is no current threat. Raising false alarm is unnecessary."

Ruth's eyes settle on me. "My proof is in a testimony, though I'd love to go back and hear from you, Callie Martin, how every-thing went down that night."

I don't need to ask her to specify which night to know she's talking about the night a third-hierarchy demon tried to burn me alive. I press my hands against the wooden bench beneath me and take in a slow breath. We've all told the same lie, but right now as I'm sitting here in front of Ruth and the council, I feel like they can all see right through me.

"How did you defeat that demon?" Ruth's eyes narrow. "And how did the vampire come into play? Was it all part of your plan?"

"My plan?" I echo, shaking my head. I look up at Tabatha and see the same tension reflected back in her eyes. "I don't know what you're talking about."

"I've examined the evidence," Ruth says. "And I'll gladly present it again. But we all know there is only one reason brimstone would be found amongst the forest ground."

A few members of the council turn to each other, speaking in whispers. The only reason brimstone would be found is if a powerful demon opened the Gates of Hell, which is exactly what happened.

And not what we reported.

"Question her as you wish, but you will do so properly." Tabatha takes a few steps forward, dark purple robes flowing behind her. "There are more pressing matters at hand right now, matters that *you* had been summoned to."

I swallow hard and let out a shaky breath. Even if this did go to trial, there's still a chance I could be exonerated for my crimes since Lucas helped save us from a demon. Without him, our chances of making it safely through the door would have been slim to none. The witches who were with us know that, and some of them are sitting behind Ruth right now.

"More pressing?" Ruth steps away from the podium. "Dear High Priestess, don't forget your place in this coven."

"I haven't but I fear you have." The flames on the candles grow brighter. "Even if this were a proper trial, you do not have all your witnesses from that night. My son, Evander, was there."

"And where is he now?"

Holy shit. Ruth doesn't know? She *was* here before they got back. It was her plan all along to accuse me of treason. But why go about it this way? It doesn't make sense, and something doesn't feel right.

And I mean something other than me being possibly sentenced to death.

Tabatha slowly shakes her head. I'm sitting behind her but can imagine the way her eyes are narrowing. The flames around us intensify again.

"My son," she starts, speaking through gritted teeth, "is possessed by a demon."

The council behind Ruth gasps, and Ruth herself looks stunned. Ruby's hand flies to her mouth and she inches to the edge of her chair, staring at Tabatha and looking like she might burst into tears.

"A demon? How did this happen?"

"The Ley line," Tabatha starts and my stomach flip-flops. The Ley line let off demonic energy because a demon from Hell opened a gate...and we've all lied about that. I feel like I'm tumbling backwards into a deep dark tunnel. I'll save Evander no matter the cost, even if that means telling the truth about what really happened.

Though I still don't know what did happen.

I don't know how I commanded the hellfire.

I don't know who the blue-eyed man is or what he wants from me.

"Which you were also made aware of." Tabatha strides forward and moves to the first step leading to the altar. "There was an influx of energy, which happens from time to time as we all know. With us coming off a Solstice, the energy was raw and powerful, and we know how that beacons other worldly creatures. The Ley line has been taken care of and the details don't matter. What matters is my son. We need to perform an exorcism. Now."

Ruth's lips press together, forming a thin line. She has some sort of secret agenda here, I'm sure of it, but she is a member of the Grand Coven and really does care about the witches under her.

"Where is he?"

"In my office," Tabatha's voice doesn't waver, and she holds Ruth's gaze. Tabatha is ruthless when it comes to protecting her family. If I weren't so scared, I'd feel emotional right now.

"Is he okay?" Ruby asks. Like Evander, she's teaching summer classes here at the Academy, and is wearing the traditional dark blue robe most professors here wear. She had a crush on Evander back in our school years, and I used to think that was part of why she didn't like me. Though I moved in with the Greystones when I was only ten, so he's always felt like an older brother to me and nothing more.

"If we can tend to him, yes." Tabatha turns, looking at everyone else in the council. Evander is well-liked and very respected amongst the coven, but even if he weren't, we couldn't turn our backs on someone in need. She turns back to Ruth. "What are your orders?"

Ruth purses her lips again and shifts her gaze from Tabatha to me and back again. "Put a temporary binding spell on Ms. Martin," she tells Ruby, who looks all too happy to oblige. "And take her into an empty office. Preferably one with warding. Then we shall handle Mr. Greystone's condition."

"But I can help," I protest.

"Help?" Ruth arches her eyebrows. "Have you performed an exorcism before as well?"

I shake my head. "No...no, of course not. But Evander is my friend and I was with him when he got possessed. The demon spoke to me."

"You were with him?"

I nod.

"Convenient."

I can't help it. I ball my fists and stand up. "You think I had something to do with him getting possessed?"

Ruth looks behind her, expecting to get full support of the council, but they know how much the Greystones mean to me. They don't know what I went through before I got here, but it's common knowledge here at Grim Gate Academy that I was mistreated by my non-magical family and that Tabatha had to come and get me out of a dire situation.

I might have stirred up trouble in my younger days, but as an adult witch, I've kept to myself and don't upset anyone. Hell, I even fight demons so they don't have to worry about it.

Ruby shakes her head. "She...she wouldn't do that. Not to him."

I meet her eyes, almost more surprised to hear her defending me than I was to be accused of treason the moment I stepped foot into the Covenstead.

"Take her and bind her powers. I assume you have a proper hagstone hex around this school somewhere?"

"Yes, ma'am," Ruby says as she gets out of her seat. Some of the smugness has worn off her face already.

"It's going to be all right," Tabatha tells me, though I'm not concerned with me right now. Evander is possessed by a demon. People don't survive demonic possession for more than a few days, and even being possessed for mere hours can cause severe internal damage.

"I'm not going to have any trouble, am I?" Ruby asks as she ushers me out of the gathering room. I turn and meet her eye.

"Seriously?"

She shrugs. "You're not really a rule follower."

I'm not in the mood to argue with her. "Evander is more important. Just take me, bind my powers, and get in there and help them."

"You're worried about him."

"Aren't you?" We cross through a large stone corridor and then move down a hall to Evander's office.

"I am. Demonic possession...it's serious. You said the demon spoke to you?" Her gait slows.

"Yes, it didn't say much. Just the usual *come back to hell with me and have power* bullshit." I leave out the part about how it was waiting to possess a person I knew to ensure I wouldn't kill them. And how it called me a half-breed and how "they" have been looking for me. "I tried to get a name, but it didn't feel like sharing."

We stop outside Evander's door. Ruby waves her hand over

the lock, muttering an incantation to unlock it. I take a seat at Evander's desk and Ruby pulls a large black box out of a wardrobe. It's full of power-binding charms and hexes, meant to be used on misbehaving students who are abusing their powers.

I look around the office and am taken back to the days when Tabatha used to occupy this very room. It's large, with gray stone walls and a massive fireplace behind the desk. Narrow windows cover the opposite wall, looking out onto the courtyard where we'd eat lunch when the weather was nice. The wall next to the desk is covered with bookshelves, and the smell of old paper and ink used to comfort me.

"How was he the last time you saw him?" Ruby pulls hagstone hexes out of the box. I'm really getting sick of that stuff...even though it doesn't seem to work for me. I can still use my powers.

"Sleeping, thanks to a sleeping spell. It hasn't been that long," I say just to make myself feel better. "If we can get the demon out of him, he'll be fine."

Ruby nods, trying but failing to hide the fear in her eyes. "You two were always close."

"He's like a brother to me. He's more of a brother than my biological brother is." As soon as the words leave my lips, I feel like it's a lie. Not about Evander, because he's always felt like a brother. We got along like siblings from the get-go. He was annoyingly protective, and I got on his nerves like any younger sister would.

What feels like a lie is saying I have a biological brother. Scott told me we weren't related. That he's not really my brother.

"You'd never put him at risk." She wraps another hex around my wrist.

"Of course not."

She goes back to the desk and closes the black box. "I thought so."

"What are you getting at?" I ask, narrowing my eyes. "You're not telling me something."

Ruby swallows hard and chews on her bottom lip. I've never

seen her rattled like this. She's always full of herself. Irritatingly confident. A stuck-up know-it-all.

The office door flies open and Ruth steps in. She flicks her wrist once she's in and the door closes behind her.

"I'll take it from here," she says, and Ruby gives her a curt nod. She looks at me once more, eyes still full of fear, and then hurries out of the office.

Ruth perches on the edge of the desk and crosses her arms, pushing the sleeves of her dress robes up over her forearms.

"I reviewed your file," she starts, and I slowly shake my head. What is she doing? Shouldn't she be in with Tabatha, helping to get the demon out of Evander?

"Okay?"

"You graduated top of your class."

I blink. "I, uh, had great teachers."

"Tell me." Her eyes narrow and she leans in. "How does a girl from a non-magical home, who didn't start here until she was ten years old, end up with such high marks?"

"This isn't important right now."

"Isn't it?" Ruth cocks an eyebrow. "Because I find it just as curious as a common witch being able to fight off a third-hierarchy demon."

"I...I don't know what you're talking about." If Lucas were here, he'd be able to hear my heart rate increasing. He'd be able to smell my fear and panic.

"Don't play dumb with me, Ms. Martin."

"I'm not. I swear, I don't know how I—"

"Cut the bullshit." She stands up, blue eyes flashing. "You are in no place to lie to me."

"I'm not lying."

"Let me remind you that your charges are dire. You seem to care for that vampire you've been spending so much time with," she says, recoiling from her own words, as if the thought of sleeping with a vampire repulses her. "It would be a shame if anything were to happen to him. After all, who will be there to remove a curse after you've been burned at the stake?"

My eyes widen and all the air leaves my lungs. She's threatening Lucas? He's old. The oldest vampire I know. It would take a very powerful witch to curse him...and Ruth is a powerful witch.

She holds my gaze. "I'm willing to throw this all out, under one condition."

My mind is racing, and I have no fucking clue what she's talking about. All I know is Lucas could be in danger and Evander *is* in danger. We need to get the demon out of him like yesterday.

"What?" I reply, desperate to appease her and deal with the consequences later. "What do you want?"

"I told you. In."

"In? In where?"

"Not where, but who." Her eyes narrow and it hits me: the Grand Coven suspected me of Satanism but didn't have enough proof to move past suspicion.

Holy shit.

Ruth wants me to get her a deal with the Devil.

CHAPTER 2

"I swear to you," I start, hands shaking. "I'm not working with the Devil."

"Please." Ruth pushes off the desk and goes to the fireplace. She waves her hands over the logs, conjuring a small fire. She purses her lips, looking at the small flames in annoyance, and waves her hand over the logs again, doubling the fire. "There's only one reason you'd find brimstone, and we both know what it is."

"Fine," I say, eyes going to the large grandfather clock in the corner by the wall. Evander is running out of time before he's at real risk for damage. "There was a third-hierarchy demon. And I fought it off, but I don't know how I did it."

"Don't lie to me!" Ruth hisses. "There is no way you could have fought one off. You're working together."

"No! I would never work with a demon."

"Lies!"

I lean back in the chair, eyes flicking down to the hagstone hexes tied around my wrists. I'm not bound to the chair, but the hexes are magically bound to me until someone takes them off. My lips part and I squeeze my eyes closed, trying hard not to freak out right now.

"I am not working with the Devil," I say slowly. "I can't get you an in with him even if I tried because I'm not in communication with him."

Ruth holds up her hand and pressure surrounds my neck as if she's choking me. "Do you think I'm stupid?"

"You probably don't want me to answer that," I choke out.

She slowly starts to make a fist with her fingers and the pressure around my neck intensifies. I gasp for air.

"Let me make this clear," she snarls. "There is no way a witch born from nonmagical heritage could possess the abilities you do unless you've been given extra power. And there's only one way you can get that extra power. So, you can either summon the Devil and tell him I'm worthy, or you will be tied up and burned. If you're lucky, you'll die of smoke inhalation before your flesh starts to melt off your bones. And then I'll have fun going after that vampire."

She releases her hand and I suck in air, coughing hard.

I don't have time for this. She's hell-bent on getting more power, and power-hungry psychos can't be reasoned with. Evander needs to be saved, and I have to go warn Lucas before he gets too worried about me and hangs around the door, awaiting my return.

"Fine," I gasp, neck aching. I swallow hard and feel my throat burn. "I'll...I'll take you to the woods and I'll summon him. But only after an exorcism has been done and Evander is okay."

Ruth considers my offer for a moment. "Okay. If you don't deliver, I will proceed with your charges."

"All you want is for me to summon him and tell him you're worthy?" I ask, desperately trying to come up with a plan. "There's not much else I can do from there. Only he can decide who he'll let in."

Ruth's eyes narrow. "The Dark Lord won't reject me."

"But if he does," I plead, "I'll still have done my part, I'll be free from the charges. You haven't filed them yet, correct?"

"Correct," she says, and it hits me even harder that blackmailing me was her plan all along. Assuming I'm working with the Devil makes sense, as much as I hate to admit it. Because like she just said, a witch shouldn't be able to fight off a powerful demon.

Or do magic while warded.

Or heal themselves.

Or have glowing eyes...like Evander said he thought he saw in the woods right before he got possessed.

My stomach gurgles with fear that I'm evil. That demon blood runs in my veins and that's why demons are after me and why they're calling me a half-breed. Why they're saying *I shouldn't be.*

But I have another question, one I can't figure out. How does she know the extent of my relationship with Lucas? Did we make it that obvious we're a couple when the other witches showed up at my house the night we escaped from the demon? I suppose it doesn't matter, though I can't help but feel violated, like someone had been spying on me and reporting back.

Just like how the vampires know about us and want me dead for it.

I suck in a breath and look at Ruth. I've been backed into a corner and my only option is to agree with her, though I won't be able to give her what she wants. I'm not working with the Devil and agreeing won't summon him. But...I have no other choice.

"I'll summon him," I say, and all my breath leaves me. I close my eyes in a long blink, trying hard to focus on anything other than the crippling anxiety that's pulsing through me. "And then it will be up to him."

Ruth smiles, eyes gleaming. "He'll be pleased with what I have to offer."

A chill runs through me and I work to keep my face neutral. "I hope so." I swallow my pounding heart. "Evander?"

Ruth rolls her eyes. "I'll go assist now."

"Let me help. I...I think I can."

"You are not getting out of those hex bracelets until I get what I want."

14

I nod, not sure if having the hex bracelets on would hinder me from summoning my old pal Lucy or not. I don't have the slightest inkling of how to fake a Satanic ritual...but I might be able to get ahold of someone who can.

"I'll need proof," I say as Ruth heads toward the office door. "Proof Evander is okay."

"Fine. I'll give you two minutes with him. Then it'll be time to hold up your end of the bargain."

She uses magic to open and close the office doors. I let my eyes fall closed and suck in air. I'm on the verge of hyperventilating, and the hexes are starting to feel oppressive, holding back my natural powers that want to be released right now. The hexes ward off witchcraft, but I have such a strong feeling I'm not really just a witch.

Forcing myself to calm the fuck down, I take a few minutes focusing on my breathing. Once my heart isn't racing and the taste of vomit has receded from my mouth, I close my eyes and think of Binx, trying to mentally call for him. It's hard to do from inside the Covenstead, and an ordinary witch probably couldn't do this.

But like Ruth said, I'm no ordinary witch.

"Come on, come on," I mutter. "Binx, can you hear me?"

I get a big fat nothing.

My thoughts shift to Lucas, to his handsome face. Eyes as blue as the ocean at night. His devilish smile.

"Get it together," I tell myself and shift my thoughts back to my black cat. Just thinking about my familiar brings me a sense of peace. I can feel him rubbing his head against me. Hear his purring. I see him clearly in my mind, sitting on the dark back porch, staring into the night.

Suddenly, his tail twitches.

Callie

Yes! We've made a connection. He can hear me.

Things are bad, I tell him.

I'm coming, he responds, voice just a harrowing echo inside my own head.

Don't be seen.

I open my eyes and feel a little dizzy. Letting out a breath, I look at the hagstone hexes on my wrists. I can't touch the hexes with my fingers, but I wonder...no, it wouldn't work. My powers of telekinesis come from being a witch. And the charms specifically block out witchcraft.

I lean back and stare out the window, feeling like eternity is crawling by. Everything is so quiet, though I don't know what I expect to hear. A group of witches shouting *the power of Christ compels you* at Evander as his head turns all the way around and he spits out pea soup at everyone?

"Please, please let him be okay," I pray to no one in particular. The image of the blue-eyed man flashes before me. "Just let Evander be okay. I'll take whatever sentences comes my way, just keep Evander safe."

I let my eyes fall shut and squeeze my fingers into the palm of my hand. Everything is going to be okay. It has to be. Evander will make a full recovery, and if he's lucky, will have no memory of the demon forcing itself inside his body.

My eyes open and the anxiety I was trying to shake off comes back tenfold. That demon specifically sought out a body that I knew. It wanted me to team up with it and seemed pretty damn convinced that if we worked together, we'd be unstoppable. I squeeze my eyes closed again.

"I'm not evil. I'm not evil," I whisper to myself.

"Of course you're not," a familiar voice echoes throughout the room.

"Binx!"

His shadow turns into cat-form and he jumps onto my lap, purring.

"I'm so fucking glad you're here," I tell him. "Ruth thinks I'm working with the Devil and wants me to arrange a meet-and-greet. Obviously I can't do that but I agreed anyway so she'd go

assist on the exorcism. Evander will be saved at least, but then I...
I...I don't know."

Binx rubs his head against me and jumps off my lap, turning back into his true form. Red eyes glow before me, and an idea takes shape. To anyone else, Binx would be terrifying. He's old and ancient and has legions of spirits under his command.

"We could trick her," I start.

"She's never met the Devil," Binx finishes.

"If we can get Pandora and Freya in on this..."

"It will work," we say at the same time.

I let out a sigh of relief, though we're far from the light at the end of the tunnel. But it's a start, at least. There's no promise the Devil will work with any witch, which is only one of the reasons the Grand Coven has outlawed Satanism.

"We're going to need Lucas," I tell Binx, hating what I'm saying. But I don't know any other way around this. "We need proof that Ruth wants to make a deal with the Devil. If he can record her doing—I don't know—anything incriminating, we can present it to the Grand Coven and get her stripped of her title and powers, which would stop her from sentencing me."

Binx nods, agreeing with me. "I will go inform the others of our plan." He shifts back into a cat and moves onto my lap again. He bites the hexes around my wrist, freeing me from the hagstone.

"Thank you," I tell him, feeling a load better from not having my powers bound. Binx rubs his head against me once more, reminding me that I'm not alone. I hug him, taking solace in his soft, sleek fur. I give him a kiss and release him, letting him jump back into shadow form to relay our message to the others.

I take the hexes and lay them out on Evander's desk. Pacing back and forth, I attempt to quiet my thoughts and fail. This plan better work. Because if it doesn't...I have no fucking clue what I'll do.

"Does she actually have evidence?" I mutter to myself, pausing by the large window. I look out at the dark, empty courtyard.

There aren't many students at Grim Gate Academy in the summer to begin with. I spent most of my summers here, with the exception of the one time I went home to see my sister.

I missed her. As nice as it was to get away from my fucking awful father and brother, I missed Abby. At first it was too risky to return home. I knew magic but wasn't strong enough to fight off my father. But the next year...that year I could have. Yet Tabatha didn't want me returning home. She accompanied me back to Chicago in late July so I could see Abby on her birthday.

I'll never forget the terrified looks on my father and Scott's faces as we all sat in the formal living room of my parents' overly ostentatious house. The thought, actually, still brings a smile to my face. It was the first time I sat in my father's company and felt like I was the one on top.

I had the advantage.

He'd called me a freak. Said I was nature's mistake.

But coming back with Tabatha...I was a witch. A witch with powers that could destroy them. My father and Scott already feared me. And Tabatha...Tabatha fucking terrified them more than any nightmare ever could.

I didn't return home on my own until I was sixteen and more than powerful enough to hold my ground. Tabatha and Evander were spending a few weeks in Europe, meeting with other Academy professors and visiting family. I was certain I could hold my own...and then I met Easton.

The charming, off-limits, bad boy my parents would have hated for me to be seen with. It was a big deal to the press that I was back home in Chicago. My father had already woven the tale that I was off in some third-world country volunteering, giving my all to the less fortunate. Being seen with someone like Easton Parker was the last thing dear old dad would have wanted for me.

I came back for the summer to spend it with my sister. I missed Abby so fucking much and our parents made it almost impossible to communicate while I was at the Academy. The day after I arrived, my father arranged an internship at a hospital.

Abby wanted to be a doctor back then, and shadowing a world-renowned trauma specialist was a dream come true.

My father did it on purpose, I know that now. I came back to see Abby and he sent her away. That's how my father is. Pretending to benefit one person only to hurt another. So I was left there, alone in that big house, for weeks until I could return to Thorne Hill.

Easton was everything I wanted and everything I didn't need. The bad boy who could piss off my parents. The rebel who could sneak me out of my bedroom window and show me how fun life without magic could be. The handsome boy who'd seen so much, who made me feel more than I could ever imagine.

And the witch hunter who was ordered to kill me.

I tear my eyes away from the courtyard, not wanting to get stuck in another memory. Though if it's about Grim Gate, there's a good chance it will be a good one. Nothing will ever replace the feeling of walking through the door for the very first time.

I felt like I was finally home, amongst other people just like me.

Only, that feeling wore off before the first year was through. Because, as Ruth said, I had talents that far surpassed the ordinary witches of Grim Gate Academy.

"Fuck," I mutter under my breath. How the hell am I supposed to fake summoning the Devil? With my powers being a little unpredictable, I have no idea what would actually happen if I did a fake summoning. I don't want to actually summon anything... let alone the Devil.

I sink down onto a velvet settee in front of the window and run my fingers over the dark purple velvet. There have only been firsthand accounts recorded about what happens when the Devil is summoned, and no one knows exactly how accurate those accounts are.

No one knows for sure what he looks like. Some reports describe him the way pop culture does. Tall, horned, with the face of a goat and the body of a lamb. Others describe him as a handsome man in a suit. We went over it briefly in my advanced-level defensive magic class, and it's one of those subjects the professors here don't like to talk about in fear it could encourage an impressionable young witch or wizard to seek out more power.

I put my head in my hands and let out a shaky breath. If there were a time to tap into whatever the hell language Lucas said he heard me speaking, it's now. Because I really am afraid I'll open a rift to the underworld when I pretend to summon the Devil.

Though if that happens, Ruth will get exactly what she wants.

Blinking, I look up at the grandfather clock and watch the seconds tick by. They turn into minutes, one slowly adding onto another. Fifteen have gone by and the halls are still silent. How long does an exorcism take? Is the demon holding on because it wants me? If I have to make another deal, I will.

Though I don't think I could get out of that one. If I agree to go to the underworld with the demon, he'll expect me to deliver and won't stop until I do.

Suddenly, the office doors fly open. Kristy runs in, panting and out of breath. She has blood splattered on her face, and her eyes are wide with fear. I shoot up.

"Evander? Is he okay?"

She shakes her head. "The exorcism…it's…it's not working."

CHAPTER 3

"What do you mean it's not working?"

She lets out a breath. "Nothing we do is weakening the demon."

Fear creeps up my spine at an alarming rate and I feel like I might pass out. I sink back onto the settee and close my eyes. It has to work. Evander has to be okay. I open my eyes and look back at the clock again. He's been possessed for a few hours now, putting him at risk for aftereffects of possession.

"I'm coming with you," I tell Kristy.

She nods and strides forward but stops. "Tabatha sent me for you. I came to undo the hexes but you—"

"Binx did it."

"How did you call Binx while you were under hexes—never mind. Let's go." She grabs my hand and we run down the hall. Tabatha's office is at the opposite side of the Covenstead, away from the school and closer to the gathering hall. I had graduated from the Academy by the time she became our High Priestess and have only been in her office a few times.

The strong smell of sage hits me as soon as we dash up the staircase that takes us to Tabatha's office. And things aren't silent anymore.

Evander screams in protest, and a collective of voices chant out a banishing spell. It's a powerful spell, said by strong witches. If that's not enough to weaken the demon...nope. I can't go there.

Kristy and I slow, taking a few seconds to catch our breaths. I have no idea what I can bring to the team that they don't already have, but I have to have faith Evander will be okay.

I flick my eyes up to the ceiling. "Help us, please."

"Are you praying?"

I slowly shake my head. "I don't know. He might not even be able to hear me."

"Who, God?"

"No...he's not God. The blue-eyed man. I don't know his name or even what he is."

"Explain later." She goes to open the door and stops. "It's not pretty in here, Cal. Are you ready?"

I swallow hard. "Yes."

She pushes her shoulders back and opens the door. Magic sizzles at my fingertips as I walk into the office behind Kristy. Things aren't playing out like they would be in a movie. Evander isn't tied to a bed, with black eyes and boils all over his face. He's not screaming at us in Latin or vomiting green puke all over the place.

He's bound to a chair and tears streak down his face. His body looks worn and tired and his expression is sad. Lost.

Desperate.

Is he in there, begging for a break? Or is the demon trying to trick us?

"Callie," the demon says through Evander's voice. "How nice of you to join us."

"Get out of him," I snarl. "Go back to hell."

Tabatha stands in front of him, with a council member on each side. Ruby and Ruth stand behind him. Ruth holds a spell book and Ruby has two sage smudge sticks. A ring of salt has been poured around the chair Evander is tied in, with white candles around the perimeter.

Kristy gives my hand a squeeze before letting go. She picks up a spell book and fills in the circle. I stand next to her, looking down at the banishing spell. The spell alone could send the demon back to Hell, but first we have to sever the ties it has on Evander, and to my knowledge, no witch has ever been able to do that.

We need a priest, and priests aren't exactly willing to work with witches. Many are still convinced we are evil and working with the Devil. Even if we did find one who would agree to perform the Rite, it would cost us precious time waiting for him to arrive.

Evander doesn't have that much time.

Now that I'm close, I can see him fighting to get the demon out, and that will wear him down fast. His eyes are bloodshot, and his cheeks flushed. I bet his skin is hot to touch too, and it wouldn't be long before a dangerously high fever were to break out, putting his whole body at risk to start shutting down.

Tabatha looks around the circle and nods. We all start chanting again while she picks up a metal bowl of herbs from a table behind us. She whispers a different incantation, invoking the powers of the herbs.

"*Auferte malum elementa invocabo,*" I say, reading the spell from the book. "*Dimittie eam mitte erranti est ultra modum.*"

The herbs ignite and dark blue smoke rises from the bowl. Tabatha hurries over and wafts the smoke around Evander. His eyes darken and he smiles, sneering at us.

"*Hic non receperint vos malum spiritus,*" I keep reading. "*Hinc ablegare invoco elementum purus. Sed vade et proficiscere et non relinquit vestigium!*"

Evander's body goes rigid and I feel magic swirling around the fingers of my right hand. I ball my fingers into a fist. Now's not the time to be taken over by my emotions. I need to hold it together and focus on sending this demon to hell. I suck in a breath, watching Evander writhe with pain as he fights against the demon.

There's nothing cinematic about this. It's so far from how exorcisms are depicted in film it leaves me most unsettled. Evander is before us, hurting and in pain. There is a demon inside of him, one that's quiet and smart and planning its next move so it can stay inside of my friend, so it can slowly kill him from the inside out.

For me.

Or...because of me, I suppose. I can hear Lucas's voice echoing in my head, telling me I can't blame myself for this. I'm not the one who forced a demon inside Evander's body. I'm not the one who summoned the demon from the pits of hell and let him run loose in Thorne Hill...only, I did.

Not directly, I know. And playing the martyr doesn't solve shit. Wallowing in guilt and shame will only set me back, but the reason the demon got out of hell was because another, more powerful demon was on a death mission.

Stop it, I tell myself. This is exactly the type of negativity a demon would want me to fall into. I take a breath and look into the demon's eyes.

"Auferte malum elementa invocabo. Dimittie eam mitte erranti est ultra modum."

Evander's head flops back and he lets out a yell. Yanking against the restraints, he jerks his head forward and back over and over, until Tabatha drops the bowl.

"Stop!" she cries. "He can't...his body can't...he needs to take a break." With tears running down her face, she goes up to her only son and places her hand on his head. *"Somnum,"* she whispers, and the sleeping spell takes effect immediately. Evander's body slumps forward, head hanging against his chest.

I can feel Ruth's eyes on me, but she's not stupid. She knows how dire the stakes are right now, and shifting her attention away from Evander will make her look heartless in the eyes of the coven. I know she's heartless, but the rest don't.

She needs them to hold her in high regard. Because once I

have proof that she forced me to perform a Satanic ritual, her own days are numbered.

"What do we do now?" Ruby asks, voice thin. She pushes her dark braids over her shoulder and pulls her robe closer around her body.

"Contact a priest," one of the council members suggests. "We don't have the power to compel a demon back to hell."

But I do.

His voice is like a whisper of wind on the back of my neck. I whirl around, eyes wide. No one is behind me, yet I know that's where the voice came from. Where *he* came from.

The blue-eyed man.

"Help us," I whisper. Kristy turns, having heard me, and narrows her eyes in question. I shake my head ever so slightly and look back at Evander. "Please, help us."

"We should all take a break," Ruth says, opening her arms to the others. "Five minutes to reground ourselves and another ten for research. There has to be a way to break through." She meets my eye as she strides past, leaving Tabatha's office. Ruby stays, arms crossed tightly over her chest, as the others filter out.

"I thought witches have performed exorcisms in the past," she says quietly.

"They have," Kristy tells her.

"Then why isn't this working?" She looks from Evander to us. "There are half a dozen witches in the room."

"The demon has a strong hold," Tabatha says, voice shaking. "But we will sever those ties."

Ruby nods but doesn't look convinced.

"You should probably get Sister Ross," Kristy says, hardly able to look at Tabatha as she speaks. "Just to be safe."

Sister Ross is Grim Gate Academy's nurse. She has the same training any RN would have, along with an extensive knowledge of magical afflictions as well as their cures.

"Good idea," I agree and take a tentative step forward. I want to comfort Tabatha, yet I fear she's going to blame me for this. In the grand scheme of things, it doesn't matter, but letting her down crushes me each and every time. I want nothing more than to make her proud, and it seems all I've done in the last few weeks is put her and the coven at risk

"I'll get her," Ruby says and rushes out of the office. She leaves the door open behind her and I hold my hand out, using magic to close it.

"I am so, so sorry," I start, tears pooling in my eyes. "If I'd known, I would have never—"

"That sort of talk won't help." Tabatha wipes away a tear. "This is not your fault, my dear."

"Then why does it feel like it is?" I slowly shake my head and look at Evander, who's still slumped forward in the chair. "It all started with that demon wanting to kill me."

"That makes you the victim," Kristy says, trying to make me feel better.

"I'm no victim," I retort, not upset with her but at the situation. "And I won't let Evander be one either. There has to be something else we can do."

Tabatha's eyes flutter closed for a second before she takes in a breath, recovering from her emotions and nods. "We can combine spells and make an even more powerful banishing spell. My only fear is that stripping the demon too fast could cause harm."

"What about holy water?" Kristy asks. "I have some at my house. I kind of stocked up when vampires first settled into Thorne Hill," she admits. "Though it doesn't do much good on them."

"Anything is worth a try at this point." Tabatha goes to Evander and presses the back of her hand to his cheek. "The fever is starting to set in."

"Sister Ross should be able to help with that." Kristy nods, needing to reassure herself as well as us.

"What if I have another way?" I bite my lip and look at Evander. His body is asleep, but the demon could still be listening. I

26

motion for Kristy and Tabatha to come over and cast a silence spell around us, making it impossible for anyone to eavesdrop.

"The demon wants me to go back to hell with it," I start. "I won't, but if I agree—"

"Making a deal with a demon is dangerous," Tabatha warns. "And making a deal with the intention of breaking it...it won't end well."

"But if I can get the demon to leave Evander's body, then maybe I can kill it."

"How?" Kristy's blonde hair falls around her face as she shakes her head. "How are you going to kill it? A demon without a body can move through the shadows. We'll have no idea who it possessed next. It could be a student."

Blue magic sparks around my fingers again. I open my fist, releasing it a few inches above my palm, and then close my fingers, reabsorbing the magic. And then an idea hits me.

An idea I know Kristy will hate, and Tabatha will flat out refuse to let me carry out. But desperate times call for desperate measures, and I'm pretty damn desperate right now.

"White light kills demons," I start, turning toward Tabatha. I hold out my hand and conjure an energy ball. "I killed a demon who possessed someone this way before."

"You've come across other demons?" Tabatha stops short. "The less I know the better."

"Callie," Kristy says softly. "The white light killed the man the demon was possessing too. Well, I think. Unless the body was already dead. He was pretty far gone." She rapidly shakes her head. "We can't risk that with Evander."

"I know." I tuck my hair behind my ear. "But the white light won't kill me. Watch." I toss the energy ball up, hold out my hands, and let it fall back onto me. The magic sizzles as it touches me, stinging slightly, but doesn't burn me. Instead, it sinks back into my body. "I can't hurt myself with my own magic."

"Callie, no," Kristy shouts, knowing where I'm going with this already. "That's a terrible idea."

"It might work."

Tabatha whirls around, facing me. "Absolutely not!"

"What other choice do we have?" I throw out my hand. "He's running out of time!"

"There's no guarantee this would even work," Kristy argues. "How can you be sure you'd even be in control of your powers?"

"I'm not sure," I admit. "But there might be a backup plan."

"There *might be* a backup plan?" Candlelight flickers across Tabatha's face. "Willingly accepting a demon into your body creates stronger ties. Exorcising this one is proving hard enough and he did not go in willingly." Tabatha puts her hand on my cheek. "I love you, my darling girl, and I admire your bravery, but this isn't the answer."

"It will work," I counter. "Even if I can't control my power, he...he'll help. Again."

"You mean that blue-eyed man you keep talking about." Kristy shakes her head.

"Yes," I tell her. "I can't explain it, but I just feel like he's watching over me. Protecting me."

"He hasn't done a very good job," Kristy says ruefully. "You were kidnapped and tortured by vampires."

"But I lived."

Kristy's eyes narrow ever so slightly, and what she doesn't say screams loud and clear. No one knows me better than her, and I can almost feel her words pressing down into me. Probably because I'm thinking the same thing and don't want to admit it to myself: I want to know who the blue-eyed man is, who I really am, so bad that I'm willing to put myself in danger.

"Look," I start, eyes flitting from Evander to Tabatha and Kristy. "If we don't do something soon, the demon will continue to sink its claws in. It wants me, and once it's in, I'll hit myself with my own magic. The demon will die, and we can all go home to bed."

"That sounds way too easy, Callie." Kristy looks at Tabatha for support.

"It does, and I'm forbidding it."

"I know I simplified it," I begin, "but we can do this safely."

"You can safely invite a demon to possess your body?" Kristy's blue eyes go wide. "Callie, think about what you just said. It could kill you from the inside out."

"That's exactly what I'm planning to do."

"Demons aren't dumb," Tabatha reminds me. "There's a chance it's already thought this through."

"And there's a chance it didn't." I nervously twist a strand of hair around my fingers. "I'm going to do this the right way—I know, I know, there isn't a right way. But we can lay down some heavy protective circles. There's one in the Goetia that—"

"Hang on." Kristy tips her head to the side as she thinks. "You just gave me an idea. Granted it might be more dangerous than your original, but theoretically, it's safer."

Tabatha, whose nerves are shot and heart is in knots, shakes her head again. "Do I even want to know?"

"Callie has a point. The demon wants her. I think if we bribe it somehow, we can get it to leave Evander's body."

"But bribing it with the promise of Callie? Absolutely not."

"What if it's not really her." Kristy inhales and looks at Evander, not trusting the silence spell. "I think we should talk in the hall once Sister Ross gets here to check on him."

I nod in agreement and Tabatha breaks the silence spell, going over to Evander. She tries to make him more comfortable by propping his feet up. Not long after, Sister Ross flies into the room, followed by Ruby. She speaks with Tabatha for a moment and then begins an assessment on Evander.

"What's your plan?" I ask as soon as we're in the hall. Tabatha casts another silence spell just to be safe.

"Astral project into the room," Kristy starts, holding up her hand so we don't stop her and tell her leaving a body while a demon is present is a terrible idea. "We'll guard your body. There are a few eleventh years here over break, right?"

"Right. Four of them."

"Perfect, one for each element." She looks at the time on her phone. "Naomi and Nicole should be here any moment. I sent them a summon as soon as I heard what Ruth was trying to sentence you with," she tells me. "They can assist the students in keeping the circle up around your body, and get Binx to come for backup."

"A demon will know I'm a projection."

"If you were just standing before him, yes. But if you were to already be there once the sleeping spell is lifted, he won't know how you got there."

"It still won't take long for it to notice the lack of life," Tabatha says.

"Not if you're standing inside a circle. I didn't think of the Goetia circles until you mentioned them, Cal. They're difficult to cast, but strong. If you're standing in it...I mean, it's a stretch, but it might work."

"Okay. So it agrees to leave Evander's body to enter mine—this sounds so sexual." I wrinkle my nose. "Then what?"

"A trapping spell." Tabatha peers in through the open doors, checking on Evander. "There's a hex-box in the magical defenses classroom. It hasn't been used it years, but should hold the demon until it can be vanquished. Ruth has perfected the invisibility spell. She can cast it on the box and it will be virtually undetectable. We can have it right next to the demon."

"Are they going to go along with this?" I ask in a hushed voice even though we've cast a silence spell. "Ruth...Ruth has it out for me." I feel bad lying, but Tabatha already has enough to be worrying about right now. She doesn't need to know a woman she's looked up to and respected for years is out for Satanic powers.

"I'll present it as my idea," Tabatha tells us as footfalls echo down the hall. Long shadows stretch before Naomi and Nicole.

"How is he?" Nicole asks, stopping right before me and throwing her arms around me in a hug.

"Hanging in there," Kristy replies. "We have a plan. Walk with me and I'll explain. We have to go wake up a couple senior students." The twins follow Kristy down the hall, and Tabatha and I go back into the office after breaking the silence spell.

Sister Ross is holding a crystal over Evander's head, reading his aura. I stay in the back of the room, watching and doing my best to keep my heart from racing and stomach from flip-flopping with nerves.

"His vital signs are good," she tells us. "I've only seen true demonic possession three other times, once when I was a young witch and twice during my studies. I have to say this case is mild compared to the others. The demon doesn't seem to have a strong hold on Evander—yet." She trades the crystal for a stethoscope and puts it to his chest, listening to his heartbeat. "How did he become possessed? Demons go after the weak."

"There was a rift in the Ley line," Tabatha says and Ruby's eyes dart to mine. I had warned her about it, told her I sensed something was off about the Ley line. If she did anything about it, I have no idea. "Callie and Evander went to repair it under my order. They were able to seal the rift but not before a demon tapped into the power and jumped into the first warm body it could find."

"So you were there?" Sister Ross asks me, and I nod. "Did you get a read on the demon? Or a name?"

"I tried," I tell her. "But of course it wouldn't tell me its name. It just said basic demon bullshit, ya know, come with me and have more power."

"It didn't attack you?"

All these questions make me feel like I'm on trial and I'm going to give something away. I'm too nervous to keep the lies straight in my mind right now, and since Sister Ross has dealt with demonic possession before, she could use any information she can get to possibly help Evander.

"No, it, uh, seemed more interested in trying to get me to agree to take power from it."

Sister Ross nods. "So, the demon itself isn't likely to have powers. That's good news for us. Just the fact that the sleeping spell is enough to knock out both Evander and the demon proves this demon isn't as strong as it's claiming to be."

The others come back, and I'm told to take a seat behind Tabatha's desk. Ruby stays near me like a babysitter as everyone talks, and I'm starting to lose my battle with my nerves. I can't hear what the others are saying, and if Ruth nixes our plan, I don't know what we'll do.

Precious minutes pass, and Evander starts to stir. Finally, Tabatha turns away from the other witches. He eyes meet mine and she nods.

We're doing this.

CHAPTER 4

I lay down on the altar in the gathering hall, carefully avoiding the candles around me. The four students Kristy and the twins woke are sitting around me, holding candles with intricate sigils carved in. They're a bit excited as well as nervous, since this is beyond any skill they've learned in school.

"Whatever you do," Naomi starts, eyes darting from student to student. "Do not break your concentration. Demons are tricksters by nature." Binx meows in agreeance and settles on my chest. I close my eyes, let out a breath, and start the spell to astral project myself out of my body.

I appear in the hall outside Tabatha's office. Kristy is right outside, waiting for me to open the door. Everything has been laid out, ready for us to try and trick a demon. Naomi's words ring in my head. Demons are natural tricksters. They're cunning and think differently than we do, putting themselves before everyone and everything.

"The box is directly in front of Evander," Kristy whispers, opening the office doors. "Four squares away." I nod and look at the rough-cut squares of stone that make up the floor of the office. I count them out, finding the spot where the box is hidden from sight. Ruth really is good at the invisibility spell. It's seamless.

I take my place in the center of the protective circle that's been drawn on the ground with white chalk. A bowl of smoldering herbs is right in front of my feet, and I have to be careful not to bump into it. Well, *not* bumping would be the problem. I'd go right through it and it would be a dead giveaway that I'm not really here.

Wax drips down the candles around the circle, and I take in one last shaky breath before looking at Tabatha, giving her the signal to start. We had to perfect our plan a bit, knowing that the demon wouldn't leave Evander's body with several other witches hanging around.

But without the other witches, there'd be no one here to do the trapping spell. I can't cast spells in astral form, and I don't think I could conjure an energy ball strong enough to kill the demon.

Kristy takes Ruby's hand and steps back into the shadows. Ruby grabs Ruth's hand, who then takes a hold of Tabatha's. Sister Ross links her fingers through Tabatha's on her other hand, and then Ruth starts chanting, casting the invisibility spell over them all. They disappear from sight and from all feeling. It's unsettling, really, to not be able to sense the witches I know are only a few yards from me.

Tabatha's voice rings out from nowhere, awakening Evander. I push my shoulders back and zero my gaze in on the demon. Evander is fighting hard against it, and his body tenses, eyes fluttering before rolling to the back of his head.

"Evander, stop!" I yell and hold up my hand. "I need to speak to the demon."

Evander's body shakes and my heart jumps to my throat. I'm not in my body but it's still reacting and feeling my emotions as if I were.

"Speak to me?" Evander's eyes darken and he tips his head up.

"Yes. I want to make a deal." I look down at the bowl of herbs and inch forward, careful not to come too close to the bowl. "Quickly, before the others come back."

The demon inside Evander smiles, flashing his teeth. It's not the way Evander really smiles, and seeing that forced look of evil joy on his face causes anger to flash through me. "Coming to your senses now, half—"

"I said we don't have time," I hiss, fighting against the urge to look behind the demon, to where the other witches are standing. "My High Priestess will be here soon, and she'd forbid it if she knew I was talking to you." I shuffle forward again. "Let him go. I'm the one you want. Save him and take me."

"Such a martyr. I'll have to beat that right out of you when we get to the pits of Hell."

"Fine. Beat me. I don't care. Just leave my friend. He's innocent in all this."

"Is he?" The demon tips his head. "I'm inside his mind. I've seen things...heard things...your precious friend might not be as innocent as you think."

"True or not, I don't care," I spit. Demons lie. Demons do anything to rattle you. That's how they work, and getting under your skin, making you second-guess everything is their tried and true method of breaking down one's spirit so they can get inside. "I'm far from innocent so who I am to judge." I shrug. "My offer stands, but only for another moment. The second that door opens, the deal is off the table. Take me."

"Your offer sounds too good to be true."

"Trust me, it's too good for you." I quickly shake my head back and forth. "But I'm done with others getting hurt because of me. Whatever you want...it's between you and me." I hold out my hands. "I'll let you in."

"Nice try." The demon looks at the circle I'm standing in. "We both know I can't pass through that warding, though I am curious to what your plan was from there. I'm smoke and shadow. I'll be gone before you have a chance to spin a spell."

Making sure I look rightfully nervous, I step out of the circle.

"There. I'm out. Now please, they'll be here any moment and I...I just want to save my friend." My hands shake and I blink back tears. I've never been good at acting but I'm really selling it right now.

I hope.

Also, I'm slightly terrified for real. So many things could go wrong, from the demon refusing to leave Evander, making us go back to attempting another exorcism. It'll be pissed then, and who knows what kind of damage it will purposely wreak on Evander's body. And if it does leave Evander's body and we—I need to stop.

Or else I really will freak the fuck out.

"You won't regret this," the demon tells me. "You and I together." The same sick smile plays on Evander's face and the demon's murky eyes glow in the candlelight. "With you behind me, I shall rule the underworld."

Evander's body starts to tremble, and his head painfully flops back. Gray smoke pours from his mouth and eyes. I hold out my hands, bracing myself. I have to sell it until the last second or else we're all at risk.

The smoke billows toward me, moving faster and faster. If I were really standing here, wind would blow my hair around my face and my skin would prickle from the pure demonic energy that's bounding near.

But the demon passes right through me. I whirl around, conjuring a small string of magic at my fingertips. It's just enough to throw down at the box, triggering the spells that have been laid out.

"I stand behind no one," I sneer.

Ruth breaks the invisibility spell and everyone steps forward, chanting. Not wanting to risk my body being a host for the demon, I pull myself out of the office and back into the gathering room.

With a gasp, my eyes fly open. Binx stands and nuzzles his

head against me, needing to check and double-check nothing came back along with me.

"I'm okay," I tell him, feeling all out of breath like I'd just ran from Tabatha's office and into the gathering hall. He moves off my chest and I slowly sit up, moving with caution so I don't get hit with a case of the dizzies that can sometimes happen after astral projecting.

"Did it work?" Nicole gives her candle to Naomi and reaches down, helping me to my feet.

"I think so," I tell her, looking around at the students. "Things were playing out as we hoped when I left. I should go there to make sure." I rub my thumb over my fingers, conjuring another string of magic. This one glows bright blue, sizzling and sparking around my hand.

"Holy shit," one of the students mumbles. "You just astral projected and can still conjure raw magic?"

"She's pretty impressive, isn't she?" Naomi winks at me. "Quite handy to have around in times like this. Play nice if you want to keep her on your good side."

I give Naomi a look, smiling as I shake my head. "Everyone's okay here?"

"I feel a little weak," one of the other students confesses.

"That's normal," Nicole tells her. "That kind of magic can take a lot out of you, and you were a little jittery before things started. The adrenaline is wearing off."

"It wears off fast," I warn them, raking my hands through my hair. "You might want to stay here—and near the circle—until we give you the all clear. I'll send Binx back after we check things out."

"And you're okay to go?" Naomi arches her brows. "Like your fan over there just said, you did just astral project."

I nod. "I'm fine. Well, not fine. But I've done more while feeling a lot shittier."

"She has a point," Nicole says, helping the girl who was dizzy sit down on the steps of the altar. "I'll bring you water once it's safe to leave. Put your head in your hands and lean forward. Focus on your breathing."

"The first time I cast a strong circle like this I almost passed out," I tell the girl after hearing two of the male students behind her snickering. I leave out that I was only twelve and had no idea what the hell I was doing. The Academy fosters what's considered "healthy competition" between the students to encourage them to be the best witches and wizards they can be. I'll be the first to admit a bit of competition can be a great motivator to do well on tests and study your ass off, but I hate the sense of needing to be the best in order to have self-worth.

"Thank you," I tell Naomi. "For coming here."

Her eyes meet mine and she gives me a small nod, saying more with that little gesture than she does with her words: we are friends. Sister witches brought together for a reason, and no matter what, through thick and thin, we have each other's backs.

"Be careful, Callie. We all know how reckless you can be." She winks, helping to ease the other students' nerves.

"I can't make any promises. But I'll send Binx back if I need you to come save me again."

I step out of the circle and rush through the gathering hall, closing the door behind me as soon as I'm through.

"*Spatiumque hanc iniuriam,*" I whisper, waving my hand over the doors. It's a simple warding, but one that would give Nicole and Naomi enough of a warning that something malicious is trying to get in. The circle hasn't been closed yet, and with their collective powers, nothing would be able to break through.

Well...not *nothing*.

But I'm not even going to think about that right now.

Binx runs along next to me, and my footsteps echo through the empty halls. My heart is already beating a million miles an hour as I race up the steps leading to Tabatha's office. I work out for this reason. You never know when you have to run away from —or in this case, run toward—a demon.

My fear is getting to me, though, making me so anxious it's

hard to think about anything else. My body is going into flight-or-fight mode already and I need to snap the fuck out of it or I'll be exhausted by the time I get to Evander.

Who's going to be okay.

He has to be.

This plan was solid...well, maybe more than slightly opaque. The demon left Evander's body. There are powerful witches in that room and hidden protective circles, plus the whole room has been outlined in salt and warded. The demon can't escape it.

Binx shadows ahead of me, slipping in through the crack under the office doors. I telekinetically throw them open, needing to see Tabatha undoing Evander's restraints. Kristy will be holding the hex-box and even asshole Ruth will be smiling triumphantly, looking smug and already planning on how she's going to take credit for this.

But that's not what I see. Not at all.

Evander is still tied to the chair, but it's been tipped over. There's a cut on his forehead, and blood pools around his head on the floor. The hex box is in pieces on the ground before him, and Kristy and Sister Ross are in a corner of the room, huddled together inside a protective circle.

My heart stops beating and falls to the floor. It's my worst fear come to life, and I duck out of the way just in time to avoid being hit by a ball of energy, thrown by Tabatha at the gray smoke that's billowing around the room.

"Callie!" she screams, making a move to run forward. Ruby grabs her arm, pulling her back and into the protective circle. Ruth is in the other circle between Kristy and Tabatha.

I turn, eyes wide, and my breath leaves me. A cold wind sweeps through the room, putting out the candles. The office goes dark and I hold my hands up, conjuring bright blue energy.

Oh shit.

I opened the door and moved the salt line. The demon can smoke right past me and possess anyone in the entire Covenstead. Binx, who's already one step ahead of me, shadows along the doorway, keeping the demon confined to the room.

I hold up my hands, lighting up the room. Where is the demon?

I spin around again, trying to get a read.

"Callie!" Kristy shouts in warning. But it's too late. The demon hurls itself at me, and I jump out of the way. My foot goes down on a broken piece of the hex-box, and I slip, landing hard against the stone floor. The magic I was holding onto is released into the air, and everything goes dark.

I can conjure more magic. It will only take a second. But that second is all the demon needs, because the next thing I know, dark smoke is swirling around me, suffocating me as it forces itself inside and possessing me.

CHAPTER 5

Everything inside me burns, like my body is covered in tiny cuts and I'm being dipped into boiling hot lemon juice. It stings and aches and pinches and stabs. My body starts to go into shock, knowing something is wrong.

I'm being poisoned. Something that's not supposed to be here *is* here, and it's threatening to take over.

Trick me, half-breed...I think not! You will stand behind me. You will do my bidding and with you, I shall rule!

The demon's voice echoes in my head. I fall back, head whacking the floor with a sickening thud. Pain radiates through me, mixing with the very real feeling that I'm dying. I fight against it, though I know it's useless. The demon is in me, and soon I'll lose my free will.

It will take over. Make me use my powers. *Kill my friends.*

"No," I say through gritted teeth. I push myself up and tendrils of yellow light rise up around my fingers. The only other time I've ever conjured yellow light was when I healed the vampire bite on my neck, and that was according to Lucas. I've never seen it before, but this...this is so much more than yellow.

It's gold and sparkling and mesmerizingly beautiful. I hold my hands up and the light brightens. The demon screams inside of me, and it's like a thousand dark voices yelling all at once. It hurts my head and makes me pitch forward. Fighting through the pain, I turn my head up and let out a breath. Tears pool in my eyes and I clench my jaw and bring one hand to my chest.

It's not the energy ball I thought I'd need to kill the demon. It's something else...something that feels as familiar as it does different. I can't explain it. I can only feel it. Conjuring this type of energy feels *right*.

"I told you," I pant. "I. Stand. Behind. No one!"

The harrowing screams inside my head grow louder and louder, deafeningly painful. My eyes fall shut as tears roll down my cheeks. Then as suddenly as the demon forced itself into me, it leaves, smoke pouring out of my mouth. Instead of leaving and trying to find another host, it sparks, looking like an electrified storm cloud.

And then it explodes.

I fall back from the force of the blow, and stay flattened on the ground until the smoke settles. Little gold glowing embers sizzle out as they land on the cool stone. Lifting my head, I blink away the smoke from my eyes and slowly sit up.

Binx shadows over, shifting into cat-form and rubbing his head against me. "Hey, buddy," I whisper, and run my hand over his sleek fur. "Kristy?"

"Cal? I'm here. Are you okay? I can't see you."

"Nobody move," Tabatha instructs. *"Ignus."* A fire roars to life in the fireplace, filling the room with light. She rushes over to Evander, and Kristy comes to me, extending a hand to pull me up.

"Is the demon gone?" Kristy asks, eyes wide.

"I think so," I tell her.

Sister Ross, Ruby, and Tabatha help Evander up. He's awake.

"Way to cut it down to the last second, sister," he coughs. I rush over, tears filling my eyes again.

"I am so, so sorry."

"Sorry?" He sits back down in the chair Ruby uprighted. "Sorry for saving us all?"

"You wouldn't have gotten possessed if you hadn't come out to help deal with the Ley line." I make a move to wipe away my tears but remember something Lucas told me. *Never be ashamed of how you feel, Callie.*

"And then we'd all be screwed." His eyes fall shut. "I need a drink."

"You and me both," I laugh and kneel down. "Are you okay?"

"Better than the demon, so I'll call it a win."

Sister Ross, who's clearly still shaken, grabs her medical bag and begins an assessment.

"What went wrong?" I ask Kristy, moving to the side to let Sister Ross work.

"The hex-box wasn't strong enough. I don't understand why, though." She shakes her head. "It should have worked."

I flit my eyes to Ruth, who's standing next to Tabatha, comforting her and probably filling her head with lies.

"I have a feeling I might know why, but I can't tell you here. Oh, that reminds me..." I look at Binx. "Can you let the twins know we're okay?"

He meows and trots out of the room. Kristy loops her arm through mine. "The demon possessed you, Callie."

"It did."

"And you...you burned it from the inside out. With golden light. I've never once seen you conjure gold light."

"As far as I know, I've only done it once before. Recently." I swallow the rising lump in my throat. "So we can add this to another thing that falls outside the range of normal witchcraft. Did I look evil doing it?"

"No. The opposite. The light...I can't explain it, and I know this is going to sound really lame, but it was so pretty. I didn't want to stop looking at it."

"I felt the same way," I confess. "I don't think this is going to help my case."

43

"Your vampire case?" she whispers and I shake my head. "What else...oh, that thing you can't tell me."

I put my head in my hands, expecting to feel exhaustion set in like it usually does after I do major magic like this.

But it doesn't.

"Callie." Ruby crosses her arms and strides over.

"Want to cuff me again?" I cock an eyebrow.

"Kind of. Though I don't think it's necessary. What you did..." She shakes her head. "How did you do that?"

"I don't know," I tell her honestly. "And I'm...I'm..." I have no idea what I am or what I should say. I'm digging myself into a hole and I'm getting tired of lying. "I'm just glad Evander is okay."

"You and me both," she says and looks me up and down. "You should get checked out."

I nod, knowing I'm going to whether I want to or not.

"And can you, uh, walk in and out of that circle?" She points to one of the protective symbols drawn on the floor.

"I'm not possessed," I sigh, though I can't blame her for being extra careful. My body feels a little sore as I walk across the room, like I just completed an intense workout. I walk into the circle, hold out my hands and spin around, and then walk back out.

"No demon," I tell her and come back over by Kristy, perching on the edge of Tabatha's desk. The office is a mess and while cleaning it is one of the last things I want to do right now, it beats standing here being watched like a zoo animal by Ruby. Waving my hand, I use magic to sweep the broken pieces of the hex-box into a pile. Kristy, following my lead, straightens a bookshelf that looks as if someone was thrown into it.

"Callie," Tabatha calls, motioning for me to come over and have a seat on the bench below the window. Sister Ross has her medical bag out, and does a quick assessment of me, taking my vitals.

"All within normal limits," she says, trading the blood pressure cuff for a crystal to read my aura. Is it just me or did Tabatha tense? I think back to that morning she sat in my living room, looked me right in the eye and said there was nothing wrong with me.

I felt like she was lying then, and I hate it. I trust Tabatha with my life. She's been more than a teacher to me since the moment she pulled me out of that medical laboratory, and I know she'd do anything to protect me.

Even keep a secret.

But the thing about secrets is they're not ours to hide. They have a way of coming out, of making themselves known at the worst possible time.

Sister Ross holds the crystal above my head and slowly sweeps it down. "Interesting," she mutters.

"What's interesting?" I ask.

"There are no disturbances in your aura."

"Isn't that a good thing?"

"Oh, of course." She holds the crystal above my heart and waits a beat. "But after a demon has possessed you, I'd expect to see traces of that energy clouding yours and you'd need a potion to help restore your natural energies. From what I'm seeing, it's like it never happened."

"Maybe because the demon wasn't in me for that long?"

"Maybe, though whatever you did to make it explode should have depleted you."

"I'm feeling really worn out," I say, though I'm not. Not like I was after commanding the hellfire. It's more like I'm unlocking part of me that's been kept under wraps my whole life, and tapping into whatever power source this is feel so damn good. "I really want to go to bed."

"You should. And while I have no reason to admit you to the infirmary, you are more than welcome to take a bed there tonight to be watched and assessed. Sometimes these things can take time and hit you hard out of the blue."

"Thanks, but I'd like to go to my house. I sleep better in my own bed." Because my undead lover will be there next to me. Naked, I'm sure.

"So do I." Sister Ross smiles and starts packing up her bag. I'm fine. Evander will be fine. The Ley line is healed, the demon gone. Things are done. Over. Yet I don't feel any relief.

My troubles are just getting started.

"Thank you all for your combined efforts," Tabatha says, and this time the emotion in her voice is apparent. She looks absolutely exhausted, and I don't want to imagine the fear she felt seeing both Evander and then me possessed by the same demon. "It's been a long night and we all need to rest. Callie and Kristy, I assume you are leaving the Covenstead for your own beds tonight?"

"Yes," we answer at the same time.

"I will walk you to the door."

"Oh, darling," Ruth coos, patting Tabatha's shoulder. "You've been through enough tonight. I can walk them."

"We're fine," I say quickly. Too quickly. "Tabatha was right. It's been a long night for everyone, and Kristy and I have walked ourselves in and out of the door many times."

Ruth puts on a pleasant smile. "I insist."

I swallow hard. At least with Kristy with me, maybe she won't try to get me to summon the Devil. Kristy looks at me out of the corner of her eye, and I can feel what she's not saying. It's weird and rude to decline someone of Ruth's status like this.

"Well, I can't say no to that." I return the fake smile, give Evander a hug, and say goodbye to Tabatha. The gathering hall is empty as we pass by, leaving me to believe Nicole and Naomi have walked the students back up to their rooms. Binx is sitting by the door, tail swishing as he waits for us.

He lets out a low growl when he sees Ruth, and Kristy tenses. I try to give her a reassuring look, letting her know I've got this under control. Ugh, but I don't want to lie.

Because I don't have this under control.

We stop and say the incantation needed to open the door. As

soon as the blue light starts to flicker into view, I give Binx the signal needed to slip out and get Pandora and Freya. I still don't think Ruth is going to try anything with Kristy right here, but I'd rather be safe than sorry.

"Thank you, Grand Mage," Kristy says and reaches for my hand so we can walk through the door together. Suddenly, Kristy's body goes limp and I fall to the ground trying to catch her.

"Kristy!" I shout as fear pulses through me. "Kristy!" My first reaction is to shake her and try to wake her up. She doesn't move. So panicked I can't think straight, I look up at Ruth and wonder why she's not helping me.

"Keep your voice down," Ruth hisses and drops an empty potion vial on the ground. It starts to roll away and I make a dive for it, pulling out the stopper and smelling the empty vial. It's a valerian root sleeping spell that she must have slipped to Kristy while I was getting assessed by Sister Ross. I didn't think anything of it when Kristy took a drink of water from the pitcher on Tabatha's desk.

"You did this!" I clutch Kristy's body. Valerian root sleeping spells are strong—dangerously strong. Unlike the sleeping spell we put on Evander, this one works magically as well as medicinally. It requires an antidote to be undone, and the amount of antidote has to equally match the amount of valerian ingested. People die from spells like this.

They're put too deep asleep and stop breathing. They're unable to be woken up and basically waste away.

"Wake her up right now!" Magic sizzles around my fingers. I jerk my hands back, so I don't burn Kristy.

"Not until I get what I want."

"You are insane." I push myself up onto my feet and the anger I'm holding back threatens to break loose. Hitting Ruth with a big energy ball would be feel so fucking good right now.

"Am I?" She tips her head to the side. "I saw what you did in there and it was spectacular. So much power just dripping from you. You killed that demon from the inside out and there's not a scratch on you or your aura. I want that power."

"You promised." I curl my fingers into a fist. "My friends would be okay if I took you to him." I sweep my hand out at Kristy. "She wasn't supposed to be part of this."

"After I saw what you did back there, I knew I needed insurance. I have the antidote, mixed up and ready. Call upon your master and once I'm granted my powers, I will hand the potion over."

I clench my jaw, not sure what to do. Terrified if I try anything, she'll further hurt Kristy, I close my eyes in a long blink and nod. "Fine. We need to go to the woods."

Binx, I call. *Be ready. Pull out all the bloody stops. She needs to go down.*

The blue light from the open door is starting to fade. Ruth strides forward and grabs my wrist, nails digging into my skin. She shoves me through the doorway, and my feet land on the soft forest floor.

She closes the door behind us and the silence of the woods surrounds me. Usually, being out here is calming. There's something about the dark woods that instantly makes me feel better. But not tonight.

My heart is racing so fast and anxiety is threatening to take over again. Every time I blink, I see Kristy lying on the ground, eyes half open and unmoving. Ruth strides forward, going to the tree where the demon tied me up and tried to burn me. The bark is still singed from the fire and the grass and weeds around the tree are just now starting to grow back.

"I can feel his power!" She puts both hands on the tree. "Call him forth."

Shit. I was hoping I could tell her I need to go to my dark altar to buy more time, but this spot makes sense. I think. Maybe? I have no fucking idea how to summon the Devil because I've never done it.

She runs her hand down the trunk of the tree and crouches

down, picking up a handful of earth. She brings it to her face and inhales, smelling the brimstone.

"Call him forth," she tells me.

I nod and go over to the tree. I put both hands on the trunk and close my eyes, listening for my familiars.

"Oh, Dark Master," I start once I feel them getting closer. "I call you forth to…to…meet another willing child of night." I step away from the tree, turn around, and hold my hands up. Maybe I can hit Ruth with an energy ball now. Knock her out and get back to the Covenstead. Kristy is all the proof I need to show I'm innocent and Ruth is the guilty one.

She used an illegal potion on an innocent member of the coven.

"I call upon you, Dark One." I hold my hands up a little higher. "Come forth and meet your willing servant."

"Nothing is happening," Ruth says after a few beats pass.

"I told you he might not think you're worthy. I held up my end of the bargain. Now give me the antidote."

"Do not lie to me." She holds out her hand and magic wraps around my throat again. I conjure an energy ball, throwing it before she squeezes her hand even tighter. I can't breathe, and I can feel my windpipe starting to crush.

"You know," she starts, tightening her hold on my neck. "There is a little bone right at the base of your neck. If broken in the right way, it will suffocate you even after I let go."

I conjure another energy ball and throw it. It hits Ruth in the shoulder. She cries out in pain but doesn't loosen her grip.

"If you kill me—" I croak out, but she continues to tighten the grip until I can't get any air. I fall to the ground, hands flying to my neck on their own accord, body taking over and trying to pull the invisible noose from around my neck.

Something whirls through the forest, moving so fast he's just a blur. Lucas stands before Ruth, appearing so suddenly he startles her. She holds up her other hand, creating a shield that he can't break through.

"Take one more step, vampire, and I'll kill her right before your eyes."

Lucas looks at me, dark blue eyes wide, and draws his fangs. "Let her go," he growls. "And I'll make your death quick."

"You're no match for me," Ruth snarls back and pulses more energy into the shield. It's loosening her hold on my neck, and I'm able to suck in a breath. My familiars shadow through the woods, drawing closer and closer.

The original plan could still work.

I pitch forward, coughing, and plant my hands on the ground. The Ley line is beneath me, and tapping into it is dangerous—obviously— but I don't see what other choice I have. I close my eyes, fighting against Ruth's hold on me, and reach down, deep down, into the ground, and take just enough from the Ley line to conjure another energy ball.

Fangs flashing, Lucas slowly advances. Ruth throws her hand out, hitting him with another wall of energy. It pushes him back, but Lucas doesn't stop.

"Let her go," he growls again. Ruth shifts her attention to him, and it's all I need to spring up, gasping for air, and throw the energy ball at her. It clips her shoulder again, but this time it singes her skin, burning through her robe.

She falls back, and Lucas rushes forward. Before he can grab her, she casts the invisibility spell on herself and disappears from view. I'm on the ground again, coughing and sucking in air.

Lucas speeds over and scoops me up, cradling me to his chest.

"Callie." He presses his lips to the top of my head. "Are you all right?"

"I will be," I croak. "Once we get that bitch."

"Did she teleport?" Lucas puts his hands on my shoulders, holding me upright as I try to recover. I shake my head, feeling the hair on the back of my neck prickle.

"Get down!" I shout, but I'm too late. Ruth conjures a string of energy and hurls it at us. Pandora shadows by at the last second, blocking us from the raw energy. It hits her hard, sparking and sizzling.

I throw an energy ball in the direction where Ruth was standing, but it flies through the forest, hitting a tree.

"It's an invisibility spell," I whisper, looking around the woods. Lucas moves to my side, holding his arms out defensively. He'll do whatever it takes to keep me safe, and while part of me wants to let him rip Ruth to shreds, I need her alive.

Kristy needs the antidote.

And a Grand Mage going missing or turning up dead...I'm already in hot water with the coven.

"Can you sense her?" I ask Lucas. Binx and Freya shadow through the woods, searching for Ruth.

"No."

"Dammit." Heart racing, I slowly look around the woods. Everything is silent. Ruth has to be standing still. There's one of her and five of us. Invisible or not, the odds are against her and she has to know it.

Pandora shadows by, already recovering. Being hit with the energy weakened her, but it takes much more than that to kill a familiar in shadow form. Especially mine, who have been taught and trained by ancient and powerful Binx.

Flames suddenly rise from the forest floor a few feet in front of us. I conjure strings of magic and my familiars shadow over. Lucas whirls around, looking behind us. He's the only one who thought this could be a distraction, and he was right.

Ruth throws a magically charged branch through the air, broken with a sharp tip.

"Lucas!" I scream and throw up my hand to stop the branch. I'm not fast enough, and the tip of the branch plunges right into Lucas's chest.

CHAPTER 6

Lucas looks down at his chest, annoyed more than anything else. "You missed," he says, and I realize that he let her stab him just to mock her. He knew it would miss his heart.

"Seriously," I hiss, watching him yank the branch out of his chest. "Scared me half to death."

"Sorry, my love." He holds the makeshift stake up and looks out into the woods. Lucas can see in the dark, and vampires have much better hearing than humans. He's looking for Ruth, and it's only a matter of time before he finds her.

And she knows it.

Binx shadows through the woods, moving so fast he's a dark blur in the night. He's trying to draw Ruth out and make her move. And it works. Lucas hears something I don't, and he throws the branch through the air like a frisbee. It hits Ruth in the head, knocking her to the ground. The invisibility spell is broken and Lucas speeds forward, grabbing Ruth by the shoulders. Fangs drawn, he goes in for a deadly bite to her neck.

"Lucas, no!" I shout and run over. "I need her alive. She gave Kristy a sleeping potion and I need the antidote."

Snarling, Lucas jerks his head back and takes both of Ruth's wrists in one hand. He pulls something out of his pocket and slips it over Ruth's head.

"Try your invisibility trick now," he sneers and spins her around, holding her arms behind her back. The hagstone the vampire Dina used on me hangs from Ruth's neck.

"Good thinking," I tell Lucas, impressed he even thought to bring it. Then again, I did have Binx brief him on what was going on. Heart still pounding, I move around Lucas and cast the magical handcuff spell Tabatha used on my father just a few days ago.

"*Ad imperium,*" I say and snap my fingers together, making the two cuffs of magic that are circling Ruth's wrist pull together. I step back and Lucas wraps one arm around me.

"You won't get away with this." Ruth shakes her head. "I'll report you. Say you attacked me."

"Go ahead," I retort. "And I'll tell them what really happened."

"And you think they'll believe you?" She narrows her eyes. "The only reason an investigation against you hasn't been started is because I said I'd handle it myself. I told you, Callie," she spits my name. "One look at your file and the Grand Coven will wonder what you are hiding. Add in how you fought off demonic possession by your own sheer will and they will take matters seriously."

"You were possessed?" Lucas asks.

"For like a minute," I tell him, giving him a look that says *We'll talk about it later.* "And let them investigate me. I've done nothing wrong."

Ruth shifts her eyes to Lucas and laughs. "Are you sure about that?"

Blue light sparks behind us and the door starts to open. "Go!" I tell Lucas. He hesitates for a second, not wanting to leave me, but speeds off. He won't go far, I'm sure.

"Help! Help me!" Ruth starts to yell before anyone is even through the door. Ruby steps out first, followed by two members of the council and Tabatha.

Motherfucker. I know how this looks.

It's not good.

Ruby starts forward, but stops before she gets to Ruth. She stands in between myself and Ruth, looking back and forth as if she's trying to make sense of things.

"Help me, my child!" Ruth tries to pull her hands out of the magical cuffs. "She attacked me."

"No, no, I didn't," I protest.

Tabatha holds up her hand. "Silence," she orders. I step back, hands shaking. Binx meows and rubs against my legs. Freya and Pandora sit patiently near the door, watching and waiting to act if need be.

"Kristy?" I ask, swallowing the lump in my throat.

"She's in the infirmary," Tabatha says and strides over to Ruth. "She will make a full recovery."

"She did it." Anger floods through me again and Binx rubs his head against my legs, telling me to calm down. I clench my jaw and stare daggers at Ruth. "She gave her the potion."

"You have no proof of that," Ruth fires back.

Ruby flicks her eyes to Ruth for half a second. "I let you into the potion room yesterday. I didn't think anything of it, of course, but after we found Kristy and realized what had been given, I went back and looked. You took what you'd need to make the sleeping potion."

"I didn't want to believe it," Tabatha says. "But then we searched your room and found the antidote." She extends her hand, holding out an empty potion vile. "One overlooked detail of this particular sleeping spell is how the victim is able to hear what's going on around them. Makes it particularly terrifying to be locked in your own body, aware of what's going on but not able to react. Kristy was able to recount everything she's heard."

"They're friends!" Ruth sputters. "Of course she'd lie for her friend! Look at what she did to me! She attacked me!"

"That's not all we found when we searched your room." Tabatha reaches into her robe and pulls a Baphomet out of her pocket. It's a Satanic object, not necessarily illegal to have, but it makes her look guilty of everything Kristy would have overheard.

Ruth was trying to force me to summon the Devil for her.

The council members look at Tabatha, waiting her command. Things are bad, and while I know I'm innocent, I know how this looks.

"I will deal with this the correct way," Tabatha says, looking pained. She pushes her shoulders back. "Ruth, you are charged with use of an illegal potion, conspiring against the coven, and practice of black magic. You are to return to the Covenstead with your powers bound until the Grand Coven arrives in the morning. And Callie." She looks me in the eye, trying to keep the emotion out of her voice.

"Until the Grand Coven reviews your case as well, I hereby suspend you from the coven and forbid you to step inside the Covenstead."

I feel like I'm falling backwards into the dark. My head moves up and down on its own accord. The suspension is temporary, and I know I'll be cleared of charges.

But what if I'm not? The coven is my family. The Covenstead is my second home. I can't lose that.

"Return to your house," Tabatha further orders me. "You will be contacted by a member of the council once things have been reviewed." The council leads Ruth back through the door, and I wait, watching everyone go through. The door seals shut behind everyone, and I go to the spot where it appears in the old tree, holding my hand out and feeling for the energy. Until Tabatha lifts my suspension, I won't be able to open the door even if I tried.

Swallowing the lump in my throat, I turn and start back toward my house. My familiars walk along next to me, and we walk in silence. Lucas is on the back porch, waiting for me to return home. He speeds forward once he sees me, and pulls me into his embrace.

I close my eyes and rest my head against his chest. The lack of a beating heart used to unsettle me, but now I find comfort in the quiet.

"Are you all right?" he asks again.

"I will be." I tip my head up. "I just want to sleep."

Lucas nods and takes my hand, leading me up the steps. I go right for the fridge, pulling out a bottle of wine and use magic to take out the cork. Not bothering with a glass, I put the bottle of Moscato to my lips and take a few big gulps.

"That's better." I set the bottle down and almost immediately feel the alcohol hit me. It's been a while since I've had anything to eat, I've been running on pure adrenaline since I was summoned to the Covenstead, and right before that Lucas drank my blood during sex. Exhaustion is going to hit me hard at any moment, and I want nothing more than to pass out and not think about anything at all.

Lucas grabs me by the waist and pulls me to him, kissing me hard. "I love you," he whispers between kisses.

"And I love you."

He pulls my hair to the side, moving his lips to my neck. I melt against him, wrapping my arms around his shoulders. The sun is starting to come up, but thanks to a spell of my own invention, the light won't hurt Lucas as long as he stays inside. He picks me up and carries me upstairs and into bed.

"Kristy was supposed to open the store," I mumble, blindly reaching for my phone on my nightstand. "She won't be able to go in."

"You're not going in, are you?"

"Someone has to open."

"You're going to run yourself ragged, Callie."

"I know," I agree, seeing no point in arguing. "It feels like we fought off supercharged demons days ago, but it was yesterday." I let out a sigh. "I'll get through a few hours until Betty comes in to take over and then I'll be home. I'll nap and rest and eat vitamins or something, okay?"

Lucas smiles, brushing my hair back. "Okay."

I set an alarm, put my phone down, and snuggle up with Lucas. I fall asleep right away.

~

I WAKE UP TO THE SMELL OF BACON AND COFFEE. FEELING LIKE I just shut my eyes a few minutes ago, I groggily sit up and throw the covers back. I really don't want to go to work today.

"You're up." Lucas walks into the room, holding a tray. "I cannot promise any of this is good." He comes to the bed and sets the tray down. He made me bacon, scrambled eggs, and toast. There's a mug of steaming black coffee as well. "I watched YouTube videos on how to cook," he admits with a smile. "It looks like it did in the video, but the smell of human food has no appeal to me."

Emotion hits me and I look at him, blinking back my feelings. "Thank you. It looks wonderful." I sit back against my pillows and dig in. There's way too much salt on the eggs and my toast is soggy with so much butter, but this is the best damn breakfast I've ever had.

"Have you ever cooked?" I ask Lucas as I pile eggs onto my toast, folding it together to make a sandwich. "When you were human, I mean. Or did women do all the cooking back then?"

"I don't know if I'd consider it actually cooking, but I provided food for myself before being captured in war. It was nothing like this, though."

I take another bite of food and look at Lucas, finding it hard to imagine him as a human. I don't know much about his human life, other than he was born in the 300s and fought as a Gladiator before being turned into a vampire and forced to fight all over again.

"Did you have a family?" I ask quietly. "When you were human?"

He shakes his head. "I wasn't married." He looks out the

window, still mesmerized by the sun. "I had two younger sisters, and our father had been killed in war when we were young. I took care of them as well as our mother."

I trade my toast for the coffee, wanting to ask more but not wanting to push Lucas. I know how painful it can be to revisit the past. Lucas continues to look out the window. "The last time I saw them was the day I went off to war, and I haven't thought about them in years."

"I'm sorry."

"Don't be. It was a very long time ago, Callie."

"Can I ask one more thing?" I set the coffee cup down and Lucas nods. "Did you know you were going to be turned into a vampire?"

"No. I didn't know vampires existed until I woke up as one." He looks at my plate. "Is the food good?"

"It is, thank you again."

"I'd like to make you dinner, though I fear anything more complicated that putting bacon in a skillet might not turn out as well."

"I'm not the best cook either," I tell him with a smile. "Unless I use magic to help me out."

"I'll buy you dinner instead."

"I'm not usually one to turn down a pizza."

He gets up, kisses the top of my head, and leaves the room. I finish eating, take a fast shower, and use magic to braid my hair. It's bright and sunny today, and will be hot like usual for this point of the summer. I go to my closet, deciding on a two-piece outfit consisting of shorts and a matching crop top. I get dressed and go down, finding Lucas putting the last of the dishes away.

"You're not wearing black today?" he asks with a smile. My outfit is beige, with overlay with multicolored flowers. "I almost didn't recognize you."

"Ha-ha. I don't wear black that often." He cocks an eyebrow. "Fine, I do. But every once in a while I like to mix it up. And it's hard to find summery clothes in black. It's hot today and I hate being sweaty when I'm at work."

"You never told me what happened last night." He sets the dish towel down and strides over, pulling me to him and pressing his pelvis against mine. I bring my hands up, resting them on his firm chest. "I got suspended from the coven."

"Fuck."

"I know."

"What does that exactly mean?" he asks.

"It means I can't get through the door if I tried. It's the step before excommunication, and anyone still active in the coven shouldn't associate with me out of fear of being suspended too."

"But you work with Kristy."

"There's some gray area. Our work isn't magical, so we can keep professional relationships, or at least that's what the Grand Coven would say." I take in a breath and turn my head up to look at Lucas. "I'll be investigated, I'm sure." I don't have to say it for him to know that we're at risk for being discovered again.

"Come to Chicago tonight." He cups my face in his hands. "We never did get to go out on another fancy date. Let me take you out tonight and then spend the rest of the week with me." He puts his lips to mine.

"That does sound good, and I do need to lay low and go on as normal. I'm not guilty so there's no need to act like it."

"Should I make us a dinner reservation tonight then?"

"Don't hate me," I start.

"I could never hate you."

"Remember that." I slip my hands under his black t-shirt. "Let me figure out what's going on with work. Kristy's stressing already, I'm sure, about this morning. I have no way of contacting her while she's at the Covenstead since I'm suspended. Phones don't work and I can't send her a message or anything." I can't bring myself to say the second part, that maybe Lucas should go to Chicago and leave me here alone.

The Grand Coven will be arriving at the Covenstead soon,

and if they come here and find a vampire at my house then Ruth's claims won't look so false. Fuck, I hate this. No one should be able to tell me who I should or shouldn't love.

Lucas makes me happy. I love him just as he loves me. We're not hurting anyone by being together, and it's just so fucking stupid that anyone has a problem with us.

"Call me when you're on your way home," Lucas starts, putting his lips to mine again. "I'll attempt to make you something to eat again."

"How did I get so lucky to have you in my life?"

He smirks. "You got drunk, attacked a vampire in my bar, and then I lied to and manipulated you to let me drive you home."

"Oh right. I almost forgot. So much for true love, right?"

He laughs and kisses me once more before I head out the door. Pandora comes with me today, and I run my hand over her sleek fur. In cat-form, she's a gorgeous calico, with eyes that look almost golden in certain sunlight. She sits on the passenger seat of my Jeep Grand Cherokee on the way into the store, and trots along next to me as I stop into Curlew's Café for a much-needed cup of coffee with a double shot of espresso.

I open the store four minutes later than normal, and three angry customers come in, huffing about having to wait out in the heat.

"You could have stayed in your cars until the fucking open sign was on," I grumble quietly so only Pandora can hear me. I love co-owning and running Novel Grounds with Kristy, but some days I really question why I went into anything that deals with the general public.

The first hour crawls by, and I finished my coffee only ten minutes in. If it weren't for the crippling anxiety, I'd be falling asleep behind the counter. I'm getting to that point of passing out when my phone rings.

It's Kristy, and I scramble to answer it.

"Hey. Are you okay?"

"I'm fine," she replies in a level tone. "Promise. Are you? Tabatha told me about the sentencing."

"I'm alive and I'm not guilty. Well, I am guilty of sleeping with Lucas but whatever, right?" I pinch the bridge of my nose. "You're really okay?"

"Yes. I woke up feeling hella hungover, but I got the antidote in time. Thanks to you."

"And you were poisoned because of me."

"Stop blaming yourself, Cal. Ruth was blackmailing you."

I nod, forgetting she can't see me. "You must be home now, right?"

"Yes, I just got back to my house. Thanks for opening for me."

"Don't even worry about it. Rest and take care of yourself and we can smile at each other in passing."

"Stop being so dramatic," she scolds. "We can talk to each other at work or in any other setting that's not the Covenstead. It sucks, but just lay low for a few days and this will be taken care of. I have a good feeling about it."

"Right. And trust me, laying low sounds heavenly right about now. The next time I get some days off, I'm going to spend them in Chicago with Lucas doing nothing but him."

"That does sound nice. I can take your shift tomorrow since you're working for me today."

"I can work tomorrow."

"I know you can, but I also know I can too. Plus, we both know I like working more than you do."

"You said it, not me," I laugh. "I'll call you later and check in. Rest, and if you need anything, send a smoke signal or something untraceable."

"I'll hook up that old CB radio I have in my closet instead."

"Sounds good. Love you, Kristy."

"Love you too, Cal."

I end the call and get back to work, ringing up a few more customers, tidying up the shelves, and sneaking bites of a granola bar in between all that. I'm watching the clock and time is going by so fucking slow.

Pandora is sitting on the counter, soaking up all the attention she can get from customers. My cats are a little famous around the shop, and people assume I'm a total crazy cat lady who spent lots of time training them to be so well-behaved. And I'm one hundred percent fine with that rumor.

She sits up, growling, and looks at the person who just walked through the door.

"You have got to be kidding me," I say, when I see demon— and witch—hunter, Easton Richards, walk through the door.

So much for lying low.

CHAPTER 7

"What are you doing here?" I close the book I was skimming and stand up, eyes darting around the store. There are a handful of other customers in here and I am not in the mood to get into anything with Easton right now.

Easton holds up his hands. "I just want to talk, I swear."

"Fine," I sigh, too tired to argue. Easton looks tired too, and though it feels like the fight in the woods happened ages ago, it was just last night. "How's Melinda?"

"She's going to make a complete recovery, thanks to you."

"And Lucas," I add pointedly, and Easton does a good job ignoring what I just said. "That's good to hear, though. You know I always liked your sister."

"I know. Which is why I wanted to thank you in person for everything."

"Thank me?" My eyebrows go up. "That's a first."

"Come on, Callie." Easton plows a hand through his hair. He's only two years older than me but looks much older. The life of a hunter is tiring, stressful, and isn't always filled with the healthiest choices. "I mean it. What you did—"

"Just me?" Some may say I'm being petty, but the guy did pretend to date me only so he could get close and kill me. He failed, obviously. But not before my teenage heart fell for him and I let him take my virginity.

"And that vampire," he mutters. "You both helped us last night and we want to thank you."

"You're welcome," I say and mean it. "I'm glad you all made it out unscathed last night." The bell above the door dings as more customers come in. "Really, I am."

He moves closer to the counter, nervously looking at Pandora. "How did you kill all the demons?" he asks in a hushed voice. "We were only gone a few hours and when I came back, they were all gone."

"Magic," I supply, knowing that's not a good answer.

"Really?" He rests his hands on the counter and leans in, hazel eyes meeting mine. He's always been attractive, and it was one of the things that pulled me in when we first met. "I know you're powerful, Callie, but it was like last night never happened."

"Oh, if only," I sigh. "Look…just don't worry about it. Don't look a gift horse in the mouth."

"What?"

"It's an old proverb that means be thankful for what you've been given."

"I've heard the proverb," he says. "But what are you telling me?"

"Nothing," I say, tension rising. "Nothing that concerns you." A line starts to form at the counter, and I hope Easton will leave in the time it takes to ring up everyone. But he doesn't. He's hanging around like a fungus, and I'm going to need an extra dose of medication to get rid of him once and for all.

I ring up the last customer and slip out around the counter, finding Easton in the self-help section. Too bad he's not reading any of the books.

"Look," I start, grabbing his arm and pulling him toward the back of the store and away from any more customers. "I was powerful when we met, but that was a decade ago. I'm much more powerful now, with powerful friends. This whole town is full of us, and if you were smart at all, you'd avoid Thorne Hill. Forever." I let out a breath, not wanting to hold onto a ten-year-old grudge. "There are a lot of witches in this town, and we're obviously able to take care of shit ourselves. There's no need to spill any blood. Get out while you can."

"Why does it sound like you're threatening me?"

"You are impossible." I roll my eyes and start to walk back to the counter. "I'm not, and you need to get your head out of your ass. Yes, you're a big bad hunter, but I'm an even bigger and badder witch, okay? Historically, we have a shitty track record, and I'm not just talking about you and me. You're a hunter in a town of witches. It's not smart to be here."

"We didn't come here to cause trouble," he says. "I swear it."

"I believe you. The demons led you here, and everyone likes to blame demons, right?"

"Right," he chuckles. "They are easy to blame, after all."

Betty comes in, smiling as she makes her way to the counter. She curiously looks at Easton and then at me.

"Hey, Betty. You're early." I look at the clock. She's not supposed to be here for another hour.

"I know." She wrinkles her nose. "I really need to find a new place to live. I love my mom, but she is driving me crazy." Betty comes around the counter and puts her to-go cup of coffee under the register.

"Oh, right. I forgot you lived at home."

Betty just nods, blinking rapidly. After being drugged in an attempted assault by her neighbor, Betty moved out of her apartment and back home with her parents. Thorne Hill is a small town and there aren't too many places to cheaply rent around here.

"And Kristy called you," I add, mostly to change the subject. "Didn't she?"

"Guilty. She said you guys both ate bad takeout and she wasn't sure how you were doing."

"I'm a little tired, but I'm fine. Thanks for coming in early."

"It's no problem," she assures me. "I'd much rather be here than listening to my mom go on and on about how I should join her Bible study to meet *nice boys*."

"I would rather be here too."

Betty looks at Easton again. He doesn't look like our typical client, as he's dressed in jeans, hiking boots, and a button up-flannel shirt worn over a gray t-shirt. It's way too hot to be dressed like that, but it's the typical garb of a hunter, who always want to be prepared for a fight with a demon or a chase through the woods.

"So you're done for the day?" Easton asks, walking down along the register.

"Yeah, I'll leave here in a bit once I get things all settled."

He runs his hand through his hair again, messing it up even more than it was before. "I was going to grab lunch and take it up to Melinda. What's good around here?"

"There's a diner two streets over that has the best burgers and fries. The milkshakes are good too, but they'd melt before you got to the hospital."

"What, you don't have a magic trick for that?"

"I'm not Elsa," I laugh. "But I might have a way to pull energy away from objects that does result in a lower temperature in the general area."

"Want to come with? Mel would love to see you."

I shouldn't spend another second with a witch hunter, but it would be nice to have a chat with Melinda…and have her promise me that they'll stay far away from Thorne Hill. Plus, she and I were kind of friends. She was the first person outside the Academy who I could talk to about magic and demons without feeling like a freak.

"Yeah. I, uh, I'll drive up behind you."

"What? Don't want to get in a car with me?" That stupid smile comes back to Easton's face.

"No, I actually don't, and it doesn't make sense to drive in and out of town. I had a really, really, *really* long night that didn't end until, well, this morning. So I'm going home after visiting Melinda."

"Fair enough. Should I go put in an order for lunch then?"

"Yeah, give me about ten minutes to wrap things up here and make sure Betty's good to take over. I want a cheeseburger with—"

"Extra pickles, no mustard, and double the cheese?"

"Yeah. I guess I haven't changed that much over the years."

He slowly shakes his head. "You have changed. A lot."

"In a good way, right?"

"You're not telekinetically throwing shit every time you get pissed off."

I cock an eyebrow. "I don't have to be pissed off to throw shit. But yes, I'm much better at controlling my, uh…my…temper," I say, trailing off when a customer comes up to the register. Easton leaves to go to the diner, and I get everything ready for a shift change. Vanessa is coming in later to help Betty close, and I wouldn't be surprised if Kristy showed up after all either.

Easton is sitting in his car outside the dinner when I pull up, and signals for me to follow him to the hospital. The nurse has Melinda up for a shower, so Easton and I sit in the waiting room, eating our food while we wait.

"So, you're dating a vampire."

I take another bite of my burger and glare at him. "Really?"

"What?"

Shaking my head, I just take another bite and stare straight ahead. I'm too tired to get into this right now.

"You're telling me you think it's a good idea to date a fucking vampire?"

"If you wanted to watch me telekinetically throw things around you could have just asked."

Easton puts his burger back in the wrapper and turns in his seat to face me. "Sore subject? I'm not the only one who thinks you shouldn't be with him then."

"Are you for fucking real right now?"

"I am. I know we had our issues, Callie, but I'm worried about you. That fucker is old and powerful. He's a killer."

"So are you."

Easton swallows hard, making his Adam's apple bob up and down. "That's different."

"Why?" Anger surges through me and it's all I can do not to blow the glass right out of the windows. I am so sick of people telling me that I shouldn't be with Lucas simply because of *what* he is. "Because the people you killed were different from you enough to justify their murders?"

"People will hear you." Easton grabs my wrist.

I yank my arm back. "Good. Killing is killing, and you can't justify it. I promise you half the people Lucas killed deserved it at least, which is more than I can say for you. You slaughtered a pack of weres."

"Werewolves, Callie. They were fucking werewolves."

"They owned a bakery!" I whisper-yell. "Vegan bakers and that was before being vegan was trendy. And you and your cult of ignorant, judgmental, sexist and backwoods hunters killed them in their sleep. Then they sent you after me. A teenage girl who didn't even know witch hunters still existed."

"If there's one thing I regret—"

"Save it." I ball up the rest of my burger, having lost my appetite. "You're no different than him, you know."

"Who?"

"My father."

Easton doesn't object for once.

I close my eyes, forcing myself to take in a breath and calm down. "Lucas knows exactly who I am. He knows what I'm capable of and he loves me for it. He doesn't look at me like I'm a freak. He's not scared of me. Doesn't think I should find a way to strip myself of my powers. He loves me for me. And I love him for the same reasons." I open my eyes and look right at Easton. "I've spent too much of my life being angry at people like you, people who fear what they don't understand, who'd rather repress and deny me of my basic rights as a human-fucking-being. But you know what? I'm not mad anymore. I just feel sorry for you. Because no matter what, you'll never be free. You live with so much hatred in your heart..."

I bring my hand to my chest. "I can't even imagine the weight you must feel. So know this. As you're lying down to sleep tonight, heart racing and mind whirling with all your hateful thoughts, body unable to relax and let go because you're so angry about things you can't control...I'll be in bed with my vampire. After he drank my blood during sex, of course. Oh, and that sex is always amazing because he's had a very long time to perfect his methods and because I love him."

The lights flicker above me, and I take it as my cue to leave. I let out another breath, feeling lighter already. I've told off my father, my brother, and Easton all within a week. I just need to check Doctor Howard off the list and I might be on my way to making a full mental recovery from my childhood trauma.

Hah.

"Tell Melinda I hope she feels better." I stand and hold my hands to my side, not caring that blue magic is sparking around my fingers. "And stay out of Thorne Hill."

∾

ALL I WANT IS A BIG GLASS OF WINE AND MY BED. PREFERABLY WITH Lucas in it, naked and next to me, of course. Though I'm too tired for sex right now. But just having him next to me makes everything better.

Seeing a truck with an *Anderson Construction* sticker on the door is the last thing I want to see when I pull into my driveway. All three of my familiars are on the porch, sunbathing like regular cats. They hold up the pretense well, but I wouldn't be surprised if the nons close to me were suspicious, especially Betty.

She seemed concerned when Pandora and I left to go to the

hospital. It's not like I can take a cat inside with me, and it's way too hot to leave a pet in the car. Really, Pandora just shadowed home, faster than anyone could notice. It's not like I could tell that to Betty, and sometimes I feel bad lying to her.

"What the hell is this?" I grumble, trying hard not to take my bad mood out on anyone who doesn't deserve it. I park in the dry grass of my side yard, leaving enough room for the trucks to pull out of the driveway.

Binx lets me know Lucas is in the dining room, sitting around the table with the construction workers. They don't know he's a vampire, and I'll have to open and close the back door quickly in order to keep his cover.

"Thanks," I tell him and hurry up the back-porch steps. I'm sweating already in the short time it took for me to go from my Jeep to the house, and I dodge in as fast as I can, hitting myself with the door in my rapid attempt to slam it shut before sunlight burns my beloved.

He'd heal immediately, but then everyone in the room would know he's a vampire. Which really wouldn't be a big deal since both Lucas and I have the ability to change memories. Though I really don't feel like dealing with anything like that today.

"Ah, sweetheart," Lucas says, standing from the table when I step into the dining room. "You're just in time."

Three men sit around the table, and blueprints of the house Lucas just bought for us are laid out in front of them. Lucas comes over and puts one hand on the small of my back. He pulls me in for a quick kiss and pushes my hair back over my shoulder.

"Are you all right?" he asks quietly.

"I will be," I huff, obviously struggling to let go of my anger. "What's going on in here?"

"We were going over the structural damage of the house."

"Is it bad?"

Lucas pulls out a chair for me to sit in. "Not as bad as I anticipated."

I sit down and look at the blueprints, remembering that we

left a headless zombie in the attic. It probably stinks to high heavens with this heat right now. "That sounds promising."

"It is," Lucas says with a smile. He bought me the house as a surprise after I rather casually mentioned that buying and fixing it up was a dream of mine. We had plans to meet with contractors and builders who specialized in restoring historic homes. I could have sworn we weren't supposed to meet today, but I'm sure Lucas moved up the meeting to try and make me happy, to try and offer a distraction from the shitstorm that is my life.

But all I want to do right now is drink myself into a stupor and pass out after watching 90s made-for-TV movies about witches.

The contractors start explaining the plan of action to me, and it doesn't take long before I'm getting excited and start thinking about the future.

About Christmas together and how I'll finally have my twelve-foot Christmas tree.

About the parties we can have in the summer, sitting outside on our patio at night with our friends before taking a midnight dip in our in-ground pool.

About waking up day after day—or night after night —together.

Forever.

Only...my forever will end.

Lucas will live on past that.

Alone.

Forever.

CHAPTER 8

"Would you like me to make you something to eat?" Lucas slips his arms around me and pulls me to his chest. The builders just left, and we're sitting on the couch in the living room.

"Maybe in a little bit." I pull my legs up and wiggle closer to him. "Can we just sit here first?"

He nods and presses his lips to mine before laying us down. My eyes fall shut and exhaustion takes over. And then I remember the zombie in the attic.

"Dammit," I mutter.

"What's wrong, my love?" Lucas runs his fingers through my hair.

"The builders are going to the house and we never took that body out of the attic."

"I did."

"When?"

"Last night when I was waiting for you to come back. I couldn't exactly sit still and do nothing."

I lift my head up and look at his handsome face. "So you buried a body?"

"Call it my therapy."

I rest my head back down against him. "I love you, Lucas."

He pulls a blanket off the back of the couch and covers us up. "I love you too. Get some rest, Callie."

Nodding, I close my eyes and readjust the way I'm lying so I can run my fingers through Lucas's hair since I know he likes it. We both end up falling asleep, and I wake up six hours later needing to use the bathroom. Lucas is literal dead weight when he sleeps, and it takes a bit of maneuvering to get out of his embrace without waking him up. The sun has set by now, and while those six hours of sleep felt wonderful, I want to crawl back under the blanket and snuggle up with Lucas again, sleeping soundly the rest of the night.

There's only one bathroom in this old house, and the stairs creak under my feet as I make my way up. After using the bathroom, I brush my teeth and pull my hair into a messy bun at the top of my head. I strip out of my clothes and head into my room to put on PJs instead.

"Now this is a sight I like to see," Lucas's voice comes from behind me. I'm standing in only my panties, and I turn around with a coy smile on my face, looking down at myself.

"It is a pretty good view."

Lucas strides forward and takes me by the waist. He kisses me, deep and passionate, making butterflies flap in my stomach and heat instantly flood through me.

"Are you still tired?" he asks, sliding his hands around to my ass.

"I'm something else at the moment."

His eyes widen. "And what is that?"

I bite my lip and hook my arms around his neck, stepping in close so my hips press against his. Feeling his large cock get hard turns me on even more than I already am. I take one of his hands and move it between my legs, showing him how hot he's making me without even trying.

That's how it is when you're in love, I suppose.

Lucas picks me up as he kisses me again. With vampire

strength, he's able to hold me with one arm as if I weigh nothing, and carries me to the bed. He sits, putting me on his lap. We move, jumbled together, until I'm straddling him, rubbing myself against his erection that's confined beneath his pants. His stupid pants that really need to come off. *Now.*

I push Lucas back onto the mattress and lower my gaze to his belt. Using magic, I undo the buckle, causing Lucas to groan with anticipation. I sink my teeth into my lower lip again, trying to force myself to bide my time. Along with feeling his dick harden against me, hearing him moaning with desire for me is enough to do me in right here and now.

"I love it when you use your magic. It's so fucking hot." He reaches for me, losing patience, and pulls me toward him while kicking off his pants. Moving fast as only a vampire can, he flips me over and puts himself between my legs. I bend my knees and curl my legs around him, bucking my hips to rub against his cock. We kiss, hard and desperate, before Lucas breaks away so I can pull his shirt over his head. Now he's gloriously naked, and if he doesn't start touching me, I'm going to explode.

He brings his head down, nuzzling my neck. I rake my fingers through his hair and give him an encouraging push, though he never needs much direction from me. Though sometimes, he likes to tease me, makes me wait and gets off on knowing how much he's driving me crazy.

Other times, like now, our desperation is mirrored and we both need to make each other come as hard and fast as we can. Yes, I enjoy when he draws it out, but it's not like we won't be doing this again later.

Drawing his fangs, Lucas grazes the sharp points over my flesh. Goosebumps break out over my skin and my whole body shudders from the chill that goes through me. He has perfect control and won't bite me until he wants to. But knowing that he could sink his teeth into me at any moment sends a jolt through me, enhancing my pleasure.

He kisses his way down, stopping at my breasts. Taking one in his mouth, he flicks his tongue over my nipple. I can feel the tips of his fangs against my skin, and if I weren't so worked up and dying for a release, I'd admire his control.

But right now, all I can think about is his head between my thighs and that skilled tongue lashing out against my clit. I'm getting wetter thinking about it, and my body begs me to push him down even more, giving me the pleasure it's so desperately craving.

Lucas slowly rolls my panties down my thighs as he continues to kiss his way down.

"I need you," I pant, giving him another push down. "Please, Lucas, make me come."

With a growl, he dives down, mouth open as he meets my core. I cry out in pleasure as his tongue darts out against my clit. My hands are in his hair and I tilt my hips up, offering myself to him. He licks and sucks my clit, getting me right on the edge of an orgasm when he turns his head to the side, sliding his hand up my thigh.

He pushes two fingers inside of me and sinks his fangs into my thigh, only inches above my pussy, at the same time. Being penetrated like this pushes me over the edge, and everything inside me tightens, getting ready for the release. He strokes my G-spot and pulls a mouthful of blood from my body, swallowing it and moving his mouth back to my clit.

I come hard against his face, and Lucas keeps his fingers inside me, stroking and rubbing me until I'm so overcome with so pleasure I don't think I can stand it. I ball my fists and press them against the mattress, mouth falling open, yet no sound escapes my lips. He turns his head again and licks up the blood that's dripping down my thigh. His mouth clamps over the wound, sucking so hard it almost hurts. Then he pulls away and moves up, wet tip of his dick resting against my stomach.

I blink my eyes open and move my hand to his face, wiping a smear of my own blood off his lips. He licks it from my fingers and lowers his head, resting his forehead against mine for a few seconds before plunging his cock balls deep inside me.

This time, a loud moan comes from deep within me, and I hook my legs around him, feeling fresh blood drip down my thigh as he thrusts in and out of me. I'm still coming down from the orgasm he just gave me, and the added sensation of his big cock filling every single inch of me is almost enough to put me in a pleasure coma.

My hands fall from his body and I can't get myself to keep my eyes open. My lips part and Lucas puts his mouth to my neck, sucking at my skin. He's retracted his fangs, not wanting to bite me anymore. He's moving so fast, fucking me so hard it's almost like his cock is vibrating inside of me.

I almost black out before we both come at nearly the same time. Panting, I feebly wrap my arms around him. He holds himself inside of me for a moment after that, and feeling his dick pulsing with the aftershock of his orgasm is one of the hottest things I've ever experienced.

"Now you should rest, my love." He gently brushes my hair out of my face.

"Yes," I breathe, agreeing with him. I'm unable to open my eyes. Or move. Lucas pulls out and moves his head back down between my thighs. He licks up the rest of the blood on my flesh and puts pressure on the bite wound, holding it until the bleeding stops. He brings me a towel after that, and I lazily clean myself up and then fall back into his arms, naked and floating on a sex-induced haze of bliss.

I SIT AT THE COUNTER, DRUMMING MY FINGERS ON THE COLD quartz top. Lucas is in the office, talking to Eliza on the phone. I know she's annoyed that he's here again, and won't be happy once she finds out there's even more witch-drama to deal with.

It's a little after ten AM and I just woke up. I haven't slept that long in forever, and my body desperately needed it. When the coffee is done brewing, I get up and pour myself a cup. I don't actually need the caffeine to wake up today, but it's such a habit I have to have it. Plus, I'm pretty sure I have a bad caffeine addiction and will get a headache if I don't have some.

I take my coffee into the dining room and look over the plans for Lucas's and my house. Construction is starting today, and I plan to go over and have a look at how things are going later. Though, I'll feel a little bad for leaving Lucas here. He's stuck in the house during the daylight, and while he doesn't admit it, he has to be bored.

The whole opposite schedules thing sucks, and even when we officially live together, it'll still be that way. The only solution would be for me to start staying up at night and sleeping during the day, which has been my schedule lately anyway.

But I have to work. Well, kind of. Lucas has told me more than once he'd be more than happy to provide for me financially, and I'm well aware of how much money he's acquired over his sixteen hundred years as a vampire.

Once the house is actually safe to be inside, we can start planning what I call the fun stuff, and I'm very much looking forward to designing my dream kitchen with enough cabinet space to house all my cooking and magical herbs. In alphabetical order, of course. I take the blueprints and a notebook into the living room, sitting at the couch and sketching out my ideas for how to arrange the layout of the kitchen.

"Do you think double ovens are overkill?" I ask Lucas when he takes a seat next to me. "I kinda want something like you have in your Chicago house, but that's just so much, ya know?"

"You're the only one the kitchen actually matters to. Have it how you want it, no expense spared."

"Do you know how dangerous that is to say? Kitchen renovations can easily exceed six figures."

"I'm expecting to invest a couple million into our house at least. Go crazy."

I smile. "Don't say I didn't warn you."

He laughs and puts his arm around me. We're sitting in the living room with sunlight streaming through the open window, talking about our future house together. It's so normal it feels weird.

"What about the other rooms?" I ask. "Is there anything you want to give input on?"

"The master bathroom."

"You don't use the bathroom," I say slowly, still having a hard time being able to grasp that concept. He drinks blood and then it just, what, absorbs into his body? It makes my head hurt if I think about it too much.

"The shower, specifically. I like large showers and a whirlpool tub."

"I think I can get on board with that. Ohh! What about one of those super fancy clawfoot whirlpool tubs?"

"As long as it's big enough for us to have sex in, I'm fine with anything."

"You're easy to please."

He nods. "I really am. Especially when it comes to you."

"Lucky for me." I smile and set the blueprints down. "Are you bored?" I ask, unable to help myself.

"Not particularly. Why, are you?"

I shrug. "When I'm busy, all I want is a day to do nothing. But then I get a day to do nothing and I feel like I should be doing something productive, and it feels even weirder when I know I should be acting like normal which makes me question what normal really is to me."

Lucas laughs. "You and normal don't really pair well together, which is something I love about you, you know."

"I do."

"If this were a normal day off, what would you be doing?"

My eyes go to the front yard. "I'd lay out in the sun and try to get a little color to my skin."

"Then go lay out in the sun."

"But you—"

"Can't? Shocking, right?"

I frown. "I feel bad."

"Are you going to wear a bikini? Or better yet tan topless?"

"I've always had a fear of getting a sunburn on my nipples. So, no to topless."

Lucas chuckles. "Go lay out and tan and I'll play the part of a stalker who watches you from behind curtained windows. I have access to my work files and have plenty to do, as well as research a new investment."

"Okay."

He kisses me before I get up and go upstairs, changing into a black two-piece swimsuit. Kristy and I haven't yet gone to Lake Michigan this summer. The water is still freezing, so we'll be strictly beach-bound, only walking knee-deep into the lake when we're dying from the heat.

Nicole and Naomi's family owns a large piece of land along the shore, and they've thrown some amazing beach parties before. I should call them later and—shit, right. I can't call them. I'm suspended from the coven and they are still active members. I swallow the lump in my throat and grab an old comforter, taking it outside to the yard to lie on.

Fifteen minutes into my tanning session, Kristy calls.

"Hey. Are you okay?" I answer.

"I am. I assume you are, but I never really know."

"Yeah. I'm fine. I'm outside tanning."

"Oh, sounds nice. It's hot out, though. Be careful."

"I will, *Mom*," I reply with a smile. "How's work? I can still come in."

"That's actually why I'm calling. I used magic to find the perfect seasonal employee to work the rest of the summer. I won't do anything without your approval, but it might be a good idea to let them cover for you until things settle down."

My stomach sinks as the gravity of the situation hits me all over again. "That's a good idea, actually. For the sake of making payroll easy, just keep them in the system as me."

"I'm pretty sure that's illegal, Cal, but I'll handle it. Are you okay not working for a while, though?"

"Yeah. Lucas has offered before to be my undead sugar daddy. I never agreed out of principle, but it's starting to look like a legitimate option given the fact I've had a hard time living a normal life lately."

"He's got a lot of money, doesn't he?"

"Probably more than even I'm aware of. It still feels like it goes against some sort of moral feminist code to just take money from him."

Kristy laughs. "It'd be one thing if you were stringing him along just for the money, and another if you were a good-for-nothing trophy wife or something like that. But you've kind of been busy saving the coven and then, oh, the whole town."

"True. And you know I can get snappy when I'm running on little sleep."

"You said it, not me," she laughs again. "So, you're fine with getting Danielle on the schedule?"

"Yes, but seriously don't hesitate if you guys need anything. I can lay low and avoid you while still working, you know."

"I do. And this will be over soon. I'm sure of it."

The lump in my throat is back again. I really want to believe her, but I have this sinking feeling it's only the beginning.

CHAPTER 9

I look at Lucas's car that's parked right in front of the porch. "If this doesn't work, you can move fast enough to come back inside before you explode, right?"

"I'd burn for a good few seconds before I'd explode."

I hike one eyebrow and look up at Lucas. He's standing next to me, and towers over my frame. I'm taller than the average woman, and Lucas is much taller than the average man. Even as a human with no special powers or enhanced strength, he was intimidating.

"That doesn't answer my question."

"Yes, I can move fast enough."

"Good," I say as I let out a breath. "Because you dying would really fucking suck, you know."

"I'd hope."

After getting everything sorted out with work, I laid out in the sun until my skin got too hot to stand it anymore, and then went inside to tell Lucas we should go to Chicago and finally have that hot date.

I showered, packed my bags, and cast the same spell on the car windows that I used in the house. My stuff is in the trunk,

81

and my familiars are in the backseat of Lucas's car, waiting to come to Chicago with us.

"I'll go out first," I tell Lucas, though he knows the plan. I've only gone over it a million times. Quickly slipping out the door, I run out to the car and get into the driver's side. Double-checking that the doors are unlocked, I look through the tinted glass and suck in my breath, holding it until Lucas zooms out of the house and into the car. His skin is smoldering from that short time in the sun, but once the door closes, he starts to heal.

"You're not going to burst into flames?" I ask.

He shakes his head and looks around his car in wonder, with a similar expression on his face to a kid walking into the Magic Kingdom at Disney World. Seeing things for the first time in the daylight seems to have that effect on him.

"Does it look that much different than it does at night?" I ask and shift the gear into drive.

"No, but it feels that much different. It's warm." He puts his hand on the dash. "And smells like sunshine."

Looking back at my familiars—and the thick blanket I stashed just in case—I let my foot fall against the pedal and drive out of town.

"THANK YOU," I TELL THE GROCERY DELIVERY GUY AND HAND HIM A hefty tip. Lucas and I have been at his Chicago mansion for about an hour now, and the first thing I did was order food. There was still stuff here from the last time I ordered, but since I plan on spending the week in the city, I figured I might as well get a head start on stuffing my face with junk food.

"Have a nice day," the young man says, pocketing the money and curiously looking inside the house. This place is huge, super fancy, and is worth the most out of all the houses on this ostentatious street in Lincoln Park. It's the last place you'd expect a super old and powerful vampire to live, and the stark and modern decor only furthers that notion.

I telekinetically close the front door and drag all the grocery bags into the kitchen. My phone rings as I'm unloading the last bit of food. It's my sister.

"Hey, Abby," I say, putting the phone on speaker and setting it on the large island counter.

"Callie. It's good hearing your voice."

"You say that like you haven't heard from me in forever."

"Well, I never know if you'll actually answer."

"Oh, right. I'm, uh…I'm sorry. Things can be kind of crazy and it's been—"

"It's okay," she says quickly. "I was wondering what you're doing tonight."

"Tonight? Nothing, actually. Why?"

"Do you and Lucas want to come over for dinner?"

I blink, letting her words sink in. "Yeah. We'd love to." A smile takes over my face.

"Are you at your place or in Chicago?" she asks.

"We're in Chicago. Just got here, actually."

"Lucas can travel during the day?"

"Yeah. There are ways for vampires to get around during daylight hours, and I kind of have a magical way of making the sunlight not hurt Lucas."

"Oh, uh. Wow." Silence falls between us for a few seconds. I pull the band from my ponytail. "So, when's a good time to come over? Phil and I both have the night and then tomorrow off."

"Once the sun goes down. Is that too late for Penny?"

"Lord no," she says with a laugh. "That kid hasn't been sleeping very well lately. It's a Wonder Week."

"What's that?"

"A growth spurt that messes with her sleep cycle, her happiness, and basically my sanity. She might be up. She might not be."

"Well, I hope she's up. Totally selfish of me, I know. But I'd love to snuggle that little girl."

"I'm sure she'll love that too."

"Do you want me to bring anything?" I ask.

"No, I've got it covered, though if you brought some wine I wouldn't object."

I laugh. "The good thing about sleeping with someone who owns a bar is basically unlimited access to alcohol of all kinds. I'll bring something expensive that I don't have to pay for."

"Sounds good. I'm making that sour cream chicken Rosita used to make. Do you remember it?"

"I do." Rosita was our nanny who doubled as a cook most nights. The last time I saw her was the day before I was sold to the highest bidder at a research laboratory. "I haven't had that in a long time. Sounds good."

"I hope I do it justice. Does Lucas need anything? I know he, uh, doesn't eat food."

"I don't think so. This is actually our first dinner party we've been invited to as a couple."

"Oh, is it weird? Being with someone who doesn't eat food?" Since Abby told me she wants to be involved in each other's lives again, she hasn't held back on her questions. It's oddly comforting to be poked and prodded about all things magic in my life. She's really trying to understand my world.

"Kind of," I admit. "Sometimes I think it would be so convenient to not have to eat but then again, I'd miss it."

"Me too. I love snacking."

"And I love wine."

"It would save me so much time."

"I know, right?" I laugh. "I hate cooking. Though, Lucas has been trying to cook for me lately. It's sweet, even though he's a terrible cook."

Abby laughs. "That's so weird to think about. I'm trying, Cal, really, but the thought of that vampire standing in front of the oven." She starts laughing again.

"He looks good in an apron."

"I think he'd look good in anything."

I close my eyes and bring a hand to my face. "He really does."

"So tonight. Right after sunset?"

"We will be there."

"Good. I miss you, sis."

"I miss you too, Abby. Especially lately."

"Has something happened?"

"Something is always happening," I confess. "I'm looking forward to a normal dinner, with normal food and normal conversation."

"I can promise you normal here. We're not that exciting."

"Sometimes that's a good thing. Because lately for me, exciting means demonic possession and evil blackmailing witches."

"I…I don't even know what to say to that."

I laugh. "Tell me we're going to talk about the weather and work and other boring stuff."

"Can we talk about magic just a little?"

"Of course. Phil's okay with it?"

"He's showing interest. I know it scares him, just like vampires do. Honestly I don't think he believed me when I told him about everything you could do."

"It's a hard pill to swallow, especially for people who haven't seen it firsthand. I still remember how unreal it felt to walk into Grim Gate Academy for the first time and see a whole new world of magic."

"I'm sure it would be. I love you, Callie, and I'm proud of you. I feel like I haven't told you that enough. But I do."

"I love you too, Abby. See you later."

I end the call, set my phone down, and put the last few cold items away before finding Lucas in his office. It looks like he's on a video chat with someone, and he's not speaking English again. He holds up his hand, letting me know it'll be a minute, and I slip back out of the office and into the kitchen while I wait.

I'm finishing up my sandwich when Lucas comes in.

"Do you care if we go over to my sister's tonight? I sort of RSVP'd for us already," I admit.

"Do you want to go?" he asks carefully, and I know what he's thinking. The last few interactions I've had with my biological family haven't ended well. But Abby is trying so damn hard, and I miss my sister, now more than ever.

"I do. It'll be nice to have a low-key night with Abby."

"Then we'll go."

I smile. "Thank you. I also said I'd bring wine, so I need to go out and get some."

"Take whatever car you'd like."

"Walking is fine. I hate finding parking."

Lucas chuckles, kisses me, and goes back into his office to work. I clean up after myself in the kitchen and then go upstairs to get a comfortable pair of shoes to walk in. I throw my purse over my shoulder and call Binx to come with me. The dress I'm wearing is black at its base, with multicolored flowers printed all over it. I add a black floppy hat and oversized sunglasses and head out, fully knowing how cliché I look walking down the street dressed like this with my black cat trotting along next to me.

And I love it.

～

I TUCK THE BOTTLE OF WINE UNDER MY ARM AND RING ABBY'S doorbell. Lucas rests his hand on the small of my back, fingers gently pressing into my skin. A few seconds pass before Abby opens the door with a smile on her face.

"Hey, sis," she says and steps to the side. "Oh, right. I have to invite you in. Please come in, Lucas."

"You've already invited him once," I say, stepping inside. "The offer stands until you rescind the invitation."

"I didn't know you could do that." Abby closes the door behind us.

"All you have to say is 'I rescind your invitation' with the intended vampire in mind," Lucas tells her. "It will force them out of the house."

"Really? And they can't get back in?"

"Not until you invite them again."

Abby shakes her head. "That's just...so weird. I don't get why you can't walk into a house uninvited. It makes no sense."

"There's ancient magic in declaring a house a home," Lucas explains, taking off his shoes after I give him a pointed look. I don't wear shoes in the house, and I know Abby wouldn't want us tracking germs all over the floor when she has a one-year-old toddling around. "It offers very basic protection, but unfortunately only against those of us who operate on those same basic principles of magic."

"And I thought medical school was complicated."

"Don't think about it too hard," I tell her. "That's what I do, at least. Especially when it comes to different dimensions. Instant headache."

"I can only imagine." She leads us into the house. "I hope you're hungry. I might have gone a little overboard on the appetizers."

"I'm starving," I tell her and she turns, looking from me to Lucas.

"Should I have bought bottled blood?" she whispers.

"No."

"I feel like I'm being rude, though. Inviting you both over for dinner and then making you watch us eat."

"I already ate," Lucas tells her and Abby's face tenses. She's trying to be okay with this, but I know it weirds her out. By Lucas saying he already ate, she knows he bit me and sucked blood out of my body, which *is* weird when I think about it too. "And human food has no appeal to me anymore. Besides, I watch Callie eat all the time."

"I do eat a lot." I give Abby a reassuring smile as we make our way through the foyer and into the kitchen. Abby lives in Lincoln Park, just minutes from Lucas. "Is Penny awake?"

"She is. Phil is giving her an emergency bath after a diaper explosion."

"Sounds fun."

"It's the second one today. She had a ton of blueberries for breakfast and the aftermath is catching up to us. How someone so little can poop so much is beyond me." She gets out two wine glasses and sets them on the counter. "Do I need to get the wine opener, or can you…"

"Do this?" I set my wine down and hold my hand over the bottle, telekinetically pulling the cork from the bottle.

"That alone makes me wish I could do magic."

I pour two glasses and take a seat at a barstool. Lucas sits next to me and rests his hand on my thigh. "How's work?"

"Busy, though I've only worked about sixteen hours since I saw you last. I'm on a pretty good rotation right now which is perfect since Phil's been doing a lot of surgery." She takes a drink. "And you're…you're okay? The last time I saw you, you were covered in blood."

"I'm fine."

"Physically, you are. But what happened?"

"It will be handled," Lucas tells her, and I take a big drink of wine. We don't know who sent the vampire bounty hunters after me or how they found out I was a witch in the first place. Lucas still has one of the vampires who hurt me locked in a cell in the basement of the bar. He pulled out her fangs, and without fresh blood, they won't be growing back anytime soon.

"Good. And you said something about demons? Is that, uh, related to the reason you came into the ER?"

"No, that's something entirely different." I swirl the red wine around in my glass and silence falls over us for a few seconds.

"So, tell me about that house you guys bought," Abby says, changing the subject. She gulps down the rest of her wine and goes to the oven, checking on the appetizers she's keeping warm.

I tell her about the plans for the restoration as I help her set the table.

"That's exciting," she says, getting another bottle of wine from a little wine fridge in the kitchen. "I can't wait to see it all finished."

"Me too. It will be a while, though. The house has to be pretty much gutted before we can even start on the fun stuff, like doing the kitchen and the bathroom. I'm also really looking forward to putting a pool and a hot tub in the backyard. And then I can have parties. Hopefully by next summer, you guys can come over and swim or something."

"I'd really like that." Abby takes a bowl of salad to the table and then comes back into the kitchen. Her phone is on the counter and starts buzzing. She picks it up and quickly ends the call, but not before I see who's calling.

"You can answer," I tell her. "I don't care."

"Mom calls all the time," she says, giving that as her reason not to answer. "Oh shit, I'm sorry. I didn't mean it like that. I know she doesn't...that you two don't..."

"It's fine, Abby. I really have made my peace."

Abby nods and looks from me to Lucas. "You must think we're terrible people."

"I do," he agrees, and I elbow him in the ribs. "You are excluded, of course."

"I don't blame you," I press. "And please, drop it before I put a memory charm on you making you forget everything that happened," I joke.

"Or turn her into a cat," Lucas adds under his breath.

"You can do that?" Abby asks.

I purse my lips and glare at Lucas. "No. Absolutely not and I've never accidentally transfigured anyone before."

Abby cocks an eyebrow and refills her glass. "I'm trying to keep my questions to a minimum because I know how annoying it can be, but what?"

"Transfiguration is a type of magic. It's the way werewolves shift and the way my familiars can take on the form of a regular animal."

"And you can transfigure people?" Her eyes are as wide as saucers.

"And objects. It's not my strongest area of magic. I'm better at conjuring."

"Don't be modest," Lucas starts. "You're incredible, Callie. Downplaying it does you no favors."

"It feels weird to brag about how I accidentally turned someone who fully deserved it into a fat orange cat."

Abby almost chokes on her wine and Phil walks into the kitchen, holding Penny close to his chest. Her curly hair is still damp from her bath, and she's wearing the cutest pink footy pajamas.

"Hey, Phil." I force a smile. "And Penny."

"Callie. Hello." He meets my eyes, returning my smile, and then looks at Lucas but doesn't risk looking at his face. "And, uh, Lucas."

I can see Abby silently yelling at Phil to behave, and I'm sure they had a strongly worded discussion before she invited me over. I'm not too sure on where Phil stands on the whole vampire assimilation movement.

"Thanks for inviting us over for dinner," I say. Penny starts to squirm out of her father's arms, whimpering for her mom. Phil makes a move to set her down but stops, realizing that she's going to have to toddle past Lucas before she gets to Abby.

For a second, nobody moves. And then Phil sets Penny on the ground, walking behind her as she makes her way over to Abby.

"Did you drive the McLaren today?" Phil asks Lucas.

"We walked today," he replies. "Want to take it out later? It hasn't been driven in a while and I don't like my cars just sitting."

Phil's eyes light up. "I, uh, yeah...I mean...it's not good to just like them sit," he sputters. "Cars? You have more than one McLaren?"

"Not in Chicago."

"Lucas has a lot of cars," I add. "I like the Chevelle the best. He's been the only owner and bought it new back in, what, the 70s?"

Lucas nods. "I still have the very first car I ever bought, actually. It's at my property in California."

"A Model T?"

"From 1910."

Phil's smile grows and he looks at Abby. "That's...that's incredible. Did you buy it here in the US? You haven't always lived here, have you?"

"No, I'm originally from what you'd call Rome today. I first came to the Americas in the late sixteenth century and then took up permanent residence here after the Civil War."

Phil slowly shakes his head. "Wow. I, uh, I don't know if Abby ever mentioned it, but I'm a bit of a history nerd. I never stopped and thought about how someone like you has lived through so much."

"I've seen the worst and best of humanity over the last thousand years."

"You were there then?" Phil takes the glass of wine Abby just poured for him. "During the Civil War?"

"Phil, chill a little," Abby says under her breath.

"It's all right," Lucas tells her as we all move into the dining room. "And I was. As a vampire, I try to avoid human affairs, but there was one night when the Confederate Army marched through my land." Lucas gets a distant look in his eye as he thinks back.

"He's not going to shut up all night," Abby warns with a smile. She slips Penny into her highchair and goes back into the kitchen to get the chicken.

"I don't think Lucas minds." I follow behind her, helping her carry out dinner. "As long as Phil doesn't start asking about his human life. Lucas doesn't seem to like to talk about it."

"You said you thought he was turned against his will, right?"

"He was. I know that now. A human paid a vampire to turn

him so he could force Lucas to fight in an underground ring. He said he didn't even know vampires were real until he became one."

"Holy shit."

"I know. It was a long time ago, but I can't imagine getting over that kind of mental trauma...like, ever."

She nods and gets a bag of shredded cheese from the fridge. "My classy girl is on a cheese and Mandarin oranges for dinner kick right now."

"That doesn't sound too bad, actually."

"At least it's not blueberries," Abby laughs. We go back into the dining room and start dinner. Everything is good, and Phil and Lucas talk about history and cars throughout the meal.

Most of Penny's food ends up on the floor by the time we're done eating, and I'm starting to see what Abby meant by the sweet little girl being crabby. Phil takes her upstairs to try to get her to bed, leaving Abby to walk us to the door.

"I had a really nice time," I tell her. "Thanks again for inviting us."

Abby beams. "I'm glad you guys came. We'll do this again," she promises.

"Yeah," I say back with a smile. "We will."

CHAPTER 10

I lift my glass up and move it half an inch, pressing it down on the table so it leaves a water ring on the surface. I repeat the process, making a pattern with the condensation.

"I never knew a glass of water could be so entertaining." Eliza slides a cocktail in front of me and leans back, crossing her arms. Lucas is in the office at the bar tonight, and I've been sitting at a table in the back for the last half-hour reading. I just finished my book and am still reeling from the cliffhanger ending. The next book doesn't come out for three months, dammit.

"Thanks," I tell Eliza, and take a sip of the cocktail. It's our first interaction since I astral projected into the bar and saw something I'll never be able to unsee. I'm sure Lucas has ordered her to try to get along with me again. We had made headway until *the incident*. "So, about what I saw—"

"Forget it." She stiffly sits down across from me. "You saw two vampires fucking. It's not much different than two humans fucking, well, only better."

"Sex with a vampire is better."

"Ew, don't put that visual in my head." She pushes a strand of her blonde hair back behind her ear. She's incredibly pretty, with soft and delicate features that remind me of Kristy in a way.

Pretty, blonde, and innocent-looking. But both Kristy and Eliza have powers you'd never suspect.

"Have you turned anyone else into a cat lately?"

"Not lately. Why, you have someone you want to be catified?"

"Catified?"

"Or any other animal. I can't promise it'll work, though."

She lets out a snort of laughter and tips her head, watching me. I've been in Chicago for three days, and the lack of communication from my coven is starting to really bother me, which is why Lucas suggested I get out of the house and go out tonight. He should be done with whatever he's doing soon.

"What about a vampire?" Eliza asks. "Do you think you could transfigure a vampire?"

"I'm not sure," I answer honestly. "Maybe? Though transfiguring them back would be much harder. You do have someone you want cursed, don't you?"

Her shoulders fall up and down in a shrug. "Not currently, but it's always good to have options."

Two guys come over to the table, sipping whiskey out of Mason jars. "We couldn't help but notice you were drinking alone," the one with a beard says.

"I know she's easy to overlook, but I'm not alone," Eliza retorts and draws her fangs. "And I don't drink."

"I told you she was one," the other guy says to beard-guy. "That's so hot."

Eliza rolls her eyes. "It is, I know."

"Can I buy you a bottle of blood then?" non-beard guy asks. "Or offer you something a little fresher?"

"No thanks, I already ate." Eliza forces another smile. She's acting annoyed, but I know she's eating the attention up.

"What about your friend?" beard-guy asks, looking at me. "Does she want a drink?"

"She's not my friend, she already has a drink, and trust me when I say she's crazy."

"I like crazy," beard-guy laughs and takes another sip of whiskey.

"Not this kind of crazy." Eliza tips her head and sniffs the air. "Speaking of crazy," she huffs, and I follow her gaze to the front of the bar. The lighting is dim already, and the energy shifts, making almost everyone stop and stare at the two redheaded bombshells that just walked in.

"Naomi and Nicole!" I exclaim, getting up so fast I almost trip over beard-guy. "What are you guys doing here?"

"We came to see you, dummy," Naomi says dryly. "And it's our half-birthday. We're going out tonight and taking you with."

"You celebrate your half-birthday?" Eliza looks Naomi up and down and then checks out Nicole. They're twins but aren't identical.

"Why not?" Naomi sinks into a chair across from Eliza and grins. "I'll take any excuse to celebrate how awesome I am."

Eliza holds her gaze for a second and then smiles back. "I like the way you think. Drinks on the house tonight. What do you want?"

"Surprise me." Naomi leans forward, raising her eyebrows. Eliza's smile grows and she gets up, moving with vampire speed to the bar. Kristy comes in the bar a minute later, throwing her arms around me as soon as she gets to the table.

"It's only been like a week and I miss you." She takes a seat next to me. "You two could have waited for me. Finding parking is a bitch around here, you know."

Naomi laughs. "We like to make an entrance."

"*You* like to make an entrance," Nicole counters. "And I agree with Kristy. I've missed you too, Callie. It's total bullshit you were suspended."

"Tabatha had to do something drastic. She's been accused of favoring me before."

"Because she does," everyone says at the same time and we all laugh.

"Have you heard anything?" I run my finger down the water glass, wiping away a few more beads of condensation.

"Nothing good," Naomi says quickly. "But we're not here to talk about that. We're here to look hot, get drunk, and live our best lives tonight."

"I can get behind that," I say.

"Good. Because that's what we're doing." Naomi looks over at the bar. "Who's the hot blonde again? I was a little distracted trying not to be eaten by zombies the last time we met."

"That's Eliza. She's Lucas's vampire daughter or whatever you'd consider her."

"Does she like to party?"

"I don't think she likes to have fun. At all." I watch Eliza come back over to the table, carrying a tray of drinks with perfect grace, impressive for how fast she's moving.

"Now I just don't believe that." Naomi picks up her drink and licks sugar off the rim before taking a drink. "This is good. I say we pregame here and then find something a little more lively."

"Pregame?" Eliza sets the rest of the drinks down on the table.

"It means drink before you go out drinking and is something college-aged people do, not us old people," Kristy laughs.

"I know what pregaming means," Eliza snaps.

"Told you she likes to have fun." Naomi leans back and smiles. "It's just too bad you can't get drunk."

"Oh, I can." Eliza puts her hands on the table, smiling in a way that shows off her fangs. She's used to being able to scare humans this way, but won't get the same reaction from me or my friends. "If the person I'm feeding from is drunk enough."

"Then come out with us. I'd love to see that."

"Really?" Nicole looks at her twin incredulously.

"What?" Naomi innocently shrugs. "Tonight is about having fun and forgetting about the bullshit going on within our own coven. Though if I drink enough tonight you might be able to convince me to start our own."

"Ugh, witches and drama." Eliza rolls her eyes again, which

96

I'm realizing is a signature move for her. "But you know what, I'm bored. Watching you four get drunk and act like idiots is better than reality TV."

"Perfect," Naomi says, picking up her drink. "Let's get this party started."

∼

"I love this song!" Kristy loops her arm though mine. We're two bars into bar hopping our way around Chicago, and if we keep drinking at the rate we are, we aren't going to make it to very many more bars after this.

Which is fine with me.

I'm having fun with my friends, and the most shocking thing of all is that I think Eliza might be having fun too. She spent the first hour making snide comments, but she either stopped or maybe I'm just drunk enough now not to notice.

"Dance with me!" I suck down the rest of my drink, not wanting to leave it unattended, and get off the leather couch I was sitting on. We're at some swanky bar that is bordering on a nightclub downtown. This place is hard to get into, and we might have used magic to put our names on the guest list. The DJ here today is someone famous, but their name rang no bell for me.

"That guy over there is totally eye-fucking you, Callie." Nicole, who's just as drunk as I am, wraps her arms around me and laughs. "Or maybe he's eye-fucking me. Because I'm standing here now."

"Where?" I lean back, obviously looking in his direction.

"No, don't look now!" Nicole giggles.

"Ohhh, he's cute!"

"You think so?"

Kristy spins in a circle, looking around for the guy. "I do! If you don't want him, I'll take him."

"Go talk to him," I say, not sure which friend I'm encouraging to go hit on the hot guy by the bar. "I need to pee." I slip out of

Nicole's arms and weave my way through the crowd to find the bathroom. I'm happily drunk, aware that I'm just about at my limit of having too much if I keep drinking.

I use the bathroom and then stop at the mirror to put on more lipstick.

"I love your hair," a very drunk girl tells me, wobbling her way out of the bathroom stall and over to the sink.

"Thank you. Yours is really pretty too."

"Aww, you think so?" She looks at herself in the mirror. "I can't get it to hold a curl like yours, though. How'd you do it?"

"Magic."

"I wish I could do magic!"

"It is very handy."

"And your dress! Oh my God, you're just so pretty." The drunk girl cups her hands around her face, looking me up and down. I changed before we went out into a tight black dress and dark purple heels.

"Thanks," I tell her again and look at myself in the mirror. "It's not very comfortable, though. Well, maybe it's just the bra." The pushup bra makes my boobs look ridiculously big, achieving the look I wanted perfectly.

I pull my phone from my purse to take a mirror selfie to send to Lucas, because right now that seems like the best idea in the world. He's either still at the bar or back at home, I'm not sure. But now that I'm thinking about him, I suddenly miss him. Specifically, his cock.

Holding my phone in my hand in anticipation for Lucas's reply to my text, I leave the bathroom and go out to find my friends. Naomi and Eliza have a group of men around them. Nicole and Kristy seemed to have given up talking to the hottie by the bar and are dancing together on the middle of the dance floor. I step to the side, letting a group of bachelorettes pass by me to get to the bathroom, and smile, looking at my friends again.

I love them so fucking much.

My heel catches on the floor and I drop my phone in an attempt to catch my balance.

"Shit," I mumble and drop to the ground to look for it. Someone walks by and kicks it under a table. Positive no one will notice, I hold out my hand and telekinetically bring it to me. Smiling triumphantly, I straighten back up. My phone dings with a text from Lucas.

"Please be a dick pic," I say out loud and then laugh. Right as I'm holding the phone up to my face to use the facial recognition to unlock it, something vibrates through the air. I lower the phone and whirl around.

The last time I was drunk in a bar and felt the energy shift like this, a vampire was feeding off an unwilling human in the basement. This, though...this doesn't feel like a vampire.

It feels bigger, which doesn't make sense. I'm drunk and confused. Yeah...that has to be it. I hold up my phone again and this time I get so far as unlocking it. Before I can read Lucas's words, the same vibration echoes through the bar. I'm not paying attention to what I'm doing as I look around again, and somehow, I've accidentally called Lucas.

"Oh, hey," I say after hearing him call my name. "I didn't mean to call you."

"I was hoping you were calling for phone sex."

I close my eyes and feel the world spin around me. "Hah, that kind of sounds nice. Though real sex would be better."

"Oh, it will be. Are you having fun?"

"I think so." I take a breath and open my eyes again, stepping back into the hall that leads to the bathroom. The hall keeps going, leading to a door with an emergency exit. The same vibrating energy pulses through the air, and I slowly start to walk toward the exit door.

"You think?" Lucas laughs. "Maybe you need more to drink."

"There's a vibration."

"Are you trying to be kinky?"

"No, it's like...it's like that scene in Jurassic Park when they're hiding in the car and the T-Rex is stomping. It makes the water in the cup ripple. Do you know what I'm talking about?"

"Yeah, I do, but I'm not following."

"I'm not really following either." I stop walking and lean against the wall. "Are you still at work?"

"Yes."

"Loser."

Lucas laughs again. "Go have fun with your friends, and don't worry about vibrating until you get back into bed with me."

"Sounds good to me." I end the call, put the phone in my purse and head back to the dance floor. I'm in the middle of a sea of people when I get that same weird feeling, but this time it's paired with another feeling, one I'm all too familiar with.

It sinks heavy in my stomach and makes my nerves tingle.

Shit. I know this feeling well and know it's usually not wrong. Because when I feel like something bad is going to happen, it always does.

CHAPTER 11

G et it together.
Tonight is all about having fun with my friends. No stress. No worry. No following creepy feelings that are probably the result of too many vodka tonics. I hold my arms out to my sides and shake my hands, ridding myself of the access energy that's making me feel all jittery.

I go back out to the main area of the bar, and Kristy pulls me onto the dance floor. Twenty minutes later, I'm hot and sweaty and still haven't shaken the feeling that something is lurking around the corner, waiting to attack.

There's a little hole-in-the-wall restaurant across the street from the bar that's open late, no doubt making a killing from all the drunk people who walk over night after night. I get a hot dog —Chicago style, of course—and a Coke simply for the caffeine. I sit on a bench along the street while I eat, watching people mill in and out of the bar.

I take my time eating, enjoying the little reprieve away from all the people at the bar. When I'm finished, I ball up the hot dog wrapper, impressed I didn't get any mustard on my dress. I throw away the wrapper and walk down to the corner to cross the street and go back inside. I'm sobering up little by little and will no doubt need to down a drink or two to catch up with my friends.

It's a little after midnight, and the line to get into the bar is longer now than it was when we got here about an hour ago. I already bespelled the bouncer and can easily walk right past everyone in line.

"Hey," some girl shouts, angry that I'm bypassing the line. I turn around to tell her to just come along with me and stop throwing a fit like a baby, but something else catches my attention.

Light from the streetlamps above us illuminate the face of a man standing at the back of the line, and I swear his eyes glowed blue for the half-second our gazes met. It wasn't quite as bright and brilliant as the blue-eyed man, but there was definitely something not human about that guy. A bit of shock crosses his face, like he's surprised I looked his way.

My breath leaves me, and I spin so fast I almost lose my balance in these stupid heels. I take off, running as fast as I can down the sidewalk.

"Hey!" I call after the man, who's briskly walking away from me. The streetlight above me starts to flicker, and I don't think I'm the one doing it. I push through people waiting in line, trying to find the man with the maybe-glowing blue eyes. It sounds crazy even to me, but I'm not willing to chalk this up to having too much to drink or a trick of the light.

I know what I felt, and now I know what I saw.

The man, who's tall with dark eyes and dark hair, moves into an alley alongside the bar. I take off, heels clicking and clacking. Loose gravel crunches under my feet, and the light dims as I move away from the building. The alley comes to a dead end between the surrounding buildings, with just enough room for a garbage truck to back up and empty the dumpster.

The door leading to the bar is locked from the inside, and the doors and windows of the building butting up to it have been boarded up. Colorful graffiti covers the plywood and I stop, looking up and down the alley.

"Hello?" I call out. There's nowhere for that man to have gone. The hair on the back of my neck starts to prickle, and the bad feeling presses down on me even stronger than before. It's hot outside, yet a chill goes through me. "Where the hell did you go?"

I can hear the bass thumping from inside the bar. Bringing my arms close to my body, I inch forward, looking at the buildings. There has to be a way inside one of these. He can't just disappear, and I know he came down here.

The dumpster, which is so full it's almost overflowing, stinks to high heaven, thanks to the heat no doubt. I cover my nose with my hair and walk around it, holding my right hand out in front of me just in case the guy is a crazy person in hiding, waiting to attack me.

But he's not behind the dumpster.

Gagging from the smell of thrown-away food left to fester in the summer heat, I hurry away from the dumpster, feeling even more confused. It's dark back here, and I know I'm missing something. I look out at the street, making sure no one is watching, and conjure a string of blue magic to light the area.

And that's when I see it, a gray feather floating on the top of a puddle. I ball my fists, turning the string of magic into an energy ball, and toss it up into the air. It hovers above me like a lightbulb, shining down on the feather.

I crouch down and pick it up. The moment my fingers make contact, something passes through me, something I can't even begin to explain to myself because it makes no sense.

The feather is familiar. Holding it in my hand is giving me a sense of peace, making me feel like everything is going to be all right.

Dirty water drips from the tip, but I don't care. I run my finger up the spine of the feather. If this were from a bird, the thing has to have wings that span at least six feet. I hold the feather up a little closer to the energy ball, needing to get a better look.

It's deep gray in color with flecks of iridescent silvers. Birds aren't that color. Hell, nothing in nature is that color. It's so beautiful, and I can't stop staring.

Loose gravel crunches under someone's feet behind me. I put out the ball of energy, shove the feather in my purse, and turn around, holding out my hand to stop whoever is coming toward me. It's a young guy, probably a few days shy of his twenty-first birthday, and is here with a fake ID, no doubt. He's staggering, with shoulder-length brown hair hanging around his face.

"Bar's that way," I tell him and point at the other end of the alley. "And if you came back here to take a piss, find another dark alley. This one is occupied."

The guy keeps staggering forward. How drunk is he?

A cold finger reaches out and moves down my spine. My hand flies to the back of my neck, reaching for whoever touched me. I whip around, heels catching on the uneven ground. My ankle twists, and I throw out a hand to stop my fall. I hit the dumpster hard, sending a shock of pain up through my wrist.

"Dammit."

The man advances and grabs my shoulders.

"Hey," I yell and bring my leg up, kneeing him hard in the balls. He doesn't even react to the pain. I telekinetically shove him away and he staggers back a few feet. He raises his head, and the dim light from above shines down on his face. The veins on his neck and cheeks are raised and swollen, appearing like black lines against his pale skin.

He's not the man I saw with glowing eyes, that's for fucking sure.

"What the hell?" I hold out my hand, creating a shield of energy to keep him from advancing toward me anymore. The guy runs toward it, eyes clouding over. He crashes against the wall of energy and then staggers back, tripping over his own feet. He falls hard against the ground, head whacking the pavement.

He doesn't get up and come at me again. Instead, his body starts to shudder, and black ooze drips from his mouth, collecting in a puddle on the ground that then starts to boil, billowing up as steam. It moves like a dark cloud, slipping through the air vents of the building next door.

"What the hell?" I repeat, staring at the man on the ground. The black veins on his face start to fade, and I shake myself. I rush forward and drop to my knees, putting my fingers to the man's neck. The bad feeling is back, and I don't need to feel the lack of pulse to know this guy is already dead.

Goosebumps break out over my skin, and I'm overtaken with the urge to run far, far away. I stand up, breathing fast, and back away from the body.

Holy shit.

Eyes on the body, I blindly bring my hand up and into my purse with the intention of getting my phone to call the police. My fingers brush over the feather, and something other than fear floods through my veins. I look at the air vent on the side of the building and then back at the body. Whatever was in him—whatever killed him—is loose and hiding inside the building.

I need to find it and kill it.

I run my fingers over the spine of the feather once more and then bring my hand out in front of me, telekinetically ripping the vent from the brick. I hike the strap of my purse up over my shoulder and conjure an energy ball, gently tossing it into the air vent. It feeds directly into the building, and I climb through, dress bunching up around my waist as I drop down several feet.

I splay my fingers and the energy ball spreads out, lighting up the room. I'm in an abandoned laundry mat, and half the washers are hanging open. Dust covers the old green tile floor, and the place smells like mold and dirty clothes.

"Come out, come out, wherever you are," I whisper to the darkness. Something rustles through a tangle of long-discarded clothing several yards ahead of me. "Gotcha."

I throw the energy ball, and a rat the size of a small cat goes sprinting away. Dammit.

"Sorry, Mrs. Rat. I hope you didn't have giant babies in there." I conjure another energy ball and walk through the laundry room and into a hall. It splits three ways, and I pause, looking up and down each way. "Where are you, fucker?" I let my eyes fall shut, listening for any sort of call to let me know to go.

But instead of some sort of intuition guiding me, my phone rings. I scramble to silence it. It's Kristy, and she's probably wondering where the hell I am. I answer at the last second, knowing she'll keep calling if I don't answer.

"Hey," I whisper. "I can't talk right now."

"Where are you?"

"In an abandoned building. Long story. Also, there's a dead body in the alley behind the bar."

"What? Did you take something?"

"No, but I did have a hot dog."

Kristy sputters something I can't make out. "Where are you?"

I inch forward, directing the energy ball to move a few feet ahead of me. "The building next to the bar. I got in through an air vent." Suddenly the floor creaks in front of me, and it's like all the air got sucked out of the room. I can't breathe, and my body starts to go cold.

The sound of horse hooves on pavement echoes around me, and my stomach painfully twists. I pitch forward, phone clattering to the ground, bracing myself from the pain. Gritting my teeth, I press my hands over my knees and force myself up. Something is coming closer and closer, and the sound of hooves turns into a low growl.

"Oh shit." I look up just in time to see a huge dog-like creature with yellow eyes lunging at me. I throw my hand up and magically throw the thing into the wall. It snarls, pulling its lips back over its fangs, and gets up, shaking its head.

It comes at me again, and I thrust my hand forward once more. The dog-creature is shoved back, but it's like I'm moving something incredibly heavy and it takes great effort just to throw the thing away from myself. Pain hits my stomach again, like someone shoved a knife, hot out of the fire, into my gut.

Another creature comes down the hall, growling. I plant my feet on the ground and hold out my other hand, ready to take them both on. The creature I'd just thrown into the wall gets up again, but doesn't advance. It stands perfectly still, yellow eyes locking with mine.

It looks like a Mastiff, but instead of sleek fur, it's covered in coarse skin and wiry hairs, much like an elephant. It opens its mouth, revealing teeth three times as long as normal dogs'. Stringy saliva drips from its mouth.

"Don't even think about it," I warn, giving it another shove. It's hard to hold the shield with this pain in my stomach, and I'm trying hard not to break my concentration and look down at myself, because now it feels like warm blood is dripping from an open wound in my abdomen.

The first dog-creature lets out a high-pitched whine and turns, running away from me.

"That's what I thought."

And then the other starts sprinting toward me. The creatures jump into the air at the same time, crashing into each other. A puff of that oozy, black smoke clouds around them, and the bigger of the two lands on the ground first, with its teeth clamped around the other's neck.

It's not killing it, but absorbing it. The two merge together as one, doubling in size.

"The fuck?" My heart speeds up and I send a final shockwave of energy forward, throwing the creature back.

And then I turn and run as fast as I can down the hall.

CHAPTER 12

I skid to a stop, throwing my hands out to keep my balance. Pressing my back up against the wall, I let out my breath and look down the hall behind me.

What the fuck just happened?

Two demonic dogs just merged into one bigger demonic dog.

Holy shit.

I bring my hand to my chest, feeling my heart racing. Calm down. I need to calm down. It's pitch black all around me, and the air is still and stale. I need to conjure an energy ball so I can see what's around me, but it'll be a dead giveaway to where I am, though I'm sure that thing can sense me somehow, and I wouldn't be surprised if it can see in the dark. Dogs can. Demons can.

Demonic dogs certainly can.

Holy shit.

The world spins around me a bit, reminding me that I'm not one hundred percent sober yet. I'd say I'm never drinking again, but if I make it through the night, I'm going to need a big glass of wine.

I plant both hands against the wall and take in a steadying

breath. Pressing my lips together, I lean forward and listen. The dog-creature is here somewhere, lurking and waiting.

And so is the black ooze.

Wait a minute…if the dog-creature is a demon, why hasn't it attacked anyone? There's a freaking bar right next door, pretty much offering up drunks like Happy Meals. As far as I know, there haven't been any reports of people mysteriously missing in this area, and no carnage has been found.

If the creature isn't holing up in this building, using it as hunting grounds then…*fuck*. It's protecting something, and I've stumbled upon something that doesn't want to be found.

But it's all good, right? Two birds and one stone and all. I'll kill that huge, demonic dog and then go after whatever it's protecting. It can't be anything serious.

Hah.

The *Game of Thrones* theme song sounds through the building, scaring me half to death. Right. I dropped my phone, and I'm sure Kristy is calling me back, wondering what the hell I was talking about. Dammit. If she comes out to investigate, she'll be walking right into a trap.

Kristy is a strong, smart witch, but doesn't have the same powers I do. Naomi and Nicole can manipulate energy and might stand a chance…if they weren't drunk.

"Shit," I whisper. Inhaling deep, I push off the wall and conjure strings of magic around my hands. They glow a brilliant blue, lighting up the hall like it's motherfucking Christmas. "Come and get me, asshole!"

I move down the hall, not sure where I'm going. I have no plan other than trying my best not to die. Though, if I cannot die *and* get to my phone, I can tall Kristy and tell her to stay away.

"Look," I start and slowly move my fingers, twisting the strings of magic around them. "I don't know what you're guarding, but I'm sure we can work something out. But let's talk first, okay?"

My heels click against the dirty tile. I'm getting close to the entrance to the laundromat again, and that same weird feeling starts to sink heavily in my stomach.

"Are you shy?" I flick my wrist and send little balls of magic floating into the air in front of me, lighting my way. "There's no need to be shy. I won't bite." I stop and look around. "I'll just blow you up with magic as soon as I get the chance," I add under my breath. "Where the fuck did you go?"

I only ripped an air vent off the building. Please don't tell me the pony-sized demon dog didn't somehow squeeze through. My phone rings again, and I freeze, moving up against the wall.

The floor creaks and a deep growl echoes through the hall. I hold my breath and put out the magic I'm holding at my fingertips. Shadows move across the hall, and the huge demonic dog growls as it walks. Ready for an attack, I peer around the corner and watch the thing sniff my phone.

It plants a giant paw on it, growling in frustration when the phone keeps ringing. If only there were a way to record this, I could get a lot of money from the phone case company for an advertisement. Keeps your phone safe against accidentally dropping it, a quick plunge into water, and colossal demon dogs.

What is that thing? And more importantly, how do I kill it?

I could conjure the biggest energy ball I can and throw it at the creature. Even if it doesn't kill it, that thing will be seriously injured. There's always the option of trying to telekinetically snap its neck, but it's already proven difficult to move it with my mind.

The phone stops ringing, and the creature growls, thick drool hanging off its mouth. It crouches down, sniffing my phone and then turns, looking down the hall. I flatten myself against the wall at the last second, but it already picked up my scent.

Okay...I can do this...I have to do this.

I hold my hands out in front of me, bringing strings of magic together to form an energy ball. The second the magic sparks around me, the creature snarls and takes off down the hall toward me. I jump away from the wall, holding the energy ball out in front of me and continue to feed it more and more magic. It's blindingly bright, swirling with bits of white and blue magic.

It's barreling toward me, gaining speed, and I hold tight to the energy ball, not releasing it until the creature is only a few yards from me. It hits the thing in the shoulder, burning its flesh. The creature lets out a high-pitched screech of pain. Its front feet fold underneath itself and it tumbles down, rolling across the floor.

It springs up, shaking its head as if it's trying to get the last bits of magic off its skin. The magic burns it like acid, and the putrid smell of burning skin and hair fills the air. The creature pushes back up to its feet and I've already got another energy ball ready for it.

It looks at me with more intelligence than a dog, eyes shifting from my face to the energy ball in my hand. Thick, black blood drips from the wound on its shoulder. It's not turning into smoke like the ooze that came out of the body, but it looks similar.

I raise my hand, aiming the energy ball right at the creature's head. With a snarl, it sprints forward, moving so fast I'm not able to get a clear shot. I throw the energy ball and miss. It hits the wall behind the creature, sizzling before going out. I dodge out of the way, and one foot lands on a piece of cardboard or something on the tile. I slip and go crashing down. Scrambling back, I throw another energy ball at the creature, knowing I'm a sitting duck down here on the floor.

The creature lifts its head and lets out a harrowing roar and then takes off. My breath leaves me in a huff and my heart is racing so fast it's pulsing through my ears. I stare at the spot where the creature stood, blinking.

Right. It knows I can hurt it, and if I can hurt it, I can kill it.

It's not here to hunt or find prey. It's here to guard something, and that's where it's going now. To protect whatever the hell is in this building. I reach up and grab onto a doorknob, pulling myself up. I'm at the back of the building again and have a lot of space to cover before I can find that thing again.

I wipe dust and dirt off my hands and push my hair back

behind my ears. Black drips of blood lead a trail down the hall, going in the opposite direction of my phone. I bite my lip, giving myself only a second to decide what to do.

I can double back and still track the creature. I need to warn my friends to get the hell out of here and then come back with a supercharged vanquishing potion. Wincing every time my stupid heels click on the floor, I move as fast as I can in this getup. I'm close to my phone when it rings again.

"Shit!" I rush forward, holding out my hand to telekinetically bring my phone to me. It's Kristy again, and I silence the call as fast as I can. There's demonic dog drool on the screen, making my phone unable to register my finger. I quickly wipe the phone off on my dress and then answer Kristy's call.

"The fuck, Callie!" she spits. "Where the hell are you?"

"I told you, I'm in the building next to the bar. Are you still at the bar?" I take a few quiet steps down the hall.

"We're out front, looking for you. Callie, there isn't a building next to the bar. It's all torn down and it's just a foundation and mess of broken boards. There's nothing there."

I come to a dead stop. "Yes, there is. I'm there right now."

"Are you sure?"

"I swear to you. It's next to the bar in the alley and—oh my God."

"What? You're freaking me out, Cal!"

"The vibrations." I put my hand on the wall and close my eyes. "I knew something felt weird, but I didn't think it could be this."

"Be what?"

"It's a glamour. Kristy, this place has been hidden from human sight." I pull my phone away from my ear and drop a pin in my location and then send it to Kristy. "There's an alley behind the bar and the building is right across from it, I promise."

I can hear Nicole's voice through the phone but can't make out what she's saying. A few seconds pass and it sounds like Kristy is running.

"I'm in the alley," she tells me. "And you're right. It feels...

weird back here. Hang on." Rustling comes through the phone and then I hear my friends chanting. "Light of the sun, dark of the night, reveal the truth before my sight."

"Seven devils," Kristy says and then it sounds like she drops the phone on the ground.

"Are you there?" I whisper, inching down the hall again. "Do you see it?"

"Yes." Her voice is shaky. "How did you see it? That doesn't matter now...you need to get out of there. Eliza is saying she can smell blood."

"Is it human?"

"What other kind of blood would it be?"

"There's something here, Kristy. Something demonic."

"Then you really need to get out of there, Callie."

My heart is still racing, and I know she's right. I'm not prepared, and my feet are really starting to hurt. "Okay. I'll meet you in the alley. I came in through the air vent. I'll come back out the same way."

"I see it. Hurry."

"I will." I end the call and put the phone back in my purse. It's a "going out" purse and is little and pretty, not holding much more than my ID, credit card, phone, and lipstick. It matched my dress much better than my usual bag, which is three times the size and always has minimal magical supplies in it.

This is the last time I choose fashion over function, I swear.

The entire building is silent as I hurry down the hall and back into the laundromat section. I push open the double doors and look around the room before stepping in. I rub my thumb over my fingers, sparking strings of magic.

I can see light coming through the open air vent, and my friends' voices floating in from the alley. I let out a breath of relief and rush across the laundromat, dropping my guard since I'm so close to getting the hell out of here.

I dropped several feet coming in through the air vent and am going to need something to climb on to get out. This room is full of crap. I'm sure I can find something. I stop several feet before I get to the air vent and grab an old laundry basket.

"Callie?" Kristy's voice comes from the alley. "Is that you?"

"Yeah. I'm trying to find something to climb on so I can get out."

"Fucking witches," Eliza huffs and zooms through the vent. "I'm only giving you a boost up so we can get the fuck out of here. Galivanting through a dirty old building might be your idea of fun, but it isn't mine."

"Trust me, it's not my idea of fun either."

"Could have fooled me." She holds out her hand to help me out the vent. "You seem to gravitate toward this sort of thing."

"It's more like it gravitates toward me." I take my purse off my shoulder and toss it out the vent and into the alley. Kristy grabs it and I put my hand on the vent, waiting for Eliza to pick me up and help me out the window.

"Try not to enjoy this." Eliza puts her hands on my waist. Right as she's about to lift me up, she stops and spins around. "What the fuck is that?"

"I don't hear anything." I let go of the vent and conjure an energy ball. "But if it's the thing that was here before…we're screwed."

"Speak for yourself." She draws her fangs and looks around the room. She can see in the dark, and right now, she's staring at something, eyes widening. Another dog-creature lunges from the dark, moving like a blur. It's half the size of the one that I hit in the shoulder with the energy ball. Did it split back apart?

Or—oh shit. There's more of them.

CHAPTER 13

The double doors fly open and the bigger of the two comes barreling in, snarling and growling, showing off rows and rows of sharp teeth. The smaller dog turns and starts to run.

"No!" I shout and hit it with an energy ball. Eliza grabs my hand and yanks me back toward the air vent, making the energy ball miss. It hits the ceiling and rains bright white light down on us. The tendrils of magic burn Eliza's skin, and she screams in pain.

I put out the magic I have burning around my fingers and grab Eliza's arm, jerking her away from the energy falling down. Lucas heals almost immediately after being burned by magic, but he's older and stronger than Eliza and is always well-fed, which affects a vampire's ability to heal quickly. I have no idea when Eliza last ate.

The bigger dog lets out a roar and then jumps on the smaller one, mouth clamping around its head. It bites down, breaking the skull, and then shudders. The smaller dog turns into black ooze that gets absorbed into the bigger creature's body, making it double in size again.

"What the actual fuck is going on?" Eliza rapidly blinks, eyes still burning from the magic.

"That thing," I pant. "I…I don't know what it is."

"No shit." She bares her fangs at the creature, he growls right back at her. It's the size of a horse now, still canine in appearance with pounds of rippling muscle under thick skin.

The creature lets out another roar, spraying us with yellow saliva.

"This dress is dry clean only," Eliza growls and rushes forward, moving with vampire speed. Like all vampires, she has super strength, but that thing is too strong. She hits it hard in the chest, making it stagger back. It snaps down at her and she dodges out of the way, narrowly avoiding being bitten. She goes to hit it again, but it moves fast and this time; it clamps its mouth down on her arm.

"Eliza!" I scream and thrust my hands forward, putting every ounce of energy I have into telekinetically throwing that thing backward. It hits the wall with a heavy thud, and drywall rains down on us. I hold out my hand, and it feels like I'm being sucked under water while trying to dead lift a thousand pounds at the same time. My ears ring and my vision starts to go hazy. "Go!"

Eliza scrambles up, zooming over to the vent. Kristy and the twins are outside in the alley still, not sure what's going on. I can barely hear their voices over the pounding of my own heartbeat in my head.

"Callie!" Eliza shouts, reaching out her hand for me to take. "Come on!"

"Go!" I yell, knowing if I look away from the creature, I'll break my concentration and will lose my hold on it. And then that thing will get Eliza and God knows who else.

"Callie!" I hear Kristy shout.

"Go!" I yell again. "Get out of here! I can't hold it for much longer."

The creature shoves itself forward, roaring and growling as it fights my hold. Its head jerks forward, fangs slashing through the air.

My hands start to shake, and my head feels like it's going to explode. I push against the creature with everything I've got, shoving it against the wall. Its head whacks back, cracking the drywall and splitting the framing. Dust billows out around it, and I know I'm getting close to losing my hold.

Narrowing my eyes, I give one final push, sending the creature through the wall. My hands fall to my sides, and the world spins around us. I let out a breath, heart hammering and ears still ringing.

"Callie, run!" Eliza yells, and this time she doesn't have to tell me twice. She's by the vent and jumps up, gracefully moving through it and into the alley. She turns around, holding out her hands. Her fingers wrap around my wrists and she starts to pull me up.

And then something grabs my ankle, jerking me back. Eliza tugs me forward, and I can feel the bones in my wrist start to separate. I cry out in pain and reach for Eliza with my other hand.

"Hang on!" she shouts as I turn around to see the dead man from the alley holding my ankle. I kick and my heels clip him in the face. He doesn't even react to the pain. The black veins are back on his face, and his eyes are dark as well, looking like they've rotted in his skull.

He twists my ankle and digs his fingernails into my skin, tearing open my flesh. The demonic dog-creature stands behind him, pulling its lips back in a snarl. Eliza pulls again, using her vampire strength, and I feel like my arm is going to rip right off my body. My arm twists, and I'm pulled from Eliza's grip. I fall hard onto the dirty tile of the laundromat, and the man drags me across the floor.

Screaming in protest, I twist around and try to hit him with an energy ball. As soon as the magic glows around my fingers, the man jerks me hard and my head falls back, hitting the tile. Pain radiates through me, causing my vision to black out for a few seconds. The man drags me through the double doors and into the hallway, where the creature is waiting. It stands before me and opens its mouth. I close my eyes, bracing for the pain.

Something crashes into the creature, sending it flying down the hall. I clamber up, ankle burning from where the man scratched me, and blink, hardly able to see through the dust haze in front of me.

Lucas plants both of his hands on the man's head and twists it around, not stopping until it snaps clean off. He throws the head on the ground and steps back, holding his arms out protectively. Panting, I bring my hands out in front of me and conjure a bright blue energy ball. The light burns Lucas's flesh, but he grits his teeth, bringing his lips back to reveal his fangs.

The dog-creature rears up right as I release the energy ball. It hits it square in the chest, burning through several layers of its skin. Lucas risks turning around and takes me in his arms.

"Callie," he breathes, eyes wide as he looks me up and down, making sure I'm okay. Then he pushes me back and sprints forward, knocking the creature to the ground and speeding back to my side. I hit it with another energy ball and the thing recoils, screeching in pain. It backs into the hall and takes off, disappearing from view.

"I'm okay," I pant, knowing what he's thinking. "All things considered."

He pushes my hair back before pulling me to him, turning away from the creature and using his own body as a shield. I can hear it growling in protest, angry that Lucas was able to throw it around like a rag doll.

"What the hell is that?" I pant, hands shaking as I reach for Lucas.

"I don't know, and I don't think we have time to find out." He scoops me up and starts forward, only to come to a sudden halt as parts of the ceiling rain down around us. We can't get through the same way we came, and when he turns, we're face to face with the creature again.

Lucas puts me down and steps in front of me, ready to sacrifice himself if it means saving me. I take in a deep breath and plant one foot firmly on the ground. My hair blows back when the creature lets out a warning growl, and I throw my hands up, creating a telekinetic shield that it crashes into when it dives right for Lucas.

I let out a yell as I push the shield against the creature.

"I...I got him..." I say through gritted teeth. "For...now."

Lucas shifts his gaze from the creature to me and back again. "Can you hit it with another energy ball?" he asks.

"I...think...so." I give the shield another shove and feel blood drip down my nose. "But I'll...have...to...let this...go...first."

"I'll hold it back."

"No!" I shout but Lucas doesn't listen. He speeds forward, moving around the shield I'm holding, and grabs the creature's back leg, yanking it away from me. My hands fall and the world spins around me. Everything is crashing down at a dizzying rate, and I know Lucas is living on borrowed time. That thing is going to turn around and attack him, ripping him to shreds that even he can't heal from.

"Lucas!" I call, but my voice dies in my throat. I hold up my hands to conjure an energy ball, but I can hardly move. My composure falters and my sore ankle twists, giving out. I fall to the ground. The creature rounds on him, teeth slashing against his chest. His skin tears open, and blood darkens his shirt.

I thrust my hand forward, using the last bit of energy I have to push the thing away from Lucas. He speeds over, catching me before I hit the ground.

His blood soaks my skin as he cradles me against him. The creature lets out another deafening roar and Lucas holds me tight, standing up but faltering. It will take him a few more seconds at least to heal, and he's losing a lot of blood rather quickly. The creature dives down on us, but smashes into an invisible wall.

"Are you doing that?"

"No," I answer Lucas. He gets to his feet, still holding me, and we turn, seeing Kristy, Naomi, and Nicole holding hands and standing in a circle, chanting.

"It's a protection spell," I explain, hearing the words in Latin. Eliza rushes forward and puts her hand on Lucas's chest, looking horrified from the blood.

"Lucas." Her eyes fill with tears.

"I'm fine," he assures her and sets me on my feet. He keeps one arm around my waist and brings his other to Eliza's cheek, caressing her face for a brief moment. I bring my head to my hands and let out my breath. The creature is detained—for now.

But that's not good enough. It has to be stopped.

Blinking, I look from Lucas and Eliza to Kristy, Nicole, and Naomi. The circle they're casting is the only thing that's holding that creature back. Once it's broken...no. I won't let myself think that way.

I inhale heavily and spin around, staring right at that thing. Face set, I march forward and throw my hands out, telekinetically jerking it into the air.

"Callie," Lucas exclaims, and Kristy breaks her concentration, looking up at me. The thing crashes forward, hitting the wall of magic laid out in front of it. I throw it back, focusing all my energy into the open wound on its chest. Whatever it is, it's strong, and it's not going to go down easy.

But I'll be damned before I let everyone I care about put themselves at risk for me. Lucas moves over, and he puts his hand on my shoulder. He's not stopping me. Not telling me this is a stupid idea and I need to tuck my tail between my legs and run.

He's letting me know he's here. He'll do whatever he can to keep me safe.

The creature jumps up, giant paws scraping against the magical wall my friends are holding up. More blood drips from my nose, and it feels like a million pounds are pressing down on me.

My heart is racing, and my ears are ringing. The world around me starts to shake, and I know I'm running out of energy.

For some reason, that stupid feather I found in the alley pops into my mind. I remember how good if felt in my hands, how sleek and soft it was and how it felt familiar at the same time.

The creature pushes forward again, and Lucas moves a step forward, ready to take that thing on if need be. Seeing him so willing to risk himself...no...I won't let it come to that.

My mouth falls open with a yell as I pull my hands apart, sinking a telekinetic hold on the creature. The wound on its chest starts to separate, and thick blood drips to the ground. Everything inside me hurts, but I don't stop. Screaming with pain, I move my hands apart and rip the creature in two.

The two halves of the creature splat onto the ground and explode into a hundred dead rats. I jerk back, vision going hazy. I lose my balance and Lucas catches me, looking at the rats with the same horrified expression I have on my face.

One of the rats twitches, squeaking and squealing as it tries to get up. Lucas sets me on the ground and rushes forward, stomping on it. He looks around for any others that are still alive to squish as well. Kristy runs to me, slipping her arms under mine and pulls me back. Nicole and Naomi stand over us, holding hands and still chanting, keeping the demon-rats from getting me.

My eyes flutter shut, and time moves slowly. Or quickly. I'm not sure, because the next thing I know, Lucas is carrying me and I'm breathing in fresh air. The thumping bass of the bar rings out next to me, and when I blink my eyes open, I realize I'm in the alley. Lucas is holding me, and my friends are looking at me with concern.

"Can you hear me, Callie?" Lucas asks, voice low.

"Yeah." The world spins and I feel like I'm drunk all over again. Visions of dead rats flash before me, and that putrid smell of death fills my nose. "Put me down. Now." He sets me on the ground, and I hurry away, moving to the dumpster. I bend over and throw up all over the pavement.

"What in the ever-loving fuck was that?" Eliza sputters.

"A hellhound," Lucas answers, gathering my hair in his hand. "Or at least it resembled the last one I saw."

"Right," I groan, wiping my mouth with the back of my hand. "You've seen one before."

"You've seen a hellhound?" Eliza asks incredulously. "Why haven't I heard about it?"

"It was many years before I made you," Lucas tells her and directs his attention to me. "We need to get her home."

"Are you okay?" Kristy asks, tentatively coming over.

"That hot dog tasted much better going in." I shudder from the foul taste in my mouth. "I need some water."

"Eliza," Lucas says pointedly, raising his eyebrows.

"Oh for fuck's sake," she groans, but isn't able to hide her fear. She rushes away, presumably going into the bar to get me a cup of water. I move away from the puddle of vomit in the alley and lean against Lucas for support.

"Leave it to you to find a hellhound on a girls' night out," Naomi quips, eyes still wide. "At least tonight was unforgettable."

The world is still spinning around me and all I want to do is lie down and take a nap. I depleted myself using that much energy.

"You kicked its ass." Nicole shuffles over. "That was...that was..."

"Incredible," Lucas finishes.

"I was going to say insane and dangerous."

"I suppose it had a little of that all mixed in." Lucas twists my hair in his hand, moving it off my back. "Are you all right, my love?"

"I don't think I'm going to puke anymore," I tell him ruefully. "The world isn't spinning as much." I sway on my feet as I turn around and look at the building. "Is it over? It...it turned into rats."

"All the rats are dead."

"Are you sure? I'll come back with my familiars and enough vanquishing potion to—"

"No," everyone says at the same time.

"You've been weakened, Callie." Lucas slips his arm around me again. "As have I. We need to go." He picks me up before I can protest and starts walking away from the alley.

"Wait," I say and push out of his arms.

"What is it?"

"The vent. I...I need to recover it."

Nicole takes Naomi's hand. "We've got this." They raise their hands together and the vent flies back onto the brick building, stuck with magic. No human will be able to get it off now.

Eliza zooms over, holding a plastic cup of water. I rinse my mouth out and then suck down the rest of the water. Lucas drove his Range Rover to the bar, and we all cram in.

"How did you find us?" Eliza asks, taking the front passenger side seat.

"I felt Callie's fear," Lucas explains, looking slightly confused himself. It's not the first time he's sensed my emotions, and it's not a normal bond for a human and vampire to have.

Whatever the reason, I'm glad he came when he did...because I don't think I could have fought that thing off without him. I take my purse from Kristy and reach inside, fingers gracing over the feather.

Shit just went down.

Tough shit.

Deep shit.

Yet for some reason, the moment my fingers make contact with the feather, everything feels like it's going to be all right.

CHAPTER 14

"I don't know anyone who can say they defeated a hellhound." Lucas sets me on his bed and moves to his knees, hands running down my calves. He starts to undo the buckles on my shoes.

"In heels and a pushup bra, no less."

He looks into my eyes and smiles. "Are you sure you're all right, Callie?" He takes one shoe off and sets it on the floor. "What happened back there was intense."

"I'm alive. You're alive and my friends are alive. Hell, even Eliza is alive. Well, I guess you and Eliza aren't, but you know what I mean."

"I do." He takes off my other shoe and then helps me to my feet again. The shower is already on, and as much as I want to clean myself up, I just want to crash into bed with a bowl of pasta.

Lucas helps me to my feet and unzips my dress. It falls to the floor, and he does his best not to react to the sight of me stripping out of my clothes. My bra and panties come off next, and we get into the shower together.

"Does it hurt?" Lucas asks, gently washing away dried blood from the scrapes on my ankle.

"A little. The balls of my feet hurt more than anything, oddly enough," I tell him, looking down at him. Warm water rushes over us both, and my heart swells in my chest. I'm too tired and too freaked out for sex right now, but I'm feeling so strongly for Lucas it's almost overwhelming.

He found me—again.

He risked his afterlife for me—again.

He's taking care of me—again.

"Do you have any of that healing balm left?" he asks, straightening back up. He towers over me and I step in, needing to feel him against me.

"Yeah, I do. And Kristy probably brought some. She's usually well prepared." My friends had intended on getting a hotel downtown for the night, sleeping off what we drank. They're here instead, as well as Eliza.

"You were incredible in there." Lucas slides his hands up and down my back.

"You always say that. I'm starting to think you just have low standards."

Lucas laughs and puts his lips to my neck. I bring my hand up to his chest. He healed by the time we got to his car, and there's not a mark left on him. His blood has dried on his skin, and now it's my turn to wash him.

Once we're both clean, we get out and get dressed. Lucas runs the towel over his hair and dresses only in gray sweatpants. No one should look that good in loungewear. I pull on black leggings and one of Lucas's white t-shirts. Leaving my hair damp and unbrushed, I go downstairs and find everyone in the living room.

My friends have changed into their PJs as well, but Eliza is wearing another pretty dress. Her hair is perfect and her makeup impeccable. I can't even get myself to look that put together with magic.

"You feeling okay?" Kristy asks, standing up when I come into the room. Binx jumps off the couch and trots over, rubbing his head against me. I pick him up and nuzzle my face into his fur.

"Yeah. I'm hungry, though, and for some reason mac and cheese sounds really good."

"That does," Kristy agrees and takes my hands in hers. She parts her lips and looks behind me at the twins. Naomi is uncharacteristically quiet, and Nicole is holding Pandora, nervously running her fingers through her fur.

"So that was a fun girls' night out," Eliza says, crossing her arms. All eyes go to her and silence falls over our little group. And then we all start laughing.

"I don't understand why it turned into rats." I sink onto the loveseat opposite the couch. Lucas takes a spot next to me, wrapping his arm around my shoulders. I let him pull me against his firm chest, finding instant relief to have my body pressed against his. "Hellhounds don't turn into anything, right?"

"I'm not well versed on them," Lucas says. "The one and only time I witnessed one it was after its mark and paid no attention to me."

He also thought it ignored him because he's just as evil as a creature from Hell. I know that's not true.

"Why was it there?" Kristy asks. "I mean, that whole building was glamoured to look like it was in the process of being torn down so it would be overlooked. What has the kind of power to cast that strong of a glamour?"

"Other witches?" Nicole suggests.

"The real question is." Naomi leans forward. "Why didn't the glamour work on Callie?"

"I don't know." I look at Lucas and shake my head. "I saw it right away. I remember thinking it was weird for that fancy bar to be next to such a shithole of a building as soon as we pulled up. And then I felt…" I trail off. I already sound crazy enough. Saying I felt compelled to go inside the building because I found a feather is enough to put me away and have my head examined.

And that man…the one with the blue eyes but not *glowing* blue eyes…it was like he was calling to me. He wanted me to find him. Maybe? Or was he trying to keep the hellhounds from escaping?

Or even lead me right to them?

"You felt what?" Kristy urges.

"There was a vibration in the air. When Kristy said there wasn't a building, it hit me what was going on."

"Why did you go back into that alley in the first place?" Eliza's blue eyes land on me.

I went back there because the man who I think dropped the feather—crazy, I know, I know—led me there. I think. "I just followed a gut feeling." It's not quite a lie. I did follow a gut feeling and it led me to the man who— "Oh shit. There's a body in that building."

"If it's been glamoured, chances are no one will find it," Naomi says like that's supposed to soothe my nerves.

"But that man...he's someone," I protest. "His family could be looking for him."

"He didn't smell very human to me," Eliza quips.

"He was human," Lucas tells her.

"Are you sure?"

"I pulled his fucking head off," Lucas replies dryly. "Trust me. He was human, but his blood had been tainted somehow."

"Like he was possessed?" Nicole asks.

"Not quiet. His blood was rancid because he was dead but was something more...like he was diseased."

CHAPTER 15

"**D**iseased?" I echo. "Like with the flu or something."

"Or something," Lucas replies. "Based on the decomposition of the body, he'd only been dead for about a day. But the blood... the blood smelled like it's been festering for much longer than that."

"That doesn't make sense." I rub my forehead. "Then again, a hellhound turning into rats doesn't either."

"Unless it was so they can scatter," Nicole guesses. "I mean, if you think about it, it makes sense. One of those giant freaky dogs walking around the streets of Chicago is sure to draw attention. But rats...they live in the sewers."

"But all the rats were dead. Unless...shit." I start to stand but Binx growls, knowing what I'm thinking. "We have to go back and make sure none got out—"

"Callie," Kristy says, voice edging on scolding. "You and Eliza almost died. Lucas got hurt too." She doesn't have to tell me that if Lucas got hurt, shit is serious. Lucas is the oldest and strongest vampire any of us have met, and is more powerful than the vampires we've read about in our history books at the Academy.

"I'll be better prepared this time, and I'll bring my familiars."

"You're supposed to be lying low," Naomi reminds me. "The

Grand Coven would have a field day if they found out you discovered another big bad lurking about the city."

"It's more like it found me," I grumble, though really, I think the man with blue eyes and the feather led me to it.

"We're trying to build a case that you're an ordinary witch with ordinary powers, excelling in one normal area, and telling them that you ripped a bloody hellhound apart with your mind is not going to help with that." She leans over and puts her hand on mine. "We know you're not ordinary." She looks at her sister and Kristy. "I think we've always known and that's why we love you. But, Callie, I'm scared for you. If the Grand Coven sentences you to death…"

"I will rip their throats out before they can lay a finger on her," Lucas promises.

"And then what?" Naomi throws her hand out. "You two will live a life of exile leaving body trails wherever you go? These things catch up with you, Cal, and I don't want that life for you or for myself."

"You don't have to be involved," I start.

"Yes, yes I do!" Naomi stands up and tears pool in her eyes. "You're like a sister to us, Callie. I couldn't stand by and watch the Grand Coven order a witch hunt for one of our own. And we both know everyone in this room will be found guilty by association. Call me selfish, but I don't want to be cast out of the coven and I certainly don't want to be tied to a stake and burned for everyone to see!"

She turns and marches out of the living room.

"Let her go," Nicole says when I get up to go after her. "Trust me, it's best to give her a bit of space before trying to reason with her."

I sink back down onto the couch and look down at Binx. "I don't want to put you guys at risk for excommunication by the Grand Coven."

"You're not," Kristy assures we. "We came here to see you. And

Naomi was right. It's all bullshit. If they kick you out for life, then I'm leaving."

"I won't let it come to that," I tell her and then look at Lucas. "And we're not murdering any witches."

"Unless they really deserve it, right?" Lucas tries.

"Let's, uh, cross that bridge when we come to it." I let out a heavy sigh and run my hand over Binx's fur.

"I think we all need to get some sleep." Kristy rubs her forehead. "And then revisit this tomorrow. From where I stand, it's over. You ripped that thing in half and all the rats are dead."

"I still feel like there's something evil in there."

"There probably is," Nicole tells me. "The energy of whatever kind of demon that was. It'll taint the earth for a while, you know."

"And no one is getting in there." Kristy sounds sure of herself only because she wants to believe it.

"No one would have with the hellhounds, but I killed them. I think."

"You ripped it in half and then it turned into dead rats." Lucas shrugs. "Seems pretty dead to me."

"Why were they there?" Nicole asks.

"I have no idea." I lean back against Lucas. "Hellhounds are sent to do a demon's bidding. Usually to collect on a deal made. That's why Lucas saw them before. A village made a deal for prosperous crops and then the hellhounds came to collect souls when the time of the contract was up."

"Do you think someone made a deal with a demon?" Nicole twists her red hair up into a messy bun. "And they were waiting to collect?"

"I suppose, but it still doesn't explain why the building was hidden with a glamour." Or why that man was heading back there. He could be just as evil as the hellhounds, yet for some reason, I know he's not. Did he want me to follow him back there?

Why?

Was it a test? Did he want them to kill me for some reason?

He seemed surprised when I saw him, like it was the last thing he expected. I turn, looking into the foyer. I dumped my purse in there as soon as we walked inside, and I want to hold the feather.

"Callie?" Kristy says, and I don't think it's the first time she's said my name. I spaced out thinking about the man and the feather. It sounds so insane when I think about it like that.

"Sorry." I bring my hands to my face and yawn. "I'm tired."

"You should sleep," Lucas urges.

"I know," I agree. "But I don't think I'll be able to fall asleep. What if some kids break in tomorrow and find *Jumanji* or something?"

"Then we'll figure out a way to stop the city from becoming a jungle." Lucas pulls me onto his lap. "But I don't think you have to worry about it. That creature is dead, I'm sure of it."

"I know."

I don't want to say it and freak my friends out, and I'm not even certain it's true myself. But I still think that hellhound was guarding something, and it's not a children's game. Whatever is hidden in that building is much, much worse.

~

"THERE ARE AUTOMATIC BLINDS THAT GO DOWN AROUND FOUR-thirty," I tell my friends. We're upstairs and ready to crash for what's left of the night. "The house is light-tight after that, so you'll have to turn on lights."

"Makes sense." Nicole tosses decorative pillows onto the ground. "This place is really nice and not what I expected for Lucas."

"Right? I thought the same thing." The guest room, like the rest of the house, is very modern.

"Saying I assumed he lived in some old gothic mansion seems stereotypical," Nicole admits. "But I kind of thought that."

"They will be living in one soon enough." Kristy leans against the doorframe.

"I do plan to have at least one room look like it could be part of the *Haunted Mansion*, but we want to keep a similar color scheme to this house, actually. I like the light gray and white."

"Me too." Nicole climbs into bed and Naomi comes out of the bathroom. She hugs me goodnight and I walk Kristy to another guest room before going into the master bedroom. Lucas is already in bed waiting for me. I get under the covers and immediately snuggle up next to him.

"I love you," I whisper as he spoons his body around mine.

"I love you too, Callie." He kisses my neck and holds me close. My eyes fall shut and then I spin around in his arms.

"You lost a lot of blood today."

"I'm fine now."

"You should eat." I push my hair back and offer my neck to him.

"I'm fine," he presses.

"What, does my blood smell rancid now too?"

"Not at all."

"They why don't you want it?" I ask. "Aren't you hungry after losing that much blood?"

"A little." He moves me onto his chest and runs his fingers up and down my back. My eyes fall shut. "I don't want to take too much from you, Callie. I will be fine and getting a few hours of extra sleep will make up for the blood I lost. It takes you longer to recover and I've drank from you recently."

He has, and he's right. If I were a normal person, I don't think our arrangement would work as well as it does. Lucas told me my blood is more filling than the average human and he doesn't need to drink as much to feel satisfied. He's a beast of a man and it's actually a wonder we've been able to sustain him only drinking my blood for as long as we have.

I haven't really let myself think about it, and I want to say I'd be okay with it...but I think it would bother me if he drank from someone else. Maybe? If he needed to eat, though, and I were unable to give him my blood, then he'd have to. It's not like he's cheating on me. He's simply feeding himself.

But feeding is rather sexual, or at least it is with us.

Ugh. It's too complicated to think about right now.

"In the morning then," I whisper.

"Yes. In the morning."

I close my eyes and drift to a sleep so deep not even the automatic blinds coming down wakes me up. Lucas is in bed next to me when I do wake up, and he's in that deep, dead, vampire-style sleep. I conjure a small energy ball so I can see my way into the bathroom.

It's ten-thirty AM and I'm sure my friends are awake. I change into a black romper, use magic to braid my hair, and go downstairs to find them. Binx is sitting at the top of the stairs, waiting for me.

"Morning, Mr. Prickle Paws," I tell him, reaching down to pick him up. I find Kristy and Nicole in the kitchen. "Hey, guys. How'd you sleep?"

"I passed out like a baby," Nicole says. "Naomi is still sleeping."

"How are you feeling?" Kristy sips her coffee. "I think I'm hungover."

"I'll be better with coffee."

"I wasn't sure if there would be food here," Nicole admits, biting into her bagel. "But then again, you live here half the time."

"I get groceries whenever I come into the city. I think the kitchen is happy to finally be used."

"Lucas probably never came in here before, did he?" Kristy adds more sugar to her coffee and circles her finger over the mug, using magic to stir it in.

"I don't think so. The house was staged before he bought it and he had them leave all the stuff here. I'm not sure why, though." I shrug. "Maybe for resale? He buys and sells properties a lot."

"There's a lot of money in that," Nicole says.

"There is," I agree and pour myself a cup of coffee. "So...who wants to go check out that old building with me this morning?"

"You're joking, right?" Kristy deadpans.

"I want to make sure the rats are really dead. And I don't have to go inside to do that. Binx already offered to check it out for me." I put the coffee pot back on the warmer.

"You're just going to look?" Nicole asks and I nod. "Then I'm in. If that thing...the rat-dog or whatever...if it's dead, then the glamour might be gone, and people will wonder where the hell that building came from."

"I didn't think about that," I tell her. "It's too early in the day to try and sort it out, but unless there are photos, people will just be confused, right?"

"Even in photos, which I'm sure there are, it'll show up as hazy," Kristy says. I take my coffee back to the island. Lucas's laptop and a folded piece of paper are on the center of the island. My name is written on the paper in his freakishly neat handwriting.

"Is it a sex note?" Nicole jokes as I pick it up. A flash drive falls from the folded paper, bouncing to the floor. She picks it up for me.

"No, it's security footage from the bar." I set the note down and open the computer. We all crowd around the computer as I stick in the flash drive. There's footage from last night, of course, as well as going back a week.

"Start with last night," Kristy says. "It was around midnight, I think."

It takes a minute or two of clicking through the different recordings until we find a camera angle that shows a bit of the alley. The building behind the bar is showing up all hazy, just like Kristy said. It makes it look like something is wrong with the camera, or that something was smeared over the lens and has distorted the way it recorded.

I rest my hand against the cool quartz counter, needing to remind myself to breathe. The man with blue eyes should be appearing any second now, followed by me. Something flashes across the screen, startling us all.

"What was that?" Kristy reaches over me and rewinds the footage, playing it back frame by frame. "Is that an outline of a man?" She stops it, right in the middle of the second-long flash. "It looks like an outline of a man."

"It kind of does," Nicole agrees.

"Yeah," I say, unable to dispute it. It does look like a man and is roughly similar to the man with blue eyes. "Keep playing it."

Kristy hits play and we see me go into the alley. The diseased man staggers past next, and then we move out of the camera view. We skip forward, slowing to real time when Kristy, the twins, and Eliza show up. We can see the backs of their heads, but the actual point of entry into the building is out of camera shot. Kristy fast forwards again, stopping when a dark shadow blurs across the screen.

"That's Lucas," I tell her.

"We go in soon after this," Nicole says. We let the footage roll in live time for a few minutes before skipping forward again. Nothing of interest happens until we come out of the building. Lucas carries me across the alley and the others follow.

"It's a good thing Lucas got the footage," Kristy says, leaning away from the computer. "Our faces are pretty clear."

"Right." Nicole nods. "If that body is found, it'll be investigated by the police. Should you have Lucas, uh, bury this one for you too?"

"Probably," I say ruefully. "He didn't seem that old, though, and probably has friends and family looking for him."

"I'm sure he does," Kristy agrees. "But he's at peace now at least." She forces a smile and goes around the island to get more coffee. "I hate saying this, but we should watch the rest of that footage, at least the alley view and see if anything weird pops up from earlier in the week."

"Sounds fun." I'm about to close the computer and go back to watching literally nothing later when I stop. Something flashes across the screen again. It's the same type of flash as before, and I know it's him.

I hit pause and slowly drag the frame back millisecond by millisecond. There's a human outline again, but this time, there's something behind him. The image is fuzzy at best, and I squint my eyes, leaning closer to the screen.

Maybe I'm seeing things, but I swear it looks like the outline of wings.

CHAPTER 16

"Evander says he's never heard of hellhounds being able to merge together or turn into rats." Kristy puts her phone in her purse. I take my eyes off the road for a second to look at her. "It sounds so crazy when I say it out loud like that."

We're on our way to the bar but have no intention of going in. The hellhound is dead, we're all pretty sure, but I need to double-check. I did wear sensible shoes, though, just in case. The combat boots actually look kinda cute with this romper too, or at least I think so. I've loaded up everything we could use as a weapon, and we're all carrying vanquishing potions.

See? I'm prepared this time.

"Did he say anything else?" Naomi asks.

"He seemed rather perplexed by the whole thing."

"Aren't we all?" I mumble.

"He said hellhounds are physical beings, brought forth from hell. They can't shapeshift like that."

"Do you think they were really hellhounds?"

Kristy holds up her phone. "He sent me this photo from a book in the library. It's what they look like. And Lucas has seen them before." She bites her lip and looks out the window. "But with the way they went from rats to hellhounds...I'm going to guess no and they were just taking on the form of something terrifying. What's more terrifying than a hellhound? I'm getting a bad feeling about this. Like a really bad feeling."

"Me too, even though it seems like it's over," Nicole says quietly. "Like whatever this is, is much bigger than we expected. It's not a demon you can rip apart and then it's gone. I feel...I feel like it has roots."

"Roots?" Naomi questions.

"Yes, roots. I can't explain it." Nicole runs her hands over Pandora's head. "She gets it, though."

If that thing does have roots, I'll rip them from the ground.

We pull up to the bar and park along the street. Bright sunlight streams down on us as we get out of the car, and my familiars shadow forward. There are a few little stores along the street and people walk up and down the sidewalk, totally unaware of everything that went on last night.

"Hey." I stop a guy walking past. "Do you know if the stores in that old building are open?" I point to the building next to the bar.

"What old—oh." He looks across the street. "Huh. For some reason I thought it was torn down. And no...it's been closed for years."

"Thanks." I lock Lucas's Range Rover and put the key fob back in my purse. The feather is in there, and I run my finger over it before pulling it out. Keeping it down at my side, I'm soothed by the feel of it in my hand.

"So, the glamour is gone." Naomi crosses her arms. "Maybe it was broken when you killed that thing."

Nicole puts on her sunglasses and goes to the crosswalk. "But do you feel that?" She holds out her hands.

"The energy is all wrong." Kristy shudders and we wait for the light to change before crossing. The bar is closed, of course, and we walk down the sidewalk in front of it. I slow when I come to the spot where the man with the bright blue eyes stood. I know I had my fair share to drink last night, but I was sobering up by the time I saw him. So why are my memories getting hazy?

"There's the camera." Nicole looks at it but doesn't point. Naomi takes her hand and together they use magic to cloud the lens, preventing it from recording us walking through the alley.

Freya, in cat-form, trots back to us. There's nothing in the building except for a bunch of dead rats and a headless body, just like we thought.

"You know it's only a matter of time before someone goes in there, right?" Kristy covers her nose with her hand. It smells like garbage in the alley. "Now that the glamour is worn off."

"I know." I move over to the air vent and telekinetically yank it from the building. Stale air rushes out, smelling like piles of dead rats.

"You are not going in there." Kristy crosses her arms. "There's no need and it's probably full of asbestos or something."

"I'm not." I crouch down, heart speeding up as I look inside. Closing my eyes, I hold out my hands and read the energy. It's not like it was last night. Not at all. There are no vibrations from strong glamours. It doesn't even feel haunted. It has a scar, like Nicole pointed out earlier, which happens when something dark and evil has tainted the aura of a specific place.

"Have Binx do one more sweep," Kristy says, tipping her head as she looks at the air vent. "Just to be sure the place is really demon-free. If there's nothing demonic, we should probably put in an anonymous call to the police so they can recover the body before it rots beyond recognition."

"Good idea," I tell her. "At least his family won't be wondering and waiting for him to come home."

"And if we can get an ID on the body, we might be able to figure out how he got mixed up in all of this in the first place."

My lips pull up in a half-smile. "What happened to not getting involved?"

Kristy loops her arm through mine. "If this thing does have roots, we need to stop it. Because roots spread."

Binx rubs against my legs and then shifts into shadow-form. Pandora joins in and they go in through the open air vent. We all stand around, watching and waiting. If there is anything in there, my familiars should be able to shadow away before falling to any harm, but I still feel a knot in my stomach as I wait. Freya is able to sense them both, though, and knows neither Binx nor Pandora are feeling any fear right now.

Only a few minutes later, they both return, letting me know that there are no traces of demons in the building.

"How do you anonymously call the police?" Nicole asks as we head back to the car.

"I'll have Lucas handle it." I open the driver's side door and take my purse off my shoulder, slipping the feather back inside. "He'll know what to do."

"Because he's dealt with a lot of dead bodies." Naomi slides into the seat behind me and Pandora jumps up and moves into the middle spot.

"He is a vampire." I pull my seatbelt on.

"He doesn't regularly kill people anymore, though," Kristy says encouragingly. "Right?"

"Not regularly." I'm getting uncomfortable with this conversation. My friends already think Lucas is going to cross a line and I won't be able to handle it. What scares me more than him doing something he can't take back is me being fine with it.

"I think it's sweet how much he looks out for you." Nicole throws me a bone and changes the tone of the conversation. "I can tell he really loves you."

"He does," I agree with a big grin on my face.

"You're moving in together." Naomi catches my eye in the rearview mirror. "Have you talked wedding plans?"

I shake my head and crank up the air conditioning. The SUV got hot and stuffy just from the few minutes it sat parked along the street.

"That hasn't come up once."

"If he proposed, what would you say?"

"Yes," I reply with no hesitation. "I'd marry him tonight if he asked me to. But Indiana doesn't recognize human-vampire marriages. Illinois doesn't either."

"Michigan does, and we live right along the state line. A nighttime beach wedding would be gorgeous."

"It would!" Nicole agrees with her sister. "Just think of the candles in the sand and the sound of waves crashing against the shore as you say your vows."

My smile comes back. "Yeah, that would be really nice."

"Should we start dropping hints?" Kristy laughs. "I can slip your ring size into a conversation."

"Right, because that wouldn't be obvious or anything."

"Can you image the rock he'd get her?" Nicole leans forward. "It'd weigh your hand down."

"He wouldn't go that overboard," I protest.

Kristy cocks an eyebrow. "He bought you a freaking house, Callie. And is having it restored for you."

"He...he just likes to see me be happy."

"Exactly," she giggles. "And in his mind, getting you the biggest, flashiest ring would make you happy."

"Then I do need you to start dropping hints. Don't get me wrong, I'd never say no to a big diamond, but let's cap the center stone at five carats."

"That's still huge."

"That's what she said," Nicole says, and we all laugh. I turn onto a busy road and smile once more. I really do have the best friends in the whole damn world.

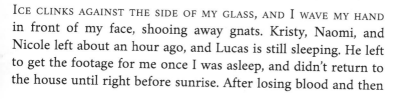

ICE CLINKS AGAINST THE SIDE OF MY GLASS, AND I WAVE MY HAND in front of my face, shooing away gnats. Kristy, Naomi, and Nicole left about an hour ago, and Lucas is still sleeping. He left to get the footage for me once I was asleep, and didn't return to the house until right before sunrise. After losing blood and then not taking any more in, he's going to sleep probably twice as long as usual, and once he's up he really should feed. There's no telling if I'll need him to come save my ass again.

I'm outside on the rooftop patio, playing catch-up on my tan, and take a big drink of ice water. My familiars have been up here with me, lounging in the sun like regular house cats. Setting my water down, I roll over onto my stomach so I can tan my back. Remembering what Lucas said about tanning topless, I lift my head and look at the houses next to me. I'm up a little higher, but there's still a good chance the neighbors could look out and see me, which I kinda don't care if they do.

It's just boobs.

I met one of the neighbors for the first time yesterday morning. I was heading out for a run the same time Mrs. Clemmot was. She's probably in her late forties and as uppity as you'd expect for someone living on this street. The only reason she stopped and introduced herself to me was because she'd only seen Lucas a handful of times and was curious about him.

Like I told Abby's friends when they asked, I said he worked in finance and was at his office a lot, which is why she only saw him coming and going at night. She seemed to buy my answer with no hesitation, though it surprises me with how nosey she was that she hadn't noticed the light-tight blinds that are always drawn during the day. Though whoever Lucas hired to put them in did a good job making them not obvious in the least.

There are trees and decorative shrubs in the front, obscuring the windows from view, and the glass on the upstairs windows is rather reflective, which makes it hard to look through to see the blinds. And I suppose it's not unusual to keep your curtains drawn when you live on a busy street like this.

Reaching behind me, I untie the strings of my top and put my head back down, soaking up every bit of sunlight. It feels so good to be outside in the heat even though I started sweating not even five minutes after stepping foot outside.

"The pool will be so nice," I mumble to my familiars. "I'll get you guys little cat rafts. You know, if you actually went in them and I got pictures it would probably go viral." Pandora scoffs, and if I looked up, I'm sure I'd see Freya rolling her eyes.

"Suit yourself. But on a hot day like this the pool will feel amazing. I wonder how hard those saltwater pools are to keep. If it's anything like a saltwater fish tank, it'll be a bitch. Though nothing would be living in it, and I wouldn't be surprised if Lucas hired someone to take care of the pool for us." I laugh at my own thoughts, imagining Kristy and I sipping sparkling rosé while watching a tall and tanned pool boy scoop leaves out of the water.

I stay outside for nearly another hour. My skin is a bit red when I go inside, and the cool air gives me an instant chill. I walk down the hall, remembering the first time I was in this house and almost got lost trying to find the door to the rooftop.

The master bedroom is on the second floor, and I pass by Eliza's room on my way there.

"You stink." She's sitting on the bed, legs stretched out in front of her, and is watching *Lifetime* movies. That's not what I expected from her.

"I do," I agree. "I was sweating like a hog out there in the sun."

"Humans are disgusting." She turns her eyes away from the TV and looks me up and down. "It's strange how you want to be tan now. I used to cover up every inch of my skin."

"Oh, right. Being tan back then meant you worked outside."

"And being rail thin meant you didn't have enough money for food. My sister was what you'd call pleasantly plump and I couldn't gain weight no matter how hard I tried."

"I didn't know you had a sister."

"There's a lot about me you don't know."

"Maybe I can get to know you," I say apprehensively. "You're rather interesting."

"Yes, I am." She looks back at the TV and I take it as my cue to keep walking. "Tonight," she starts, and I stop. "If you can pull yourself off my maker for an hour or so, we can hang out and…

talk," she spits out her words like she can't believe what she's saying.

"Really? I'd love that! And statistically speaking, the chances of getting attacked by another demon are pretty low. I'll bring vanquishing potions just in case."

She doesn't take her eyes off the TV, but I can tell she's trying not to smile. "Given what I saw last night, I don't think you need any potions." A commercial for adult diapers comes on and she flicks her eyes to me. "As much as I hate to admit it, you were pretty fucking badass last night."

"Thank you." I smile. "Maybe me, you, Lucas, and Dom—"

"No."

"You don't know what I was going to ask."

She crosses her arms. "No double date."

"It could be fun."

"Would you go on a date with your father?"

I make a face. "No, but my father is an arrogant asshole."

Eliza purses her lips. "You've met Lucas. He can be an arrogant asshole as well as the best of them."

"He is a tad protective."

"A tad?"

I can't help but laugh. "I see your point. It's still a little confusing to me when I think about your relationship with him. When we first met, I thought you two were a couple."

"I can see how you'd think that. But we never have been."

"I know. Lucas told me."

She just nods and goes back to watching TV. Peeling a strand of sweaty hair from my neck, I continue down the hall and quietly open the master bedroom door. Lucas is still in bed, and his naked body is gloriously sprawled out on the mattress. I close the door behind me, and the room goes dark again.

I tiptoe into the bathroom and take a quick shower. Wrapped only in a towel, I leave the bathroom and climb into bed. Lucas stirs, reaching for me in the dark.

"I can still smell the sunshine on your skin," he whispers and pulls me to him.

"Is that a nice way of saying I still smell like sweat?"

"No." With vampire speed, he moves on top of me, parting my bare thighs and pressing himself in between. I bend my legs up and run my nails over his back. "You smell delicious."

"You need to eat."

"I do."

The room is pitch black and I can't see a thing in front of me. The sensory deprivation would be freaky if I were with anyone but Lucas. Arching my back, I press my core against his. He puts his lips to my neck. His fangs are already drawn and scrape against my skin. Kissing his way down, he puts one leg over his shoulder and dives back in between my legs, tongue lashing out against my clit.

Moaning, I reach down and tangle my fingers through his hair. He slides his hands under my butt, lifting me off the mattress. My other leg goes over his shoulders and I can feel an orgasm coming on already. He's not teasing me, not drawing it out like usual. He wants to feed but won't until he makes me come. Vampires are all about doing what feels good, and while Lucas definitely does what feels good for him, he always prioritizes my pleasure.

My body shudders, getting closer and closer. Lucas sets me back on the mattress and pushes his fingers inside me, going right to that sweet spot that makes me come almost instantly. I cry out with pleasure, writhing against him. He keeps his mouth on me, licking and sucking, until I come for the second time. My pussy spasms wildly and my ears ring as stars dot my vision. Lucas moves on top of me, pushing his large cock inside and fucking me hard and fast.

Wrapping one arm around me, he brings his head down and sinks his fangs into my neck, lapping up the blood that pours out. He groans as he drinks my blood, and I curl my legs around him, rocking my hips along with his.

He clamps his mouth around the bite and sucks hard. I don't think I'll ever get used to the sensation of blood being pulled out of my vein like this. Most of the time, I'm overcome with pleasure which more or less blocks out the pain. Though every once in a while, a little voice in the back of my mind wants to scream that something is wrong. That I'm losing blood at a scary fast rate and if Lucas doesn't stop, I won't have enough left.

But I trust Lucas completely. He'll never lose control.

Swallowing a mouthful of blood, he drives his cock into me, holding it there for a second as he takes in one last drink of blood. He keeps his mouth over the wound on my neck as he comes, licking up the blood that seeps out but not sucking out more.

Cock pulsing inside of me, Lucas gently puts two fingers over the bite on my neck.

"Your blood," Lucas starts, licking the last bit of it off his lips. "It tastes like the sun."

I smile. "I'll have to lay out and tan more often then. I was topless this time."

"I wish I could see that."

"I can lay around topless inside."

"I mean you in the sun." He presses a little harder against the bite wounds, needing to apply pressure for a good minute before the bleeding stops.

I rake my fingers through his messy hair. I accidentally cast a spell to make windows filter out the harmful light of the sun. And I know moonstone absorbs enough sunlight to burn him.

"Maybe you can. I might be able to figure out a way."

"I can, through the window."

"I know, but I mean I might be able to figure out a way for you to day-walk."

And if I did figure out a way to allow a vampire to walk in the sunlight, the Grand Coven would have my head for sure.

CHAPTER 17

I feel a little dizzy when I sit up, which Lucas warned me about. Anytime he drinks a decent amount of my blood, he always babies me for the next few hours while my body heals.

"Are you all right, my love?" Lucas pulls his sweatpants back on and speeds over. I sit back down on the mattress and blink a few times.

"Yeah. Just dizzy like you said."

"Lie back down. I'll bring you water."

"I can get it."

"I know." He's already grabbing the blanket to tuck me back in. "And I can too." He kisses my forehead and speeds out of the room, returning a few seconds later with a glass of water. I take a big drink and set it on the nightstand.

"Do you have to work tonight?"

"I'm done going over the bookkeeping, but I did plan on going in. I allowed Dina to feed last night so her fangs would grow back. I plan to rip them out again after I question her."

"What if she gives you answers?"

"I'll still rip them out, as I will continue to do for the rest of her afterlife. She bit you. Tasted your blood. She hurt you." Anger flashes in Lucas's eyes, and to anyone else, he'd look terrifying right now. "I will find out who sent her and do the same to them."

"I almost forgot vampire bounty hunters were after me." I reach for my water again and take another drink. "What does that say about my life? It's so full of danger and drama that I forgot a group of vampires are against assimilation and want me dead."

"They want you for something, but not dead. Not yet at least."

"The Grand Coven knows we're together. Those rogue vamps know. The Vampire Council will find out soon enough." I let out a snort of laughter. "Breaking us apart might be the only thing the Grand Coven and the VC ever agree on."

"That would be a first."

I finish the water and slowly get up and go to the dresser to get myself a pair of underwear. Most of my clothes are at my house in Thorne Hill and I usually pack just enough for a few days at a time when I come here. It's kind of annoying, but I don't have enough clothes to split evenly between both houses.

We'll be together in Thorne Hill soon enough.

I put the black romper I'd worn earlier back on and go into the bathroom to brush out my hair. Lucas and I go downstairs together, and I head right into the kitchen. I need to eat after he drinks my blood, or I'll start to feel sick later.

"Do you want me to cook for you?" he asks.

"Why do I get the feeling you want to cook?"

"It's a challenge," he says with a smile. "I've mastered toast now."

"You have," I laugh. "And sure, that would be really sweet. I'm still craving mac and cheese and there's a box of it in the pantry."

Lucas turns, having to look around the kitchen for the pantry. I don't think he's ever opened it before.

"You think you can handle it?" I ask as he reads the instructions on the box.

"This is rather simple."

"You say that now," I tease and sit at the island counter. My purse is on the barstool next to me, and the feather is inside. I pull it out, stroking the spine with my finger. Lucas turns, opening and closing his cabinets.

"The pots are in the lazy Susan," I tell him, tucking the feather under the counter. "It's that corner cabinet over there." I point to it, finding it amusing that he has no idea where anything is in his own kitchen.

I keep the feather in my lap and steal a glance down at it, like a kid sneaking looks at a cell phone in class. I don't know why I want to keep this a secret. Maybe because I can't explain why I like it?

"What are you doing?" Eliza comes into the kitchen, stopping short when she sees Lucas at the stove.

"Making Callie lunch." Lucas fills the pot with water and sets it on the stove.

"But that's human food."

"She's human."

Eliza wrinkles her nose. "Speaking of lunch, mine is on the way. Then I'm going to bed."

"Clean up after yourself," Lucas tells her, and I snicker. She really is like his fully grown child. Giving Lucas an annoyed glare, Eliza saunters off, waiting for, well, I'm not sure.

"Eliza doesn't drink bottled blood, right?" I ask.

"No, I won't allow it." Lucas steps back and stares at the pot of water, waiting for it to boil.

"So, when she said her lunch is coming here, she means a person?"

"Yes. There is a service to order from. You pick who you want, and they come to you."

"I've heard of that." I run the feather over the inside of my palm. "And the protests against it."

"Your father led one of the biggest."

"Ugh, don't even bring him up." I shudder. "I say what people want to do with their own bodies is their own choice. As long as they're not hurting anyone, right?"

"I've always agreed with that."

I stick the feather back in my purse when Lucas isn't looking and get up, going over to the pot. "I can cheat." Holding my hands over it, I magically bring the water to a boil.

Lucas smiles and dumps the noodles into the pot. "Get some wine and sit down. I'll bring you the food when it's done."

I don't have the heart to tell him if I drank wine right now, I'd be drunk after two sips. He's trying hard to be involved in every aspect of my life. Teaching himself how to cook means more to me than I expected.

Pouring myself another cup of coffee, I go back to the counter and look through Pinterest, showing Lucas different ideas for the kitchen. We've been in Chicago for a few days and I'm looking forward to going back to Thorne Hill to see how much progress has been done on the house.

"I wish they could put the pool in now," I joke. "But I know it would end up being a mess of dust and scrap and whatever else they take out of the house."

"Once the structural damage has been fixed, it shouldn't be too messy. Maybe by the fall."

"It's too cold in the fall for me to swim."

"How cold is too cold for you?"

"It kind of depends. If the water is warm and the sun is out, probably like seventy-five. We could get a hot tub and use it year-round."

"Okay," he agrees right away.

"And a stable full of white ponies," I add just to see what he'll say.

"Wouldn't you rather have a horse? You're too tall for a pony." He turns around with a smile. "And white doesn't suit you. You need a black horse, like a Friesian."

"Ohhh, those are pretty. I took riding lessons before my father sold me to science, and someone at the stable had a pair of Friesians. I was a kid then, obviously, and I remember them being huge."

"If you want horses, I'll get you horses. It's been a while since I've owned any."

"I didn't know you even liked horses."

"In my human life, we depended on them. As a vampire, I could cover more ground on my own, but still traveled on horseback. I owned racehorses for years but got out of the business."

"How come?"

"I didn't like seeing the horses mistreated. I might have drained a few owners and thought it was best to find a new interest to invest my time and money into."

"Wait a minute." I hold up my hand. "You *killed* humans who mistreated their horses?"

"Yes," he says as if he can't see the issue with it.

"Just when I thought I couldn't love you more…" I laugh and the doorbell rings. "I'll get it," I call to Eliza, not sure how she was planning on answering the door. Though if this is a vampire meal delivery service, I'm sure they're used to walking into houses during daytime hours.

"Send her upstairs," Eliza tells me and speeds up the curved staircase. I give her another few seconds to move out of the sun before opening the door.

"Hi," I say awkwardly to the woman standing on the porch. She's wearing a tight red dress, big hoop earrings, and heels so tall I'm not sure how she can balance. If she got up this morning and decided to look like a cheap hooker, she succeeded. The neighbors will be talking today, that's for sure. "Come in."

She smiles and steps inside. "Wow, this place is sweet. Should I take off my shoes?"

I close the door behind her. "Uh, probably. They don't look very comfortable."

"I got those Botox shots in my feet and don't feel pain anymore."

"That's a thing?"

"Oh yeah! I can give you the number of a doc who'll come

right out to your house and do it." She's too chipper. Way too fucking chipper for someone who's about to be bitten.

"Uh, no thanks." I sweep my hand out at the stairs. "She's upstairs. The door should be open."

"Thanks, honey!" The woman jogs up the stairs and I'm left staring. Shaking myself, I go back into the kitchen.

"If I did cocaine and you drank from me, it would effect you, right?" I ask Lucas.

"Depends on how much you did and how much I drink." His brows push together. "Why? Do you have some?"

"Gross, no. But that meal-on-heels that just got here for Eliza is very hyper. I'm not saying she's on drugs, it just crossed my mind."

"She probably took a B12 shot before she got here. Most do." Lucas opens another cabinet and pulls out vitamins. "Speaking of, you should take these."

I fill up my cup with water to wash down the B12 and iron supplements. "I have a favor to ask you." I toss the pills in my mouth and take a drink of water. One gets stuck on my tongue and Lucas looks at me with a blank stare as I gag and cough. I hold up my hand, letting him know I'm okay. I take another drink and finally get the pill down.

"If it's sex, yes."

"It's not sex. It has to do with a dead body, though."

"You want me to bury the body from last night?"

"The opposite. I want the police to find it so he can be ID'd. His family will be notified then."

Lucas stirs the macaroni and sticks his finger in the boiling water to test to see if they're soft enough.

"That fast-healing thing must be nice," I grumble.

"It is." He turns off the burner and takes the pot over to the sink.

"You need a colander."

"A what?"

"Actually…I don't think you have one. And I have a way around it. Tip it in the sink and I'll hold it."

"But you'll burn—oh, with magic."

"Comes in handy from time to time." Lucas drains the water and then adds the milk, butter, and cheese powder.

"You call this cheese?"

"I do. Some don't. Nevertheless, it's a staple in most American homes. It was the one thing Evander could make when we were kids. Tabatha wouldn't let us use the stove when she wasn't home until he was like thirteen. But we could use magic to boil water, so we ate it all the time."

"Why did you return home to the Martins after you lived with Tabatha and Evander?" Lucas mixes everything up and then dishes half of it onto a plate for me. And then he gives me a fork.

That is not how you eat mac and cheese. He'll learn eventually.

"I only went back a few times, and it wasn't until I could defend myself that I stayed alone. Mostly, I wanted to see Abby. I was worried she'd be mistreated or something. She doesn't have powers, but without me taking the spot, she kind of became a black sheep. Most visits were only a day trip with Tabatha there with me, but one summer when I was sixteen, Tabatha and Evander were visiting family and I didn't want to intrude."

"I take it your family treated you like shit then too."

"Oh, of course. My father tried to keep me out of the house, but then someone tipped off the press that I was back, and that's when my father spun that stupid tale about me being off in a third world country, devoting my life to the less fortunate. He had no choice but to let me stay at the house or else it would look bad. I just wanted to spend time with Abby, but she chose an internship at a hospital over hanging out with me. Now I know she agreed because she was scared of our father, but at the time it felt like a betrayal. That's actually what made us lose contact."

"She's really making an effort now."

"Yeah, she is and it's nice." Lucas kisses the top of my head and leaves the kitchen. I blow on my mac and cheese to cool it down. My familiars trot into the room, wanting some for themselves.

"It's hot," I warn, getting up to give them each a bowl. I trade my fork for a spoon while I'm up as well.

"It's done." Lucas comes back into the room holding a cell phone.

"What's done?"

"I tipped off the police that there is a body inside the building."

"You just called?" I take my seat at the island. "From your phone?"

"It's a burner. I keep a few for instances like this."

"For instances like calling in and reporting a body."

Lucas nods. "Yeah."

I laugh. "We are so normal it hurts."

CHAPTER 18

W hen Eliza said we'd hang out and talk tonight, I assumed she meant at the house or maybe even a coffee house, even though she doesn't drink coffee. I didn't expect to be sitting at a table at the back of Taproom again, waiting for her to find time to come over as she tends the bar.

Which is fine, actually. This place is familiar, and I cast a circle around myself to keep people from coming over and talking to me. Lucas is in the basement torturing Dina, and I've been debating if I should go down and join him.

He's probably more effective without me there. And sitting here by myself, I get to hold my feather.

"I've officially lost it," I whisper to myself and put the feather in my purse before I start calling it *my precious*. I open the internet on my phone and do another search to see if any articles have been written yet about the headless body. Is murder so common here in Chicago this guy doesn't even get a mention?

"We can talk now." Eliza sits down across from me and looks at the time on her phone. "You have ten minutes."

"Good thing I wrote down a list of questions."

"You're joking."

"I am, actually. I thought we'd hang out more like friends, not like an interview. But since I'm on the clock, I'll start. What do you like to do for fun?"

"Now why does it sound like you're hitting on me?"

"Wishful thinking on your part," I spit back and Eliza smiles.

"Fine. Lately I've been on the hunt for particular antique items. There aren't many flea markets open after dark, though. Makes it hard."

"What are you looking for? I can go," I offer, and Eliza just stares at me. "It's not like I have much else to do these days. I'd like to stay busy to keep me distracted."

"From demons?"

"Well, yeah, but on how I'm not part of my coven right now and how that lying bitch, Ruth, has weaseled her way into the Grand Coven."

Eliza presses her lips together and inhales, looking disturbingly human. "That must be hard. I've never belonged to a group like that, but I can imagine how tightly bonded you all are."

"Thank you. And yeah…I'm not close with every single person in the coven. There are too many for that. But the Coven-stead and the Academy…that's my home."

"You really went to witch school?"

I nod. "I'm not supposed to tell vampires about it."

"One of the first things I heard you say was how you have a tendency to do the opposite of what's good for you."

"Hah, isn't that the truth."

"How old are you?"

"Twenty-five."

"You'll be dead before you figure out how to do what's good for you."

"That's probably true," I agree ruefully. "Either from old age or murder."

"My money is on murder."

I laugh and then Eliza does too. "There's a neat antique store in Thorne Hill," I tell her. "The owner is scared of vampires and closes right at sunset."

"Closing at sunset is too late to avoid vampires."

"I know. There are only two vampires in Thorne Hill right now."

"Must be young vampires. Most older ones would know to stay away from witches."

"They are young. Probably turned within the last ten years or so. I've stayed away, and they haven't caused any trouble."

"What about the people in Thorne Hill." Eliza rests her hands on the table. "It's not just witches."

"Over the years, the nons have grown to outnumber us, which is great for business."

"You call them *nons*? Why?"

"It's short for non-magical people."

"Makes sense. And they have no idea they live amongst a town full of magic?"

"I'm sure some have seen things or at the very least felt things," I explain. "They're drawn to the town because of the Ley line. In its natural state, it emits positive energy that makes Thorne Hill a great place to live."

"It has a certain quaintness to it," Eliza admits. "The place you call the Covenstead...how does that work?"

"It's this whole hidden magical dimension thing that's super complicated."

"Sounds like it." She looks back at the bar and draws her fangs. My heart skips a beat, thinking something is wrong, but then I see Dominic walking in. Monica, his human girlfriend, is on his arm.

"So, are you two together?" I ask carefully.

"Sometimes we are. Sometimes we aren't." Eliza stands and smooths her pastel pink dress. "Tonight, we will be. Good talk, Callie. We'll have to do this again."

I turn my head down, feeling a little bad that I don't want to talk to Monica. She seemed pretty head over heels for Dominic, and even told me she thought they were fated to be together or something like that. And he and Eliza are secretly fucking on the side.

Talk about awkward.

The feather ends up in my hands again, and I spend a good ten minutes just staring at it. It's shiny in the weirdest way, and the way the light reflects off it is as hypnotizing as watching dark waves lap against the ocean's shore.

I don't know how much time passes. A minute? Five? Twenty? I zone out, heart rate slowing and blood pressure dropping. I'm completely relaxed, and I bring the feather to my face, thinking of the blue-eyed man in the woods who saved me from the demon.

Feeling Lucas's presence before I see him, I open my eyes and watch him walk through the bar. The crowd parts and everyone looks at him with a mixture of awe and fear.

And lust.

Though it doesn't bother me that every single female in the bar and even a handful of the men want to fuck Lucas. There's only one person he wants to hook up with, and I still feel so lucky that it's me.

My heart leaps in my chest and a smile comes to my face. The room dims as he draws near, and all that I see, all that matters, is him. The feather falls from my hands, gently floating to the table.

He slides into the booth next to me, snaking one arm around my shoulders. Pulling me to him, he kisses me, deep and passionate, and I'm completely aware of the jealous stares and hateful glances being thrown my way.

"Hello to you too," I say, breathless when we break apart. He kisses me once more, tongue pushing into my mouth, and then holds me against his chest. There's no telling me how much he wants to take me home and fuck me or anything of the sort, making me think whatever information he got out of Dina is bad.

"Lucas," I breathe, tipping my head up. His face is flecked with blood, and I don't have to ask to know it's not his. "What'd you find out?"

"Let's go home."

"Uh, okay."

"To Thorne Hill."

"I'm trying to avoid everyone there, remember?" I push away so I can look him in the eyes. "What's going on? What did she say?"

Lucas's dark blue eyes cloud over. "They've been watching you."

"Vampires?" I winkle my nose. "How rude." I do my best Michelle Tanner impersonation.

"This is serious, Callie."

"I know, which is what triggered my mature response."

Lucas scoots me closer, holding me tight like he's afraid someone is going to come in and snatch me right out of his arms. "I don't know who tipped them off, but as soon as they knew you were a witch, you were of most importance to them."

"Who's them?"

"I didn't get any names, and I'm afraid my temper got the best of me. It will be a while before Dina will be answering any questions."

"Oh. Well, we'll...we'll, uh, figure it out. And if I can handle a hellhound that was really made up of a hundred rats, I think I can take on a few vampires, and don't get all defensive over that. I could kick your ass if I really wanted to."

"You could try," he says back, unable to help himself. "And I don't think it's just a few vampires."

"Between you and my familiars, I think any vamp who tries to kill me has another thing coming."

"That's the thing, Callie." He cups my face with one hand and tips my chin up to his. "I didn't get a straight answer—yet—but they don't want to kill you."

"Then what do they want?"

"They want to use you."

CHAPTER 19

"**U**se me?" I echo. "Use me for what?"

"I'm not quite sure, but I won't rest until I find out."

My heart speeds up and my throat tightens. I'm on the verge of freaking out again, and everything seems too overwhelming. I wish my water was wine. Or whiskey. Yes, tonight is a whiskey kind of night.

"What's this?" Lucas picks up the feather.

"Oh, that old thing." I take it from him and suddenly everything seems hopeful. I'll get back into the coven. I'm not guilty of anything. We'll find and kill the vampires, which will result in shutting down a dangerous gang as well.

"Callie?"

I blink, tearing my eyes away from the feather. I zoned out again. "I, uh, I found it and it seems special."

Lucas leans in and smells it. "It smells weird."

"Weird is a little vague. Care to explain?"

He sniffs it again. "I can't. It doesn't smell like a bird."

"I don't think it's from one."

Lucas's eyes meet mine. "What, you think it's from a unicorn or something?"

"Of course not. Unicorns don't have wings. That would be a Pegasus. Too bad they don't exist in this world anymore."

"You think they existed at one point?"

"I know they did. What, in the sixteen hundred years you've been undead, you've never once heard the lore?"

"I did, but it's just that. Lore."

"I read about it in school."

He plays with my hair, twisting it around his fingers. "Do I need to explain how not everything you read is true?"

"It was an old textbook, not a mythical creatures website some sweaty fat dude runs out of his mother's basement."

"Nice visual."

"I try to keep it real."

"You don't want to go back to Thorne Hill yet?" Lucas asks.

"Oh, I do. I miss it, but I don't want to cause any trouble. Well, any more trouble." I want to look through my Book of Shadows, which I left hidden in a magically locked box in my bedroom. It belonged to another witch before her death, and Tabatha gave it to me since I didn't come from a long line of witches who had books to pass down generation to generation.

There's nothing in my book about demons made up of rats. There's not much in my book about demons in general. Most of the information about demons was added by me, and I've never so much as heard of a demon bursting apart into dead rats.

What I need to do is go to the library at the Academy and go through every single book about demons and black magic I can find.

Obviously, I can't, and my only other option would be to send Kristy there. No one would know we're looking into this together, and honestly it wouldn't surprise me to get a call from Kristy in the morning telling me she already went in to look for info about the mystery demon.

An alert goes off on my phone, letting me know an article was posted about a decapitation here in Chicago.

"This might be our guy." I unlock my phone and stare at the

screen impatiently as the article loads. "It just says a body was found and asked for anyone with info to call in." I set my phone down. "They haven't released a name yet."

"What are you going to do when you do get his name?"

"Old-fashioned police work?" I bring my shoulders up in a shrug. "I suppose I'll start with questioning his friends and family, see if they noticed anything demonic. Then I plan to break into his house and look to see if he was into any sort of Satanic cults. I'll use magic, of course, so no one will catch me."

"That's a solid plan. Question them at night and I will hold them spellbound, compelling them to tell the truth."

"How come you can't hold other vampires spellbound?" I close my fingers around the end of the feather.

"For the same reason your spells don't always work on vampires. We're dead. The magic doesn't work the same."

"Shame. I have this sex-slave spell I really want to put on you."

A growl comes from deep within Lucas's throat and he brings his lips to my neck. "You don't need a spell for that."

"I know I don't." Now I do expect him to tell me how much he wants to take me home and fuck me. My phone rings, and I have to tear myself away from Lucas to see who's calling and if it's worth answering.

It's Kristy.

I grab the phone, answering her call right away. "Hey, you okay?"

"I'm fine."

"Thank goodness. What's up?"

"The Grand Coven is here again."

My heart moves up to my throat. "Please tell me you're calling with good news about that."

"I am. Well, kind of. They want you to come to a hearing to review your case. I was only able to get a few words in with Evander, but he seemed optimistic. They found no reason to suspect you of Satanism like Ruth tried to accuse you of."

I let out a breath of relief. "And the bad news?"

"They know Lucas has seen the location of the door. But," she adds quickly, "they also know he only went there to help assist us to safety and then stayed and helped you fight off the demon. That's still a punishable offense, but we think the fact that he saved us will hold up with the council."

"What about Ruth?"

"She's still being held with her powers bound."

Sensing my heart beating faster with anxiety, Lucas rubs my back. I let out another breath and lean into his hand.

"When is the hearing?"

"That's why I called. They want to do it tonight."

"I'm in Chicago."

"I know. I told them you were visiting your sister, and it checked out."

"Thank you, Kristy."

"Do you think you could be here by the witching hour?"

Lucas nods. "I can get you there fast."

"You shouldn't go," I tell him slowly, hating that I'm saying it. "Or at least not to my house." Resting my head in my hand, I let my eyes fall shut. It's nearing ten thirty and in theory, we could get to Thorne Hill before midnight. If we hit traffic, that will be a different story.

"I'll be there," I tell Kristy. "Alone."

"THE GRAND COVEN CAN'T GET MAD THAT YOU'RE HERE." I OPEN the door to Novel Grounds and turn on the light. "Vampires have as much right to live in this town as the non. There are two vampires who live downtown somewhere already."

"I'm surprised they didn't discourage it." Lucas follows me through the store.

"I don't think these vampires know the bad blood between witches and vampires, and as far as the rest of the world knows, we're just an ordinary small town full of ordinary people. If it got out somehow that residents here didn't want vampires to move in, it could bring unwanted attention to us."

"Does it bother you?"

I wave my hand over my office door, unlocking it. "Does what bother me?"

"Having to hide who you are from the world?"

I shake my head. "No. People can hardly handle the fact that vampires exist. Knowing magic is real, they'd go insane."

"But that has nothing to do with what you want."

"Sure it does." I turn on the light to the office. It's nothing fancy, and it's pretty small. "People will either want to kill me or want me to do spells for them. I'd rather just be left alone."

"You can cast spells for that, like you did at the bar tonight."

"True." I turn and lock eyes with Lucas. We made it to Thorne Hill in just under an hour. Lucas is good at speeding thirty miles over the limit while weaving in and out of traffic. I put a good luck spell on us not to crash and burn and the drive still terrified me. "Really, though, I just want to be accepted. I'm so tired of having to explain and rationalize things to people." I let my purse fall off my shoulder and go over to Lucas, sliding my arms up around his shoulders. "Like us. It's nobody's fucking business, and I am so over being told how I feel is wrong. It's not. There is nothing wrong about us at all."

Lucas's large hands land on my hips and he brings them to his. "You are the only thing that's right about me, Callie. You brought me out of the darkness, and I don't just mean that literally. I died over a thousand years ago and part of me never left the grave. And then I met you."

My eyes fall shut, trying to dam up the tears that threaten to fall.

"You brought me back to life, and I'd go through another thousand years of pain and darkness if that's what it would take to be with you."

I slit my eyes open and see that he looks just as emotional as I'm feeling.

"I love you now." He brings his lips to mine. "As I will tomorrow. And the day after that. For the rest of my existence, Callie, I will always love you." He kisses me hard, tongue pushing past my lips. I'm weak against him, resolve lost and crumbled on the floor.

I don't care about the hearing.

I don't care about being removed from the coven for the rest of my life.

All I care about is Lucas and how he makes me feel. How I don't think I could survive without him. My life was full of pain and betrayal. Of heartbreak and tears.

I've always loved being a witch, but it took a long time to learn to love myself. And Lucas...Lucas accepts and embraces every imperfect part of me.

"And I'll love you," I pant between kisses. "I don't care what happens tonight. I'm not letting anyone get between us." I hold onto him like my life depends on it. In some ways it entirely does. "I won't let it come to that. Whatever happens tonight...I won't let them even attempt to keep us apart."

His fingers dance over the marks on my neck where he sank his fangs in yesterday. I put Kristy's extra-strength healing balm on them, fading them fast but not fast enough. I'll put more on when I leave the shop, and then hopefully makeup and wearing my hair in a braid over my shoulder will be enough to keep them from being noticed.

"I'll call you when I get back to my house." My words choke up in my throat. If I stay here, I'll be with Lucas. If I leave... there's no telling what could happen.

CHAPTER 20

"Holy shit, it's good to see you." I throw my arms around Evander, feeling a shade better just to be near him. "How are you?"

"I'm fine. There were no demonic side effects."

"Thank goodness."

"No, thank *you*." He releases me and takes my hand, turning to say the incantation to open the door. My suspension has been temporally lifted, allowing me to pass through.

"*Invoco elementum terrae. Invoco elemuntum aeris,*" I chant another with Evander. "*Invoco elemuntum aqua. Invoco elemuntum ignis.*" The empty space in the large tree flickers blue. Still holding my hand, Evander and I walk through, emerging into the Covenstead.

It's obvious right away shit is going down tonight.

"Our entire coven is pissed about this," he whispers to me, taking his hand from mine and wrapping it protectively around my shoulders.

"At me?"

"No, at the Grand Coven. We all know what you did, Callie. You saved us from a demon. You were the first one to notice the Ley line had been tainted. And you saved my life."

"When you say it like that, I sound pretty awesome."

"You have your flaws," he laughs. "But we are lucky to have you and everyone in the coven knows it. Persecuting you is wrong. You haven't endangered anyone, and we all know it." He gives me a squeeze. "We have your back."

We go into the gathering hall and my stomach clenches. Three members of the Grand Coven are seated to one side, with an empty chair in the middle of the altar for me. A handful of council members are seated as well, with half being from my own coven and the rest from another to weigh in as unbiased opinions.

Tabatha is seated in the first row, a stricken look on her face. Kristy and the twins are seated two rows behind her, and I can't bring myself to even look at them. Kristy is freaking out, I'm sure of it. I undo the ties of my cloak as I walk down the aisle, eyes set on the chair on the altar.

"Callista Martin," Albert, a Grand Master, stands and beckons me to the chair. My heart is all flutters of nerves inside my chest. Once I'm seated, another member of the Grand Coven brings over a black candle. I take it with one hand and hold my other over top of it.

"You have been brought forth before the council today to address the accusations against you. Do you swear to powers of the coven to stand before us and tell the truth, the whole truth, and nothing but the truth?"

The flame grows taller, heating the palm of my hand. "I do."

"Very well." Albert gives a curt nod and the candle is taken from me. He goes to the podium and every witch and wizard in the gathering hall holds their breath. "You have been accused of willingly leading a vampire to the location of your coven's sacred door. How do you plead?"

I press my hands against my thighs and let my eyes fall shut for a second. "Guilty."

Almost everyone in the gathering hall gasps, and even Albert looks shocked.

167

"You admit that you took a vampire to the location of the door?" he repeats.

"Yes. I did."

"You do realize that is an offense punishable by fire, do you not?"

"I do," I say, fighting to find my voice. "And I would do it again if I had to."

The witches from the other coven's council lean together, whispering. They don't know the details of what happened, and I sound pretty insane and totally guilty right now.

"She admits guilt to her crime," another Grand Master booms throughout the hall. "Per witch-law the trial is over, and her punishment shall be dealt with."

"There were extenuating circumstances." A witch from my council stands up. "I'd like to testify on her behalf."

"As do I." Evander rises, eyes set on me.

Kristy shoots up next. "As do I."

"As do we," Nicole and Naomi say at the same time.

"Me too," Brooke, the young witch we helped escape through the door says, much to her mother's chagrin. "She saved us."

Her father stands up next, followed by the girl's brother and then her mother. Tabatha meets my eye and gives me a small nod. She's not allowed to testify on my behalf, but the look on her face says it all. *We've got you, Callie.*

I swallow the lump of emotion rising in my throat and watch several other witches stand, willing to testify for me.

"I'll testify." Ruby Darrows stands, holding her head high. She doesn't specify if she's testifying for or against me. My money is on *against*.

Albert nods and holds out his hand, pointing to Ruby. "I call you forth, Ruby Darrows. Let the council know she is a professor here at Grim Gate Academy." Ruby sidesteps out of the pew and comes up to the altar. She goes to the podium and is given the black candle, being sworn in to tell the truth.

"Please explain the nature of your relationship with Callista Martin," Albert orders.

"I've known Callista—or Callie, as we call her—since her first year here at the Academy."

"Would you consider the two of you friends?"

"Quite the opposite, actually. Callie and I had our fair share of differences throughout the years." She's looking at the council next to me. "During our years at the Academy, Callie was quite the troublemaker, as she continues to be today."

I shift my weight in the chair, sweat dripping down between my breasts. The fuck, Ruby?

"But I know without a doubt, Callie Martin would never bring harm to her coven. I testify on her behalf. I was not there that night, but I heard from the witches who were that the vampire assisted Callie and risked his own afterlife to keep demons at bay so the door could be opened."

The other coven's council members whisper amongst themselves.

"And tell me," Albert goes on. "Do you believe it was absolutely necessary for the vampire to be there?"

"Like I said, I wasn't there," Ruby presses and I'm pretty sure Hell just froze over. She's defending me? Maybe I do have a chance at getting out of here alive. "But from what I was told, yes. As we all know, vampires possess strength and senses we do not. The vampire was the first to realize demons were headed toward the door and alerted Callie and her familiars to assist in protecting the witches who needed to escape to the Covenstead."

Albert speaks with the other two members of the Grand Coven and then dismisses Ruby. He calls forth Brooke next, and she clutches her mother's hand the whole way to the altar.

"What is your name, darling?" Albert asks Brooke and crouches down to her level. His eyes are kind, unlike Ruth's. I'm trying not to lump him in the same shit-list as Ruth. They sat on the Grand Council together, but that doesn't mean he's an asshat too.

"Brooke."

"And how do you know Callie?"

"I've seen her at gatherings." Brooke looks at me and I give her a small smile.

"Do you know the night Ruby was talking about?" he asks and Brooke nods. "Can you tell the council what happened?"

"It's okay," her mother encourages.

"We went to Callie's house because it was safe and closer to the door than our house. We were waiting."

"What were you waiting for?"

Brooke looks at her mom, who reminds her they were waiting for Evander to show up with backup. "Callie and her friend got there first."

"The vampire?"

Brooke nods again. "He said he's never had pizza."

A few people laugh and Brooke gets embarrassed.

"How sad for him. I do love a good pizza. Now, Brooke, I know it was a scary night, but can you tell us what happened in the woods?"

"There were people. With black eyes. They tried to get into the door and Callie and her friend fought them off. They were like superheroes."

"Did the vampire scare you? It's all right if he did. Vampires scare me."

A human lawyer might have considered that leading the witness. I edge forward, waiting on Brooke's words.

"No. He was very handsome," she says, and everyone laughs this time. She blushes. "He was funny too."

"You never once felt frightened of him?"

She shakes her head. "Nope."

"Thank you, Brooke. You were very helpful."

She's dismissed and one of the witches on the council who was with us that night gives her testimony next. It's similar to Brooke's but in more detail, telling everyone what happened and how hard it was to hold the circle of protection against the demons.

"I think we've heard enough," Albert concedes. "The vampire played a vital role in helping the witches and wizards escape as well as fighting off the demons." He surveys the council. "I have to say this is no ordinary case. Never in my years have I heard of a vampire joining an alliance with a witch. I have made my conclusion, and if the council agrees, I would like to move forth clearing Callista Martin of all charges."

The two other Grand Coven members stand, dismissing the council to another room where they can discuss my fate. Nine times out of then, the jury rules in favor of the Grand Master who leads the trial, but all it will take is one witch to refuse to forgive me for associating with vampires.

And even if I am cleared, I will be risking everything by staying with Lucas, but that's a risk I'm more than willing to take.

Because life without Lucas isn't worth living at all.

I can feel the coven's eyes on me, and I'm sure there are a few out there who think I was wrong to let a vampire help me. But Lucas isn't like other vampires, not anymore at least. Folding my hands in my lap, I watch wax drip down the candles on the altar. It shouldn't take long for the council to reach an agreement. There's no evidence to go over, as we take our word seriously. Our words cast spells, after all.

Tabatha avoids my gaze and the feeling like she's hiding something comes back. I focus on the dripping wax again, trying to stay calm. Another minute ticks by.

And then another.

And another.

All I can think about is the longer this takes, the more likely it means people don't agree on my punishment.

Finally, the council comes back out with Grand Master Albert leading the way. His face is expressionless, and my heart immediately hammers in my chest.

"We have reached a decision." He pauses for dramatic effect, which annoys me more now than it does when they do that on eliminations rounds on cheesy reality TV shows. "Callista Martin has shown great heroism toward her coven. She has proven deep devotion to protecting the sacred Covenstead and risked her very own life to ensure others live. Bringing a vampire to the door is a great offense, and we cannot overlook the danger of a vampire knowing the perfect hunting spot for unsuspecting witches."

I feel like I'm going to throw up. Lucas isn't a danger, and I want to jump up and shout it at the entire coven. I press my nails into my palm to hide that I'm shaking.

"Many of us dream of a world full of peaceful coexistence but we must not forget who our enemies are."

Yep. Definitely throwing up.

"That vampire is not our enemy."

A collective gasp whispers throughout the coven. My own jaw drops. What?

"I do not condone any witch being in the presence of any vampires. Never trust a vampire. It's one of the first things we are taught, is it not? The charges against Callista Martin are hereby dropped." He leans on the podium and looks at me. "Under one condition."

I swallow hard and nod my head.

"You are not to consort with vampires ever again. If you are caught, your High Priestess will punish you as the law states."

CHAPTER 21

B reathe in.
     Hold it.
Breathe out.

My vision is dotted with stars. The wooden arms of the chair bite into my skin from me gripping them so hard. I'm not going to never see Lucas again. That's not an option. At all. The threat means nothing to me because there is no way in hell I'm letting anything get between me and the man I love.

What upsets me is knowing what would happen to Tabatha if she's caught withholding punishment. She knows Lucas isn't just some vampire I hung out with for a while and just happened to be around when demons attacked.

She knows we're in a committed relationship together. That we're planning on living together as soon as the house is done.

She knows that I'm in love with him and that there is no fucking way I'm losing him.

"Callie." Kristy hurries through the crowd of witches leaving the gathering hall and hurries up the altar steps. I'm still sitting in the chair even though I've been dismissed. The Grand Coven and council are gone, and Tabatha followed after them needing to do her role as High Priestess.

"Are you okay?"

"Why wouldn't I be?" I blink several times and stand up, smiling at my best friend. "They cleared my name. I'm not going to burn to death."

"Yeah but they also…"

"Forbid me from seeing Lucas?"

"Yes." Her face falls. "I'm so sorry."

"Don't be."

"But you…Are you sure you're okay?"

I start down the stairs. "I'm fine. Really."

"Bottling up your emotions isn't good."

"I'm not bottling up anything. *I'm fine*. I just want to go home and be with my boyfriend now."

"But you can't."

"I couldn't before, either. It's a stupid fucking law. How can a legal system tell me who I should or shouldn't love? What does the fucking law fucking know about fucking love?"

Kristy loops her arm through mine. "There's that anger I was waiting for. I agree. It's stupid. Really stupid and old-fashioned and wrong. Vamps and witches were at war a thousand years ago and it's time to let the past go. Hell, even the US and Germany are allies now."

"Right? It's just so fucking stupid and I'm going to do something about it. I just…I don't know what I'm going to do yet."

"Start with doing Lucas." Her lips pull up into a half smile. "That seems to put you in a good mood."

"It does." We slow, not wanting to be within earshot of anyone ahead of us. "Do you think it's wrong we're together?"

"No, not at all. I used to think it was weird, but then I saw how much he cares for you and makes you happy. He gets you, almost as well as I do. You've been my best friend for fifteen years, Cal. No one will ever be good enough for you, but Lucas… he comes pretty close to checking all the boxes. I do have to take a few points away because he can't take you to Disney World. I know how much you love Splash Mountain."

"We could always go at night."

"Good point. I'll give him some points back then."

I rest my head against hers. "Thank you for being my best friend. Has it really been fifteen years? We're getting so old."

"Tell me about it. Though you don't look like you've aged a day since your last birthday."

"I'm telling you, it's all the wine I drink. And probably the exercising. I do run a lot. Not lately, though. It's too fucking hot outside."

It's late and I'm tired, feeling the strain on my emotions from the trial. Meeting at the witching hour is typical for us even though most of the members of the coven hold regular jobs with daytime hours.

"Who's opening tomorrow?" I ask as we step behind another group of witches to step through the door.

"Me," Kristy groans.

"I'm off probation now. I can come back to work."

"I kind of gave all your shifts to Dani, the new girl, for the rest of the summer. It was the only way I could get a temporary replacement. She wanted hours so she'd have as much money as possible before leaving for college this fall. Stay home, day drink and enjoy your sugar daddy."

"Oh, I plan to." We step through the door and I'm greeted by my familiars.

"Your plan to get four-wheelers to ride to your house isn't a bad one," Kirsty says after we've hiked half a mile through the woods.

"Right? Once the temp drops, we'll be saying that even more."

"You'll be even farther from the door when you get into the new house, won't you?" she asks.

"Yeah, so I really will need to invest in a four-wheeler or a team of horses."

"Ohhh, get horses! You know how much I love them."

"I already causally mentioned to Lucas that having horses would be cool, so don't be surprised when he builds me a barn."

"I'm trying really hard not to be jealous, but I'm a little jealous," Kristy laughs.

"Don't be. I can be your sugar-friend, mooching off her own sugar daddy."

"I like the sound of that." We keep walking through the woods until we get to my house. Kristy usually parks here and walks through the woods with me instead of going through the forest the way most of the other witches do, who are coming from town.

"Be careful, Callie. I can't…I can't lose you."

"You won't," I promise. "Lucas and I have always been forbidden, so it's like nothing changed. But what I do want to know…" I let out a breath and feel a chill come over me. "Is how Ruth found out about us in the first place. Tabatha never mentioned Lucas when she told the Grand Coven about that night."

"You're right. I wonder how she knew."

"Someone had to have tipped her off. But I don't know why. I'm not really that involved in the coven, and Lucas—"

"What?"

"The vampire bounty hunters. They knew we were together too."

"You don't think Ruth was working with them, do you?"

"No, or at least probably not. It doesn't really make sense. The only reason she brought up the vampire stuff was to blackmail me into getting her onto Satan's good side." I let out a breath. "I'm too tired to think about this and I slept in this morning."

"Go inside, enjoy your naked vampire, and rest. But please, Callie, be careful."

I'm on my second glass of wine when Lucas pulls into the driveway. He parks his black Mercedes in the driveway and gets out, moving with vampire speed up to the front porch.

"What's that smell?" he asks, making a face.

"Lavender, lemon, and eucalyptus oil." I motion to the diffuser I have on the porch next to me. "It keeps mosquitoes away. You don't like it?"

"It's very strong."

I look into my wine glass for bugs. I don't see any, and I'm getting tipsy enough not to care as long as I drink them down fast enough. Finishing the last bit of wine, I set my glass down and get up. "Who has a stronger sense of smell: a vampire or a German Shepherd."

"The dog, thankfully."

"Really?"

"Yes, though really, I'm glad. The world smells enough as it is."

"True, and I'm glad too because I do human things in the bathroom occasionally."

Lucas laughs. "I know you're alive, my love." He picks me up and kisses me, pressing my back against the front door. I called him when the trial was over, letting him know to come over and not to worry about finding BBQ Callie in the yard. Then I hung up and started drinking away my problems.

It's a terrible coping mechanism, and one that I started way too young. We all have our vices, and I know this will catch up to me sooner or later.

"How drunk do I have to be for you to get drunk too?" I ask between kisses.

"It depends." Lucas draws his fangs and grazes them over my flesh.

"On what?"

"On how much I take from you." He stops kissing me and looks in my eyes. "I won't take too much. I love you, Callie Martin, and I will never hurt you."

"Anne."

"Anne?"

"It's my middle name. Callista Anne Martin."

"Martin is your father's last name."

"I know." I feel like I weigh nothing at all as Lucas easily holds me up. "But it's mine too."

"For now." Lucas doesn't give me a second to think. He kisses me hard again, tongue entering my mouth. Heat rushes through me and I don't have time to process what he just said.

"Let's go inside." I grab the hem of his shirt and inch it up. No one from the coven has reason to go by my house tonight, and it's far enough away from the road it would be impossible to sense that Lucas was a vampire even if someone did drive by. Still... fuck. I hate this.

Moving with vampire speed, Lucas carries me in and lays me down on the couch. I curl my legs up around him and we go right back to where we left off.

"I should..." I start, trailing off as Lucas bunches up my dress. "Put an extra—ohhh." He slides his hand up my thigh and sweeps his fingers over my clit. "Wa..warding on...on...the house."

"Are you expecting more demons?" His fingers slip under my panties. "I'll kill them just for interrupting us."

"Not demons, but witches."

Lucas stops stroking me. "Why are you warding against witches?"

My eyes fall shut and suddenly I can't breathe. Lucas moves off of me and I get up, going into the kitchen for more wine.

"I thought the trial went well." Lucas watches me forgo a wine glass and put the bottle to my lips. "Yet you're drinking like you want to forget something."

"Oh, I do. I want to forget that the Grand Coven forbid me to see you or any other vampire ever again, because it's not like I'm going to listen." I swallow another mouthful, tipping the bottle up too fast and causing myself to choke. Classy, I know. I cough and wine drips down my face.

Lucas takes the bottle from me. Widening his legs, he rests one hand on the small of my back and urges me to him. He cups one of his large hands around my chin and tips my head up to his.

"Who do I have to kill?"

"I honestly don't know if you're joking right now."

"It depends on what you want."

"I want us to move into that old house and live happily ever after," I say with no hesitation. "And more wine."

"You weren't supposed to be with me before and it never bothered you."

"Yeah, and I still don't really give a fuck what the Grand Coven says. But this time…Tabatha is responsible for dishing out a punishment if I'm discovered to be in communication with vampires. She already knows about us and if it gets out she's aware but hasn't done anything about it, she'll be stripped of her title of High Priestess and cast out of the coven. It's not just me I'm risking, it's her, and she's the last person I want to put in danger like that."

Lucas's brow furrows and he holds me closer.

"I just don't know what to do." Tears fall down my face and Lucas gently wipes them away. "I love you and nothing will ever come between us. But being together in Thorne Hill…I just don't know." Unable to hold back any longer, I start crying. I'm tired, stressed, and terrified of hurting those I love.

"It'll be okay," Lucas soothes. "Somehow…it will."

Sniffling, I nod and press my face against his chest. "Sorry for getting tears all over your shirt."

"I guess I have to take it off."

I turn my head up to see his cheeky grin. "That would be for the best." Breaking apart, I grab a napkin from the counter to blot my eyes and blow my nose. Lucas has his shirt off and pours me another glass of wine, and seeing him standing in my little kitchen half naked while offering me booze is one of the best things that could happen tonight.

The second-best will happen when his pants come off.

"I think it would be entertaining to see you drunk." I take a big drink of wine. "How long does it last?"

"That would also depend on how much I drank, much like it would for you, but not nearly as long." Lucas sits at the island counter and scoots the other stool out for me. "Do you want to talk about the trial?"

I take another big drink of wine and set the glass down. Instead of sitting on the stool, I climb onto Lucas's lap.

"No. I want to drink and have sex until the sun comes up."

His eyebrows go up. "I can be of assistance with that."

"I figured you would." I fold my arms around him and rock my hips. Lucas pulls my dress up and I bring my hands down over his chest. My fingers rest on the button of his jeans. He picks me up, sets me on the counter, and takes off his pants.

I bite my lip, eyes going to his large cock, and then lean back so Lucas can strip me of my underwear. He tosses them on the ground and moves in, parting my thighs with his hand.

"Touch yourself," he growls and steps back. "I want to watch you make yourself come."

"But I'm sitting on the counter." I feel like I'm on display and it almost makes me nervous.

"I know."

Then I see the lust in Lucas's eyes. Parting my lips, I bunch up my dress, moving it off my thighs. I let out a breath and sweep my hand over my chest, slowing moving it between my legs. Lucas draws his fangs as he watches me circle my fingers over my clit. It feels better when he touches me, though that look in his eyes and the precum that's dotting the tip of his cock is turning me on so much it won't take long before I come.

"You are so fucking hot," he groans, wrapping his fingers around his cock. My eyes fall shut and I'm getting close to coming and Lucas knows it. He advances, pulling my hand from between my legs and putting my fingers in his mouth, tasting me.

Then he drops his hand down and finishes what I started, and the moment the orgasm rolls over me, he brings me to him, lining his cock up with my entrance. I buck my hips and that's all he needs to know I'm ready for him to enter me.

Holding me to him, he sits back on the barstool. My legs hang down around him and he grips my waist. The stool creaks under us as I rock my hips, moving faster and faster and feeling him fill every inch of me.

I moan loudly as I come again, my pussy tightening around his cock. Lucas comes right after that, and puts his mouth to my neck. His fangs dig into my skin but don't break through. He holds me tight against him, and we stay together like that for a moment after we're done.

"Think of all the places we'll have to check off our sex list in the new house," I pant.

"As soon as it's safe for you to be in there, we should get started."

"I agree." I rake my fingers through his hair. "I'm excited to check it out tomorrow and see how much work they got done while we were in Chicago."

"I am as well."

He kisses me and then we get up, going upstairs to shower. I finish my wine on the way and wobble up the stairs.

"You're drunk, Callie."

"Strange. Wonder how that happened."

I turn on the shower, knowing it needs a minute to warm up. "Are you hungry now?"

"You just want to get me drunk." He grabs two towels from the cabinet under the sink. "And you say I'm a bad influence."

"I'm really curious to what you'd be like drunk," I admit and test the water. It's still cold. "And they say drunk sex is better than regular sex."

"We never have *regular sex*."

"No, we don't, and I fucking love it." I go to get into the shower and almost lose my balance. Lucas catches me and helps me in. We quickly wash up and then go into my bedroom. It's been a few days since I've slept in my own bed and it hits me how homesick I was.

Not just for this bed in this house, but for *home*.

Home is Thorne Hill.

Home is the Covenstead.

And home is with Lucas.

CHAPTER 22

The world spins around me and I'm not sure what's making it spin faster. The fact that I just came a record amount of times or that I'm one and a half bottles of wine deep into the night.

Lucas brings his head up from between my legs and splays his fingers over my stomach. We're in my bed, having sex for the second time tonight. I meant it when I said I wanted him to fuck me until the sun came up.

The aftershock of the intense climax is still pulsing through me, and I let my head fall to the side, gasping for air. Lucas kisses the inside of my thigh, and I try to move my leg but don't know how. It's a wonder I didn't forget how to breathe, really.

Lucas kisses his way up to my neck. His fangs are out, and they press into my skin without cutting into me. I open my mouth, having every intention of asking him if he's hungry, but I'm unable to form words.

"Breathe, my love."

"Mmmhhh," I moan and slit my eyes open. Lucas lays down next to me and kisses my neck.

"Are…are you hungry?" I finally pant.

"I might have worked up an appetite."

"Drink me," I groan and tip my head to offer up my neck. I turn the wrong way and end up hitting my head against Lucas's. I laugh and he moves back down between my thighs. He kisses the inside of my thigh before sinking his fangs into me. He hungrily laps up my blood and then moves on top of me, driving his cock inside me. He fucks me hard and fast, and goes back for more blood after he comes.

The world is still spinning when he collapses in bed next to me.

"Am I still bleeding?" I bring my hand down to feel for blood, and am surprised to find none. Lucas isn't a messy eater.

"You clot fast." He envelopes me in my arms.

"Is that good?"

"I don't know." He nuzzles his head in my hair. "You're less likely to bleed out that way."

I spin in his embrace and hook my leg over his. The flesh around his bite is tender, and will be that way until the morning. The wounds hurt for a good day or so, but I kind of like it.

"I'll get you a towel," he says but makes no attempt to get up, which is fine by me. A few minutes pass and he gets up, but lacks his usual grace. I'm close to drifting to sleep, but seeing him stagger makes me shoot up.

"Are you drunk?"

He brings his hand to his forehead. "I, uh, feel the alcohol from your blood."

"I feel like I need to document this moment," I laugh. "But my phone is downstairs."

Lucas bumps into the doorframe on his way to the bathroom, making me laugh. He zooms back and into bed. I clean myself up and twist, moving onto Lucas.

"Do you want to go buy shit off of Instagram ads now? I do that when I'm drunk sometimes."

"No," he laughs. "I want to have sex with you again."

"Already?"

"I'm a vampire. I really can fuck you all night." He flips me over, pinning my body between his and the mattress. "You are beautiful." His lips meet mine. "We should go on vacation."

"We should. Like a cruise!"

"If that's what you want."

"You'd hate it, wouldn't you?" I run my hands up and down his back. "It's all sunny and oceany."

"I like the ocean. And the sun. Too bad it'll burn me."

"Yeah," I laugh. "Too bad."

"You name the place and we'll go. You know I'll do anything for you, Callie." His words slur a little and it's fucking adorable.

"Kristy was talking about Disney World earlier and I want to go back. Tabatha used to take me and Evander when we were kids. We loved it. It's magical without real magic."

Lucas lets out a snort of laughter. "Then we'll go." He rests his head against mine and closes his eyes. His phone rings, echoing up the stairs.

"It's Eliza," he sighs. She has her own ringtone and he knows it's her calling. "She's so needy sometimes."

Now it's my turn to laugh. "She just loves you."

"Obviously."

I playfully smack him. "She worries."

"Too much."

"Go answer! She's finally starting to like me and when you ignore her for me, she gets jealous."

Lucas grumbles but gets up, zooming out of the room and then back into bed with me. I snuggle up next to him, not realizing he's FaceTiming Eliza.

"Nice tits," she answers.

"I know, right?" Lucas laughs and spins around, grabbing my boobs.

"Stop!" I protest, laughing and reaching for the covers. Lucas tickles me and I squeal as I push him away.

"What the fuck is going on?" Eliza's voice crackles through the phone. "I'm going to hang up."

"But you called." Lucas lets me go and plops down on his back, holding the phone up so Eliza can see his face.

"Um, no. You called me."

"Only because you called first," Lucas counters and gets distracted with my boobs again.

"Lucas, stop!" I laugh.

"I don't want to." He drops the phone and snakes his arms around me. Eliza's voice is muffled, but I hear her saying she's going to hang up. I reach around Lucas for the phone.

"What's up?" I ask, trying to hold the phone up but end up smashing it against Lucas's back. He turns back around and takes the phone from me.

"Because she's nosey," he answers. "She's always been nosey. Nosey little vampire."

"Are you drunk?" Eliza's blue eyes widen.

"Maybe."

Eliza lets out an annoyed sigh. "I'm glad you're not dead, Callie. Have fun with him. He's obnoxious when he's had alcoholic blood. Be glad it'll wear off fast." She ends the call.

"She's right." Lucas drops the phone onto the mattress and spoons his body around mine.

"That you're obnoxious?"

"No," he laughs. "That it wears off fast. Why, you think I'm obnoxious?"

"If I did, I wouldn't tell you." I twist around in his embrace and kiss him. "I'm tired."

"You've had a long day. Let's both get some sleep."

I sit up just enough to glare at the window. Bright sunlight is shining through and birds are happily chirping. I hold out my hand and telekinetically close the blinds.

"Thanks," Lucas mumbles, still half asleep. "I prefer the dark."

"Me too when I'm hungover." I flop down and let my eyes fall shut. I drank a lot and then Lucas drank from me. I feel like shit right now and want to go back to sleep. But I'm so thirsty and I have to pee.

Dammit.

Mentally groaning, I stagger out of bed and into the bathroom. I gulp down water right from the faucet and use the toilet. Then I drag my butt back into bed and snuggle up with Lucas. He's dead asleep, skin cold, and perfectly still. I'm hot and have a stomachache. Curling up against his cool body feels good. Binx is sleeping on my pillow and Freya and Pandora are sleeping on piles of laundry on the floor, looking so much like normal cats it's almost funny.

I fall asleep, and when I wake up again three hours later, Lucas isn't in bed with me anymore. The smell of coffee fills the air, and I push myself up, smiling. This time when I get up, I don't feel quite as shitty, but I'm going to need to drink a gallon of water before I feel back to normal.

"Morning."

"Good morning, my love." Lucas takes a mug down from the cabinet. "You feeling all right?"

"Let me have some coffee first and then I'll answer that."

He laughs and pours me coffee. I take it to the island counter. "You don't feel hungover, do you? I mean, you can't."

"Right. Even if I drank you dry, I'd heal before the alcohol affected me in that way."

"Another perk to being immortal."

"Or you could just not drink so much."

"Where's the fun in that?" I bring my coffee to my lips.

"It's going to be okay," he says softly. "I won't lie to you and tell you I know how or why, but I'll find a way. You are mine, Callie. I won't let anyone take you from me."

"Do you think vampires and witches will ever get along?"

"Maybe," he says after a moment of hesitation. "We share a common enemy."

"Humans," we say at the same time.

"Though most witches blend into the human world seamlessly. Even you do."

"What's that supposed to mean, even I do?"

Lucas makes a face. "You're the least human human I've ever met."

I sink my teeth into my lip and shake my head. "What if I'm not really human?"

"You're at least partly human or else I wouldn't be able to drink your blood."

"Right. I suppose it doesn't matter, right?"

"We both know it matters to you. I love you no matter what, but I can't blame you for wanting to find out more."

My fingers loop through the handle of the coffee cup. "I think Tabatha knows something and is keeping it from me."

"What makes you say that?"

"Back when the demon attacked me in the spring...back when I was called a half-breed for the first time, I asked her and she couldn't look at me when she answered. And it was more like this feeling." I bring my hand to my chest. "Because deep down I know I'm not fully a witch. And you said it yourself: I don't smell like my family. Is it because they're not really my family?"

"Wouldn't it be a good thing if they weren't?"

"Oh, I'd love to not be related to my asshole father, but Abby..."

"She'd still be your sister."

"I should call her. Or at least text and say hi." Right on cue, my phone rings. "If that's Abby I'm adding premonition to my list of powers."

It's not Abby, but someone from work. I have a mild panic attack that I was supposed to go in and open today and Kristy forgot to tell me with everything else going on last night.

"Hey, Callie." It's Betty. "Sorry to bug you on vacation, but someone came in looking for you, and when I said you weren't here, she asked for your number. I didn't want to just give it out."

"Thanks. Who is it?"

"She said her name was Melinda Richards. Do you know her?"

The fuck? Melinda is in Thorne Hill? At my store? I should have hung around at the hospital and relayed the message. I'm betting that fuck-off of a brother didn't even tell her to stay away.

"Yeah, I do. Is she there? I'll talk to her."

Betty hands the phone over. "Hey, Callie. It's Mel. I'm sorry to get ahold of you this way but I had no other way of finding you."

"What's going on?"

"Work has kept us really busy. Lots of late nights at the office," she says, and I know what that's code for.

"In Thorne Hill? This is my town and—"

"No, in Chicago, but we need help. The books, are um, more complicated that we thought." She can't go into more detail with Betty standing there. "We need help."

"How bad is it?"

"Everyone who's, um, read it has died. Died with excitement for the next one."

"How many?"

"Ten in the last month. There's probably more. You know I wouldn't ask for help if it wasn't necessary."

"I do." My mind whirls. Melinda wouldn't ask for help unless she had no other option. I shouldn't be talking with hunters, and she's risking it all by asking me for help.

"Hey, your friend just walked away to help someone," Melinda says, letting me know she can talk freely. "I've never seen anything like this before." She's talking fast, needing to get me all the details before Betty comes back over and hears. "This demon...we have no idea what it is. It's been moving from one abandoned building to the next, and anytime someone gets near, they've been found dead by the next day. There have been ten deaths we've connected to this demon, but there could be as many as twenty-seven."

"You couldn't confirm the other seventeen?"

"No. The bodies were chewed to bits by rats."

"Rats?"

"Yeah. Like hundreds of rats, according to the coroner's reports."

"Fuck." I slap my hand against my forehead. "Do you remember where that big white house was in the woods?"

"Yeah, I do."

"There's another old house on the same street. All brick with a white Jeep parked out front. Come here and we'll go over everything."

"Thank you." The call ends and I throw my head back.

"Who was that?"

"Melinda, the hunter who got her leg slashed by a demon in the woods."

"And you invited her here?" Lucas asks incredulously. "You think that's a good idea?"

"Oh, I know it's a terrible idea. It's not a trap or anything, at least I don't think so. I'm already breaking witch law by having you here. Why not throw in witch hunters into the mix?"

"Callie," Lucas starts but I stop him.

"She said this demon is hiding in abandoned buildings and some of the bodies found were consumed by rats. Sound familiar?"

CHAPTER 23

Shielding the sun from my eyes with my hand, I watch a gray Jeep Wrangler bump down my gravel driveway. Melinda is alone and on crutches. She waves as she gets out, hobbling toward the house.

"Thank you for meeting with me," she says as I help her up the stairs and into the house. She's not lying about wanting to come here to talk about a case. The warding wouldn't have let her pass if she had ill-intent to be here.

"Of course. What do you need? A vanquishing potion?"

"I wish, but I have a feeling this is going to take more than that."

I open the front door and let her in first. All of my familiars are sitting on the stairs, growling at Melinda.

"Guys, be nice."

"It's okay. It's smart of them not to trust me or anyone they don't know." Melinda rests her crutches against the wall and takes off her shoes. Leaving the crutches, she limps into the living room and almost screams when she sees Lucas. "What? H-how? I thought he was a vampire!"

"I am." Lucas draws his fangs and zooms to us, towering over Melinda.

"Put your fangs away and sit down," I scold. "She's not even armed."

"I am. I have a gun in my backpack. And three knives. And vesta powder."

"See?" Lucas retracts his fangs.

"It's habit." Melinda tries to hold her ground and not look scared, but anyone with half a brain would be terrified of Lucas. He could kill you before you even knew what was happening.

"Let's all sit down, okay?" I hold out my hand and Lucas lets out a growl but comes with me and sits on the couch.

"How are you out during the day?" Melinda takes her backpack off and puts it on the coffee table, not taking her eyes off Lucas.

"Magic," he says simply.

Melinda shifts her eyes to me and nods. "That's, um…"

"Incredible?" Lucas supplies for her, knowing that was not at all the word she was going to use.

"Sure."

"Tell me about this demon," I say, and she takes files out of her backpack. They're stolen police reports, and she lays them out on the coffee table.

"We don't know much, just that it seems to be hiding, waiting for victims to come to it rather than seeking them out and hunting."

"Are these all hunters?" Lucas picks up three of the files and flips through them.

"No, but three hunters have been killed trying to take the demon out."

"How were they killed? The same way as the nons—sorry, as the victims?"

Melinda sorts through her files until she gets to the hunter's reports. "One had his stomach chewed open—" she grimaces "—by rats. While he was alive. The other was from blunt force trauma to the head and the last was filed as having a heart attack, much like the other victims. I know anyone can drop dead from a heart attack with no warning, but it was unlikely everyone did."

"Maybe the demon feeds from the fourth chakra. It would cause heart attacks. And the others were killed before they could kill the demon."

"It's a good theory, and one we thought of too."

Lucas closes a file and tosses it back on the coffee table. "Why are you here?"

"Because we need help. I don't want to watch anyone else die, and we have no idea what we're up against."

If it's the same thing that was in the building next to the bar, then we don't either.

"It's more than that." Lucas leans in and catches Melinda's eye. He has her spellbound in an instant. "Tell me the truth. Why are you here?"

"Easton is going after the demon tonight. I don't want my brother to die."

Lucas breaks his hold. "Fucking knew it."

Melinda shakes her head. "I'm sorry, Callie. I would have told you but...but I know you guys have had your differences and I'm scared." Her face falls. "He's the only family I have left, and you know how stubborn he is. He won't listen to me and it's not like I can go along and help."

"If you're dealing with what I think you are, then you're all as good as dead." And if it's the same thing from before...maybe... just maybe the man with the blue eyes will be there again. I don't care how small of a chance it is that I'll see him again, but I'm taking it. "Do you know where Easton was going tonight?" I look at Lucas. "We fought it off before, and it requires a lot of strength and magic."

"Yeah." She digs another paper out of her bag. "We think it's here. The hunter who was tracking it hasn't been heard from. I'm sure he's...um..."

"Dead and being eaten bit by bit by rats?" Lucas fills in and I elbow him. "I know where this is," I say, looking at the address Melinda has scribbled on a piece of paper. "It's near the lake."

"Callie, can we talk in the kitchen?" Lucas is already standing, reaching for my hand. "You think this is a good idea?" he asks as soon as we're out of the living room.

"It sounds like the same thing we fought off."

"Exactly. We barely made it out of there alive. If I hadn't shown up—"

"But you did, and this time I'll have you with me."

"Why not let them deal with it?" He motions toward Melinda.

"Because they'll die. This is what I do, Lucas," I remind him. "I have the power to stop these things." I know he doesn't really get why I continue to put myself at risk, but who else can fight demons? "And maybe it's crazy to think it's my destiny or whatever, but I can't just keep on living my life like everything is okay, well, far from okay given the shit that's going on, but you know what I mean. Innocent people will die. And that thing...not even Evander had heard of anything like that. One was bad enough. If there are more..."

"It could be bad for business," he finally relents. "I won't make money if people are dying."

"Good attitude." I stand on my toes and hook my hands on his shoulders. His hesitation for me to hunt demons comes from a place of concern and worry. Demon hunting is dangerous, there's no way around it. Lower-level demons usually aren't an issue for me, but then again, an unsuspecting woman can pepper-spray me in the face which resulted in me being kidnapped.

"We'll go in there with firepower and will be much more prepared than the last time."

He plants his hands firmly on my hips and bends his head down to mine.

"There's something I didn't tell you," I start, thinking of the feather and the man with blue eyes.

"Yeah?"

My mouth opens but I can't bring myself to say it. I know

how crazy it sounds, and if Lucas knew part of the reason I want to take on a demon that almost killed me was to *maybe* see some guy who looked at me like I wasn't supposed to see him, he'd refuse to let me go. Not that it would matter in the end since I'd ultimately do what I want, but we have enough relationship drama right now.

We don't need to be fighting on top of everything else.

"I had the feeling those dog-rat hellhound things were guarding something, and I think whatever it is guarding is biding its time for a reason. Maybe it's weak and has to grow strong before it can attack. It makes sense if you think about it. Why glamour the building? If it needs to feed off human energy, having people either be lured in or wander in on their own is kind of necessary."

Lucas thinks for a moment. "That does make sense. Hiding the building from humans seems counterproductive."

"Exactly. And if it moved from empty building to empty building, maybe the glamour was a last-ditch effort at keeping itself hidden. And then I found it and now it's pissed. But that means if that thing was guarding something then it's still out there."

Lucas rests his forehead against mine. "Then we'll find it."

∿

I DOUBLE-KNOT THE LACES OF MY COMBAT BOOTS AND SLIDE THE knife into a sheath on my belt.

"Something dead is inside," Lucas tells me, smelling the air. "The blood smells human."

"Great." I look at the building looming ahead. We're right along Lake Michigan on the outskirts of Chicago. "At least we can assume we found the missing hunter."

Binx winds around my feet and the sounds of the lake echo against the large empty warehouse.

"Ready?" Lucas holds out his hand.

"I am." I link my fingers through his, heart fluttering. "Thanks for coming with."

"You don't have to thank me, Callie. You know I enjoy ripping things apart second only to as much I enjoy being with you."

"The couple that slays demons together…" I start and laugh, trying to cover up my nerves. I downplayed this the entire way here. Rats turning into demonic dogs from Hell? We can handle that. Demonic dogs from Hell merging into one giant hellhound?

Been there, done that.

We got this.

Right?

Right…

The building is boarded up, and the smell of rotted wood and animal droppings is strong before Lucas yanks the plywood off the door, letting us in. I bring my hand to my face, covering my nose. Binx shadows in ahead of us and Lucas steps in first, holding out his hand and helping me over the rubble.

This place was most recently a restaurant that closed five years ago when the owner got in trouble with the IRS. It's been empty since then and if it weren't for the steel mill run off in the background, I'm sure this place would have been snatched up quickly.

"Can you tell where the smell of blood is coming from?"

"Yes," Lucas says. "We're getting close."

Binx checks out the hall ahead of us and comes back, not wanting to leave me in case a demon dog attacks. Lucas and I carefully pick our way down the main hall, which splits the first floor down the middle. The restaurant portion is on the side that faces the water, and the other side is full of storage.

"It's so quiet in here," I whisper. "And yes, I know I'm jinxing us. I'm doing it on purpose."

"You know I don't believe in jinxes." Lucas tears another boarded door off the wall as if it was nothing at all. He drops it to the ground and dust flies up in the air. I wave my hand in my face and cough.

Stepping through the doorway, we find a staircase. We're halfway up when something clatters above us.

"Still don't believe in jinxes?" I whisper to Lucas. He reaches behind him for my hand. I slip my left hand into his, conjuring an energy ball with my other hand. Binx goes ahead of us, shadowing over broken floorboards. Lucas stops, turning to scoop me up so he can jump over the last three steps, which are warped and water-damaged, and look like they will cave away if we were to step on them.

I put out the energy ball so I don't burn his flesh as we move up the rest of the stairs. Lucas puts me down and I conjure up a string of magic, twisting it between my fingers. It's dark up here, with no light coming in from outside.

"Wait." I reach for Lucas, hooking my fingers around his. I hold up my other hand, the energy ball glowing bright above us. "Do you feel that?"

Lucas slowly shakes his head. "I smell blood, though. It's fresh."

"Shit." Bad energy presses into me, surrounding me like humidity and making it hard to breathe. Where is the man with the blue eyes? If that demon-creature-thing is here, why isn't he? A chill runs down my spine and I suddenly get an overwhelming feeling that we shouldn't be here, and it was a mistake to hunt this demon.

I push my fears away and give Lucas's hand a squeeze. If there is a demon out there killing people, it has to be stopped. And there's no one I'd rather go into battle with than Lucas.

"There's something in the next room," Lucas tells me, voice barely audible. "I can hear it moving."

"Does it sound human?"

Lucas waits a beat. "Maybe. It's shuffling, like it's dragging a foot."

"Binx, go check it out," I tell my familiar. His dark shadow disappears, slipping through a crack in the wall. No sooner does he vanish from sight, something else moves behind us. Lucas whirls around and dashes in front of me, protecting me from whatever is lurking in the dark.

Whatever it is lunges at him. I hold up my hand and the blue string of magic I'm holding turns bright white. The creature lets out a shriek of pain, and Lucas shoves it away. It hits the wall and falls apart into a dozen wriggling pieces.

"Fucking rats again!" I throw the energy ball at them and they go up in flames. Lucas hurries over to me, fangs bared. "If this demon wants to confuse the hell out of me, he's succeeding."

Lucas looks at the smoldering pile of dead rats. "Something about this is familiar."

"Deranged creatures turning into rats?"

His brow furrows. "No...the smell of the blood and the rats." He shakes his head and takes my hand again. My heart is racing and adrenaline floods through me.

"Do you hear anything else?" I flick my eyes to Lucas's face. "There's no way this is over yet."

"No," he agrees. "It was too easy. Almost like it was testing us."

"And now that it knows it's up against a vampire and a witch, they're going to pull out all the big guns." I close my eyes and shake my head. "Let's just hope it's not hellhounds again."

The floorboards creak and Lucas turns, looking at something I can't see in the dark.

"I was wrong," he starts. "You did jinx us."

CHAPTER 24

A low growl rumbles through the dark. Lucas, growling back, pulls his lips up over his fangs and sprints forward. I conjure an energy ball, lighting up the room. Long shadows are cast on the walls, and that thing is only yards from us. It looks just like the other hellhounds, and blood-tinged saliva drips from its yellowed fangs.

"Lucas, duck!" I yell, bringing my hands together, feeding the energy ball. It glows bigger and brighter. I throw the energy ball at the creature, aiming for its shoulder on purpose. It hits right where I wanted and burns through the creature's skin and down to the muscle.

I don't waste any time. Planting my foot down, I thrust my hand forward and throw it against the wall behind it. It cracks against the drywall, splintering the frame, and then slumps to the ground.

Lucas moves so fast I can't tell what he's doing until a sickening crack of bones rings out, twisting the creature's head around. As soon as he drops it, the thing explodes into rats, all dead expect one.

"Wait," I yell as Lucas goes to stomp on it. The thing writhes around on the ground, trying to get off its back. "It might go back to—I don't know—a home base or something."

Lucas nods. "A pied piper, so to speak."

"Binx," I call, thinking we might need him to shadow through small spaces. "Where are you?" The rat struggles to get to its feet and starts to limp away, jumping over the bodies of other rats.

My familiar shadows down the hall.

"Follow it," I tell him, and he takes off, slipping through another crack in the wall.

"Can you sense him?" Lucas asks and I nod, raising a finger and pointing to the wall.

"They're in there. Binx says they're moving down."

Lucas picks me up and jumps down the stairs in one leap. We're back in the restaurant portion of the building, in the main dining hall. White sheets cover the tables, and chairs are stacked against the wall. I mentally call out to Binx, getting a feel for him.

"The kitchen."

Lucas takes my hand and starts forward. We're in the middle of the large room when something jumps down from the ceiling, landing on Lucas's back. He falls to the ground and I jerk back, bumping into a table. I throw out my hand at the last second, sending a wave of energy at whatever the hell is on Lucas.

The creature has a strong hold on him, and instead of being blown off Lucas's back, it pulls him with as the magic shoves it back. They tumble through a glass window and fall several feet onto a warped and broken deck.

"Lucas!" Strings of magic sizzle around my fingers and I take off, running after them. I skid to a stop at the broken window. The glass is jagged and sharp. Heart in my throat, I freeze for a second, taken over with panic.

Then I shake myself, grab a dusty sheet from the table and throw it over the glass. Glass still bites into the palm of my hand, but I make it out more or less unscathed. Every nerve in my body is on edge, and I'm breathing so hard I'm on the verge of hyperventilating.

Where is Lucas?

The thought that something happened to him shakes me to my very core. I whirl around, trying to force myself to calm down. I'm standing on the deck that overlooks part of the lake. It's overcast tonight, and the moon offers little light. Water laps at the shore, and the smell of dead fish permeates the air.

"Lucas!" I call again, feeling like I might pass out. Then I notice the trail of blood on the ground. Sucking in a breath, I follow the blood down the deck. It turns, going around the back of the building.

Lucas is there, surrounded by three creatures that I think are people at first. Then I get closer and realize they are covered in the same thick gray skin the hellhounds were. The boards creak and crack under my feet, and one of the creatures turns. Where a human face should have been is just a mouth, large and round, with four rows of razor-sharp teeth.

Lucas takes advantage of the distraction. He grabs the creature and uses it as a weapon against the other, hitting its head into the back of another. The two creatures let out horrible shrieks of pain, and their cries reverberate off the building.

They're too close to Lucas to throw an energy ball. If I hit him with one, it could kill him. The one creature that didn't just get its head bashed in makes a move for Lucas and I throw out my hand, telekinetically throwing it over the side of the deck, leaving the two human-ish monsters to deal with. They reach for each other, and I know what they're doing.

So does Lucas. He punches his fist through the one's chest and pulls out its heart. Only, the heart is a rat. Startled, Lucas drops it do the ground. One of the creatures starts to turn into black ooze, merging into the other.

"Oh, shit." I take off, running down the wobbly deck as fast as I can. Lucas grabs the creature by the arms and jerks it around. Raising my hand, I conjure up a small energy ball of bright white light.

The creature opens its mouth, roaring at me as it grows in

size. Lucas pins it against him, holding it in place. I release the energy ball when I'm only a few feet from the creature, and it goes right into its mouth. Its body shudders as the light goes down, burning it from the inside out.

Lucas lets go and jumps back, and I turn, just in time to cover my face and miss being covered in smoldering rat guts.

"Callie." Lucas is before me, hands landing on my shoulders. "Are you okay?"

"I am." I straighten up and look him over. "Are you?"

"Yes, they didn't try to kill me," he rushes out and pulls me to him, protectively wrapping me in an embrace. "They wanted me out of there."

"Because of whatever they're guarding."

"Or to get you alone." He releases me and looks over the deck at the water below. "It's not there."

"It probably went back inside." I close my eyes and feel for Binx. "The basement. Binx is in the basement."

"Of course."

We step over the smoking rat parts and go back to the broken window. Lucas jumps in first, moving with fluid grace. He breaks away the rest of the glass and folds the sheet, covering the bottom part of the window for me. He pulls me up with ease.

"To the basement." I hold out my hand to conjure another energy ball, wanting to be ready and needing the light to see. Lucas walks behind me, on the lookout for any more of those creatures.

We go through the dining area and into the main hall again.

"The smell of human blood is getting stronger," Lucas tells me.

"Fresh blood?"

"No."

I splay my fingers, and the blue light brightens above me, illuminating crude graffiti drawn on the walls. Binx shadows out of the dark, red eyes glowing.

"You found it?" I ask him.

"Yes," he says, voice deep and booming even when he whispers.

"What is it?"

"Demon. An old and powerful one."

The energy ball flickers from my own nerves. "Okay...we...we need a plan." I look at Lucas. "You don't happen to have one, do you?"

"Kill it."

"Yeah, but how?" I swallow hard, mind racing. The last and only time I went up against a powerful demon, I killed it with its own hellfire. So, unless the demon in the basement plans to burn this whole place down, I have no bloody clue what to do.

"We can hit it with everything we've got," Lucas suggests. "Rip its heart out. Break its neck. Hit it with energy balls. One of those would at least slow it down." His eyes go to the dagger hanging on my waist. "The blade is enchanted, right?"

"Right."

"Will it hold the demon?"

"Maybe for a few seconds if we're lucky. The demon in the woods...nothing hurt it. Not even its own demon blade."

"White light. You were able to get demonic energy to retreat from the Ley line by hitting it with white light. If I hold the demon, you can burn it with white light."

"I might burn you in the process." I squeeze my eyes shut as I think. "The Goetia circle might work."

"What is that?"

"A very strong circle of protection that just might hold the demon long enough for me to hit him with white light. It might work, actually. If you can get it into the circle, I'll have a good shot at blowing the fucker up."

The floorboards creak behind us and a voice rings out in the dark. "But where's the fun in that?"

CHAPTER 25

L ucas speeds forward, fangs out, and lunges at the demon. Black eyes gleaming, the demon sneers and holds out a hand, throwing Lucas back and through a wall. Binx goes after it next, and the demon raises its other hand, stopping my familiar in his tracks.

He slowly lowers his hand, and Binx's shadow is forced to the ground, slipping through a crack in the floorboards.

"No!" I cry and reach for my familiar. My mouth falls open and I bring both hands up, throwing them out at the demon. He's shoved back just enough to lose his hold on Binx. In an instant, my familiar is back by my side, circling around me.

"I don't want to hurt him," the demon says. He's in the hunter's body, and thick, dark veins web across his face. Being in a human body and not being in its true form means we have a shot at killing it. "He could be very useful."

I throw out my hand again, hitting the demon with another wall of energy. This time he counters me, throwing up a shield of his own. Like a shockwave, it hits me hard in the chest, making it hard to breathe. I gasp for air but recover fast, conjuring a string of blue energy. I throw it at the demon, who doesn't even attempt to move out of the way.

He holds up his hand, touching the energy. It burns his skin and makes him wince in pain, but he's more interested than hurt.

"We've been waiting for one that is worthy." He looks at his fingers where the magic just burned him. "No one is strong enough. But you…you…what are you?"

"She's mine," Lucas growls, coming from seemingly nowhere. He barrels toward the demon and grabs it around the neck, twisting its head around. I hear the neck bones cracking and watch the man's head spin unnaturally around on his body, but it does little to slow the demon. It shakes Lucas off and then throws him into a wall again. Lucas's body bends unnaturally and I start toward him, enchanted dagger in my hand.

"Not so fast." The demon rounds on me, flicking his wrist and pushing me back. The dagger falls from my hands, clattering to the ground as I'm shoved back against the wall. The pressure builds, feeling like a million hands are holding me in place. Suffocating me. Squishing me. Everything hurts and my insides start to burn. It's not hellfire but it hurts just as much. Where is the blue-eyed man this time?

If you're going to show up, now's the time.

"What are you?" the demon draws closer. "You smell human but you're so much more."

"I'm a witch, dumbass," I croak out. "You're not much of a demon if you can't tell that."

"Witches are humans at their core. Big weakness, if you ask me. But you…you're something more and it's like I was expecting a snack but got a whole dang meal!" His dark eyes drill into mine. "You might be what we need."

"I am so tired of demons telling me that," I say through gritted teeth. "I'm not going to be your unwilling bride in Hell."

"In Hell? We want the opposite." The demon takes a slow step forward. Binx shadows at him but stops at the last minute, going around the demon almost as if he's afraid of crashing into him. Binx has never backed down from a fight. He'd die protecting me and it's not like him to—the dagger isn't on the ground anymore. He's taking it to Lucas.

The demon is possessing a human body. Right. The demon is fueling it with its own powers, but like he said, humans at their core are weak. I curl my fingers into a fist, getting ready to hit it with an energy ball.

"We have to put you to the test first." The demon grabs my hand and I lose the string of magic I was building. He presses his fingernail into the skin on my wrist and drags it down, scratching me.

"Ow!" I jerk my arm back. I'm not even bleeding. "That kind of hurt."

The demon steps back, watching. "What are you?" he asks again, tipping his head to the side.

"I told you, she's mine." Lucas slashes the dagger through the air, cutting the demon's throat. Thick, dark blood oozes out and the demon brings his hand up to try and stop the bleeding.

Binx shadows around the demon, knocking it to the ground. Lucas jumps on top and drives the dagger deep into its chest. The demon, still able to use its powers, telekinetically throws Lucas and pulls the dagger from its chest. He raises it up to bring it down on Binx.

"No!" I shout and thrust both hands out at the same time. The demon slides back, human body weakening more and more as time goes on. Breaking out of the demon's hold, I fall forward onto my knees. Lucas is there again, dagger in hand. He stands over the demon, fangs drawn and lips pulled back in a snarl.

I push up onto my feet as Lucas cuts the demon's head off, skin smoldering from the enchanted dagger. Once the last of the spinal cord is cut through, the demon leaves the body in a dark gray cloud.

"Not so fast, fucker." I hold my hand in front of me, conjuring a bright ball of white light. I throw it at the demon, burning it before it can jump into another warm body. I throw another energy ball at it, and the whole thing sizzles and sparks before exploding.

I let my hands fall to my sides and suck in air. Binx shifts into cat-form and weaves around my legs. Lucas is covered in blood but hugs me anyway, hand going to the top of my head. He balls my hair in his fist and kisses me.

"I'm fine," I tell him, knowing he's going to ask. "Are you?"

"Yes. My wounds have already healed. You...you don't have a scratch on you?"

"Just one." I show him the red welt on my wrist. "After all that, the demon just clawed me like a sissy baby." I rest my head against Lucas's chest. The demon is dead, but things still aren't adding up.

The demon wasn't in its true form, yet was being guarded by those things. Was it controlling them? Did it create them? But more importantly...are they gone now that the demon is dead?

"There's still one of those creatures out there," I remind Lucas. He runs his hands down my arms.

"We'll kill it."

Binx shadows off to check the rest of the basement, trying to locate the creature. Lucas keeps his hand in mine after we break apart.

"That's the hunter." My eyes go to the headless body a few feet from us. I've seen my fair share of demon-related deaths, but this is making my stomach clench. "I think."

Lucas lets go of my hand and checks the body for ID. He finds a wallet, and I conjure a small string of magic so I can see the name.

"Melinda didn't say who it was, but this has to be him. I mean, who other than hunters wear flannel in summer?"

Lucas hands me the wallet. "You should give it to her."

"I know," I sigh. "I'm sure she knew he was already dead, but having to tell her..."

Lucas looks at the body for a moment and then turns back to me. "I don't hear anything else in here, my love."

"Good." My eyes fall shut in a long blink as a sharp headache suddenly comes on. "I don't even know its name."

"Does it matter if it's dead?"

"I keep a record of the demons I've vanquished in my book. You know, for the future generation of—" I cut off, realizing what I'm saying.

Lucas and I can never have a family.

And now is *not* the time to even entertain thoughts related to that.

"Knowing its name would help me understand why it's here and if I should expect more."

"Is there a way to find out?"

The sharp pain comes back in a wave. I squeeze my eyes shut again and it passes as quickly as it came on. "Not that I know of. That explosion was pretty final, though. I don't have anything to resurrect if I tried."

"That's probably a good thing."

"Probably." My stomach tightens and for a few seconds, I think I'm going to throw up. The sick feeling passes, and I look up at Lucas's face. "You heard what it said, didn't you? That I'm not human."

"I did," he says and I'm so thankful he didn't feed me the "demons are liars" line. "I meant what I said earlier. It doesn't matter what you are, Callie. Who you are is what counts, and you're the single most amazing person in this whole fucking world."

Binx comes back, letting me know he didn't sense anything at all in the rest of the building.

"Let's get out of here. I really want tacos." My eyes go to the headless body on the floor. Bits of demon dust my hair. Lucas is covered in blood, some of it his own but most the demon's.

And I'm thinking about fucking tacos.

"I've heard humans at the bar talk about a taco cart. I'll take you."

"We should probably get cleaned up first." I shove the wallet into the back pocket of my jeans. Lucas guides me through the dark building, and we go out through a set of double doors in the back, emerging onto the deck. At one point, it offered outside eating right along the lake.

The headache comes on strong again and Lucas can sense it. He turns to put his arm around me when he suddenly stops. A dark figure rises from the shadows and points a gun at us.

My heart stops and I don't have time to react. A shot is fired, ringing out into the night.

CHAPTER 26

I know from the time I hear the gunshot to the time I feel it hit me is less than a second. Yet the pain never comes, and Lucas is in front of me, growling. Another shot is fired, hitting him in the stomach.

Fighting through the pain, Lucas speeds forward and grabs the gunman's hand, snapping his wrist back. The bones break and the gun clatters to the ground. Using my powers, I throw the gun off the deck and into the lake. Funny, how facing demons and creatures made up of hundreds of rats scares me, but having someone point a gun at me scares me even more.

My eyes go to Lucas, who has the gunman pushed up against the wall of the building. His fingers are wrapped around his throat, fangs glinting and eyes full of anger. He's not mad he got shot—twice—but that someone aimed the gun at me and pulled the trigger.

"Hey!" another man shouts, running down the deck. "Let him go!" He's holding a pistol in one hand and points it at Lucas. I recognize his voice before he comes into view. *You have got to be fucking kidding me.* I throw out my hand, knocking Easton back. I'm glad he listened to his sister and stayed away. I'm sure he thought I couldn't do it, that he'd need to run in here and save me from the big bad demon.

There is no way anyone without powers could have faced that thing and come out alive.

"Callie?" Easton slows to a stop. "What are you doing?"

"What you couldn't, apparently." I drop my hand. "You're not supposed to be here. Didn't Melinda tell you to stay away?"

"She did." His eyes go from me to Lucas, and he raises his gun again.

"Don't point your gun at him," I run my thumb over my fingers, conjuring a string of white magic. I let it go into the air, lighting up the area of the deck we're on. "And you really need to learn to listen. Like I said, we got this."

"Be glad we did show up. There were two fucking huge demonic dogs at the entrance to the property."

"So that's where the others were." Lucas slides the gunman down the wall so his feet are back on the ground. The bullet wounds are still bleeding, and his shirt is soaked with dark red blood. He's standing, not acting as if the pain is bothering him at all, yet the sight of his chest and stomach all bloody like that makes me want to panic.

If he were alive, well...he wouldn't be for much longer.

"Other?" Easton echoes. "There's more?"

"Did you kill them?" I ask, ignoring his question. "The demon dogs. Are they still out there?"

"We got one and then the other exploded."

"Into rats?"

"Yes." The look on his face reads he's just as confused as we are. "Dead rats."

"Killing the demon must have killed the rats," Lucas tells me, looking over his shoulder. He lets go of the gunman and zooms back to my side.

"You were right about the demon being some sort of pied piper to them."

Binx shadows around Easton, knocking the gun out of his

hand. Lucas darts forward, grabbing the gun and coming back to my side so fast it was like he didn't even move at all. Binx shifts into cat-form and rubs against my legs.

"Are you okay?" I turn to Lucas, putting my hand on his chest. My fingers become slick with blood.

"I'm fine, my love."

"Are the bullets still in there?"

"Yes, but I can feel them being pushed out."

"You're okay, though?"

Lucas, not caring that we have an audience, cups my face with both his large hands and puts his lips to mine. "I will be."

I suck in a shaky breath. The headache is getting worse and I'm feeling so drained and depleted. Seeing Lucas get shot, even though I *know* he's a vampire, shook me.

"You took a bullet for me."

"I'd take a hundred for you."

I clench my jaw and flatten my hand over the wound in his chest, wanting to stop the bleeding. The wounds won't heal until the bullets are out, and while his body will heal itself and push them out, I can get them out a lot faster.

"Brace yourself," I tell him and telekinetically pull the bullet from his chest. Lucas lets out a grunt, body tensing. The bullet went through his sternum and I have to pull it back out the way it came. I look away, hoping I don't pass out or throw up. Finally, the first bullet clatters to the ground. The second comes out smoother, not having to be removed through bone.

He will be fine, just like he said. He's already healing, and it doesn't seem like it hurts that much. Either that or Lucas is really good at keeping a poker face.

Easton and the gunman watch us, and it's obvious from the look on their faces they've never seen anything like this before. Even in the life of a hunter, watching someone telekinetically pull bullets out of a vampire's chest isn't something you see every day.

I hope I never have to do this again.

"What do you mean, he took a bullet for you?" Easton asks, eyes flitting from me to the gunman.

"He shot at us," I say. "We were just walking down the deck after killing the demon you couldn't."

"I thought they were demons," the other hunter spits out. "This place has been crawling with demonic energy for the last few days. And after seeing that…that thing by the gate I didn't think it was possible for humans to still be alive in here."

"You're lucky it was just us." I turn away from Lucas to stare daggers at Mr. Shoot First, Aim Later. "Demons occupying the place or not, innocent humans could have been here."

The hunter messed up, and he knows it. He was freaked out and let his emotions get the best of him. He cradles his wrist to his chest and gives Easton a dubious look.

"So, what they say is true. You are friends with a witch and a vampire."

"We're not friends," Easton and I say at the same time.

"Kill the fuckers!" the gunman shouts and Binx growls. Sitting by my feet and swishing his tail, he drops his shield a bit and lets his eyes glow red in the dark. The gunman stiffens. Most hunters have been taught that witches are the evil villains fairy tales paint us out to be.

We're killers. Evil. Will eat your babies and kill your pets.

It's so far from the truth it's comical.

"What the hell are you waiting for? That fanger broke my wrist."

Lucas speeds forward, fingers wrapping around the gunman's throat again. "You're lucky that's all I did. You tried to kill the woman I love. I'd do the same to you, but that death would be too quick."

"Get control of your attack dog." Easton pulls out a knife. The tip of the blade has been dipped in a special kind of holy oil, working almost as well as my enchanted dagger. *Almost.*

"Guys!" I yell and Binx shifts back into shadow form, circling around Easton again. Lucas snarls at the gunman, fangs up in his face, and shoves him hard against the side of the building. I bring my hand to my head, rubbing my temple. The headache is back, and I can hear my own heart beating in my ears. "This isn't going to solve anything! Lucas, Binx, and I would kick your ass before you knew what was happening, so save it, okay? We all came here with the same intention of killed that rat-bastard of a demon and it seems like he's gone. It's over. So let's go home, okay?"

Begrudgingly, Lucas lets go of the gunman. Binx comes back to my side, taking the form of a pretty black cat. Easton doesn't lower the knife. Letting out an annoyed sigh, I pull the wallet from my pocket. "If Arnold Keller was a friend, I'm sorry. The demon possessed him. He was gone before we got there."

Easton takes the wallet and flips it open, looking at the ID. "It's the missing hunter."

"How long has he been missing?" My throat feels thick when I swallow and I'm starting to get really dizzy. I guess seeing Lucas shot and bloody is catching up with me after all.

"Two days."

"The body looks farther gone than two days, didn't it?" I ask Lucas.

"Yes, it was deteriorated enough to have been dead for a week."

"I saw Arnie the morning he went missing," the gunman tells Easton. "What the hell did they do to him?"

"We did nothing," Lucas presses, sounding annoyed with the hunter. "Your friend was possessed by a demon. That can speed up the rate of decay. Human bodies can't handle demonic possession for long."

"Once the body is dead, the rate of decomposition can be accelerated," Easton says. "We've seen it before." His eyes go to me again, and I can tell he's torn. If I wasn't feeling so sick right now, I might feel sorry for him. Being a human born into the life of demon hunting isn't easy. It's isolating and lonely and dangerous. Going after things with powers when you don't have any yourself is just stupid too, if you ask me.

The group hunters run with are their family, and often their real families have been picked off by demons over the years. Easton's group of hunter buddies is like what the coven is to me. They can stop running with him and Melinda, refuse to help them or give them places to stay while traveling around on hunting trips.

Letting a witch walk free is an offense big enough to make that happen. Letting a witch and a vampire walk…they'd never talk to him again. But he'd be alive, not sentenced to death. That is one thing witches could learn from hunters. They value human life above anything…though then again, they don't consider witches to be humans.

"He's in there if you want to get the body. I'm sorry for your loss," I add, manners coming through even now. "Now, I want to go home. If either of you try anything as we walk away, so help me God, I will curse you both."

"We can't let them—" the gunman starts.

"We can," Easton interrupts. "These are the two that saved Melinda. I owe them that at least, and then our debt is paid. If I see them again, I'll kill them."

The hunter with the broken wrist isn't satisfied with Easton's response, but he knows he's seriously out-powered here.

"You should probably burn all the dead rats," I add, taking Lucas's hand. "Just to be safe." I flick my fingers and slide the gun back over to Easton, trying to show a gesture of goodwill. He won't shoot me, and he knows shooting Lucas will only result in pissing us all off.

The deck leads down a rickety set of stairs and then continues along the water, turning into a dock. One rusty boat is tied up at it, and the smell of human feces and pee is strong coming off the water. I suppose living in there would beat being homeless, though the boat doesn't look occupied right now.

I blink, looking back at the dark water. And then I see him. The outline of the man with the blue eyes. He's standing in the boat and is gone the second I see him.

"Hang on." I pull my hand from Lucas's and hold up my finger, signaling for him to stay put. I tiptoe down the dock. "I saw you," I whisper into the dark. "Twice. Who are you?"

"Callie, what are you doing?" Lucas calls from the deck, taking a few steps down the dock. The old wooden boards groan in protest under his weight.

"I thought I..." I trail off, dizziness crashing down on me like a heavy fist. I step back and the boards crack under my feet. I throw out my hands, and I swear I feel feathers brush against my finger.

But it doesn't matter, because I stumble back and fall into the dark water.

CHAPTER 27

"You can't leave well enough alone, can you?" Lucas sits on the deck, holding me in his lap. He was there the second after I plunged into Lake Michigan, pulling me from the water and back onto dry land.

"It's one of my many faults." I shiver. "Why is the water always so fucking cold?"

Lucas brushes my hair back, and Binx meows, gently pawing me. "What did you see out there?"

"The man with the blue eyes."

"The one you said saved you from the demon in the woods?"

"No, that's the Blue-Eyed Man. This guy isn't as...as ethereal looking. He's more like a regular man but has blue eyes."

"Did you hit your head?" Lucas runs his hand over my head.

"No, I'm fine." I push out of his arms and stand. The dizziness is back, and Lucas steadies me.

"I'm taking you home."

I want to protest and go back out onto the dock, demanding the man with blue eyes come out and face me. Why lurk around like a creep? If he wants to attack me, then do it already.

Lucas picks me up and races over the grounds, not stopping until we're by his car. I get in the passenger side and Binx jumps up on my lap. The headache is getting worse and all I want to do is sleep.

"Do you want me to get you food?" Lucas asks, turning the heat on instead of the air conditioning. I'm so, so cold, and I have a feeling it's not from the plunge into the cool water.

"I'll find something at your house, but thanks."

Lucas rests one hand on my thigh. "We're taking that vacation, I promise."

"Can we leave in the morning?"

He laughs. "If that's what you want."

"I want a week without demons and witch-trials and people trying to kill me."

"Let's go to Paris. You'll love the nightlife there."

"I've never been to Paris." I rest my head back against the seat. "And they're much more open to vampires over there."

"They are. Vampires have almost equal rights to their human citizens."

"Right, I remember hearing that. And they were one of the first countries to legalize vampire-human marriages too."

Lucas runs his hand up and down my thigh. I can feel him looking at me, but the pain in my head intensifies and I close my eyes, fearing I'm going to puke all over Lucas's car. I turn down the heat, which is making me feel even sicker, and start shivering. It takes over half an hour to drive back to Lucas's house in Lincoln Park.

We go right up for a shower, and Lucas pulls his bloody shirt over his head and throws it in the garbage.

"How many items of clothes have we gotten rid of because of blood?" I mumble, stripping out of my clothes. Losing my balance, Lucas catches me at the last second before I fall on the marble floor.

"Are you feeling all right, Callie?" He looks into my eyes, searching for an answer.

"I'm tired," I admit. "Really tired and I have a headache."

"Aspirin," he starts, not sounding sure of himself. "That's what humans take for headaches, right?"

"Not so much anymore. I usually take Advil instead. Aspirin can thin your blood so it's probably not a good thing for me to take."

"I will get you some."

"Shower with me first?"

"Of course." Lucas helps me strip out of the rest of my clothes and get into the shower. I feel a little better once we're both clean. I run my hand over his chest. There's not even a mark on him.

"You need to eat. You lost a lot of blood. Again."

"I'm not drinking from you tonight."

"Do you need to drink from somebody else?" I tip my head up, eyes shut to keep the water out.

"No." He turns the temperature of the water up a little more for me. "I don't want anyone else's blood. Nothing tastes as good as you do, Callie."

"You told me before that vampires aren't usually monogamous."

"Correct."

"But you are with me."

"You're an exception to a lot of rules." His hands slide over my body and he holds me close, kissing the top of my head. "Now let's get you into bed." He shuts off the shower and wraps a towel around my body.

"You're so good to me," I say when he lays me down in his bed after drying me off.

"And you're too good for me." He smiles and plants a kiss on my forehead. "You're hot."

"Mmmhh, yeah I am."

"No, I mean that literally. You're hotter than usual."

"Maybe because we were in a hot shower?"

"Perhaps." Lucas puts his hand to my forehead. "Do you want me to get you anything?"

"Just some water."

Lucas hurries out of the room and comes back with a glass of ice water. I suck it down and then fall back into bed. I'm so dizzy and something just feels off. I can't explain it. Binx curls up next to me, and I lay on my side, arms wrapped around my familiar, and fall asleep.

~

I WAKE UP WITH A SORE THROAT AND AN ACHE IN MY CHEST THAT gets worse when I breathe. Binx is stretched out next to me, taking up a surprising amount of space for how small he is in cat-form. The master bedroom doors are open, and I hear Lucas talking to someone downstairs. The house is dark, and I have no idea what time it is. I feel like I only slept for a few hours and then at the same time days might have passed.

I use the bathroom and am startled by my appearance. My eyes are bloodshot, like I spent the night drinking, and dark purple circles hang under them. I must have used more energy than I thought last night killing that demon. Pulling on underwear and a t-shirt dress, I go downstairs to find Lucas.

"Hey," I say, seeing Eliza sitting cross-legged on the couch in the living room. My voice comes out scratchy and hoarse.

"I heard you had a fun night."

"It was riveting." I clear my throat, trying to get rid of the nasty feeling. I swallow hard and just make it worse. "What time is it?"

"Ten AM. Almost my bedtime."

"Oh, I didn't realize I slept that long."

Eliza tips her head, looking at me. "You look like you could use more sleep."

"Yeah," I agree. "I think I'll take a nap later. Where did Lucas go?"

"In his office, but don't bother him. He's in the middle of something."

"Care to elaborate?"

"Not really. Business bores me." She picks up her phone and texts someone, fingers moving with impressive speed. Binx comes down the stairs and beats me into the kitchen, ready for me to make him breakfast.

I plug in the coffee pot first and sink down at the island counter with my head in my hands. Man, I feel like shit. The last time I felt a magic-hangover like this was when I used the hellfire to kill the demon. Last night was intense, but nowhere near the level of *I'm going to die* as the night in the woods.

Then again, I haven't had the best habits lately and Lucas has been drinking from me almost nightly. We knew it would catch up with me sooner or later. I hoped it would be later.

I chug the coffee to help pull me from the fog my brain is in, and then scramble eggs to share with Binx. There's one package of frozen sausage left in the freezer, and I pop it in the microwave.

Eating usually makes me feel better after a night of drinking and especially after Lucas has drank a lot of my blood. My body craves protein and water, and I just consumed plenty of that. Lucas is still in the office and it sounds like he's on the phone. I don't want to bother him, so I get my phone from my purse and call Evander.

The call goes to his voicemail right away, which usually means he's at the Academy. My mind is so fuzzy I don't even know what day of the week it is, but if it's a weekday then he's teaching a summer class right now.

"Hey," I say to his voicemail. "Remember that weird rat-demon-dog-whatever the fuck thing Kristy told you about? We fought off more yesterday and then killed a real demon. I think it's over, but something feels weird about it. It just doesn't make sense. Call me when you get a chance and I'll assign tons of research for you to do on my behalf. Love you, bye!" I end the call and go into the kitchen for more water. My throat feels raw and my chest hurts even more when I take in a deep breath.

I down another glass, blink a few times, and tell myself I'll be back to normal soon. Maybe after another nap. Sitting at the island counter again, I rest my head on the cool quartz and groan.

"What's wrong with you?" Eliza sits next to me, setting down a little bag full of nail polish.

"I don't know," grumble.

"You sound terrible." She looks through bottles of nail polish and picks out a bright pink color.

"I feel terrible."

"Are you sick?"

The thought hadn't occurred to me because I haven't been sick in years. I actually don't remember the last time I had a cold. I've always had a strong immune system and only ended up in the infirmary at school because of injuries, not illness.

"Maybe. It hurts to breathe, kinda like it did when I inhaled the smoke from the hellfire."

"Did you inhale smoke last night?"

"No, but it was pretty dusty inside that old building."

Lucas comes into the kitchen, smiling when he sees me. He comes right over and puts his hand to my forehead. "You're still hotter than normal."

"I am?"

He looks into my eyes. "Why would you be hotter than normal?"

"It's called a fever," Eliza quips. "Have you been dead for that long? Humans get fevers. It happens when they're sick."

"You're sick?" Lucas is suddenly concerned.

"I'm feeling a little rundown, and with everything that's been going on, I'm actually not surprised I got a cold."

"What can I do to make you better?"

"Watch a movie with me?" I suggest. "I'm tired and want to go back to sleep."

"What about the medicine?"

"Oh, right. Yeah, something for my headache would be nice."

Lucas turns to Eliza. "Have Monica bring over everything necessary to care for a human with a cold."

"Lucas," I say a little sternly. "It's a cold. They last for a few days and then I'll be back to normal. It's not like I'm dying or anything."

His jaw tenses. "Fine. Have her bring Advil then."

"I can go get it," I say though I don't feel like moving from this bar stool.

"No, you need to rest. You were hot last night, but you're even hotter now."

Eliza calls Monica, putting the call on speaker.

"Eliza, hey! Hi! How are you?" Monica answers.

"I'm fine. I need you to run an errand for me."

"Sure, of course! What do you need?" Monica has no idea her vampire boyfriend is fucking Eliza and part of me feels like I should tell her. But a bigger part wants to stay out of it.

"Advil and a thermometer."

I turn my head and cough, and it instantly burns through my chest, like I'm breathing fire. There's phlegm in my lungs, and I can't get it up. I cough again, and even I know I can't deny how awful I sound.

"And cough medicine. Something strong so I don't have to listen to that anymore."

"Sure. Who's sick? I mean, never mind. I know it's none of my business." She's been groomed on how to interact with vampires and it's kind of sad. That, and I'm sure Lucas has held her spellbound on more than one occasion. "And where do you want me to bring this?"

"Lucas's house on North Orchard."

Monica hesitates and I remember her saying she's still a little afraid of Lucas and doesn't want to go into his house out of fear that he'd be mad at her for it.

"Oh…okay. I'll be there in twenty minutes."

"Thank you," I add before Eliza can hang up. Lucas takes me upstairs, tucking me in bed like a baby. I'm not going to lie, it's nice right now. I'm coughing hard again, and my throat burns. I know colds can hit you all of a sudden, but do they get this bad in only a few hours?

Lucas fluffs the pillows for me again and sits next to me, looking intently at something on his phone.

"This says you should sleep sitting up." He grabs another pillow to stick behind me. "And drink water. I'll get you more." Leaving his phone on the bed, he zooms out of the room. I pick it up and feel warm and fuzzy inside when I see that he Googled "how to take care of someone with a cold." Medical treatment has changed a lot since he was last alive, and he's told me before that he never cared for a human the way he cares for me.

"I'll find a delivery service to bring you chicken noodle soup." He comes into the room and gives me the water. "It said that helps too."

"It does, but I'm not hungry right now." I take a sip of water and set it on the nightstand. "I'm tired and I'm sure once I take a nap I'll wake up and feel better."

"I hope you do." He slips back under the covers and I lean on him, eyes falling shut. "What are your symptoms?"

I lift my head up just enough to look into his eye. "Every human knows not to look up symptoms on the internet. You'll fall down the WebMD rabbit hole of thinking you have a rare jungle disease you contracted from infected fruit or something like that."

"But what if you do? How will you know?"

I rest my head on his chest again. "I don't get sick very often," I start. "But normal people will power through it at home first, doing the basics. Resting, taking over-the-counter meds, and drinking lots of water. Usually after a few days, you either feel better or you don't. And if you don't, you go to the doctor for medicine."

"And if that doesn't work?"

"Lucas, stop worrying. I have a cold. The stress of everything paired with the lack of sleep finally got to me." Heat creeps down my neck, but my body is chilled. I cough again, feeling more phlegm getting all sticky inside my lungs. I sit up, coughing so hard it's hard to breathe. I bring a hand to my chest, lungs burning.

Lucas, looking a little panicked, sits up with me and grabs the glass of water. Once I can breathe again, I take a drink and fall back against the pillows.

"You feel hotter." Lucas puts his hand to my forehead. "From what I read online, you should have a low-grade fever with a cold. What I'm feeling is a significant temperature difference than how you usually are."

A shiver runs through me and I curl my legs up against my body. "Can you turn the heated blanket on?"

"You have a fever, you shouldn't bundle up or use the heated blanket."

"Just for a minute?" I ask, shivering harder. Lucas leans over and presses a button.

"I'm keeping it on low." He folds the blanket around me and encases me in his arms. "You're trembling."

"You get chills when you have a cold."

"I don't think this is just a cold."

It doesn't feel like it, granted I haven't been sick in forever. Maybe I'm just a big baby? And nothing else can come on that fast. Most illnesses take time. You feel crappy for a day or two and it slowly gets worse.

Well, unless it really is some rare jungle disease.

Lucas holds me, gently running his fingers up and down my arm. I'm coughing nonstop now, and each time I inhale it hurts worse than the last. The doorbell rings, and a minute later, Eliza comes upstairs holding a bag. She takes out a bottle of Advil and turns on the thermometer.

"Look this way," she says, and I'm surprised by the gentleness in her voice. Maybe I look as bad as I feel.

"One-oh-three point four," she reads.

"That's not a low-grade fever."

"No, it's not." I reach for the Advil and start coughing again. Eliza opens the bottle and gives me two pills. I wash them down with water and lay back down only to sit up again because I'm coughing.

"How long does that stuff take to work?" Eliza picks up the bottle and reads the words on the side.

"About twenty minutes," Lucas answers. "Or at least that's what one website said."

Eliza nods and goes out of the room, leaving me alone with Lucas. He holds me against his chest, keeping me upright.

"Try and get some sleep. I'm taking your temperature again in nineteen minutes."

Every time I get close to falling asleep, I start coughing. It's incredibly frustrating, and I'm feeling worse and worse by the minute. I don't understand what's happening.

I'm never sick.

And what I thought was a cold is something else, I just know it.

"Callie?" Lucas whispers. "Are you awake?"

"Yeah."

"It's time to take your temperature again." The thermometer beeps and he puts it to my forehead.

"What's the verdict?"

"One-oh-three point seven. It's going up."

"Maybe from the blanket?"

"Maybe." He puts the thermometer down and turns the heated blanket off. It hasn't done anything to rid me of the chills anyway. Groaning, I snuggle up against Lucas, shivering hard. My joints ache and my head is still pounding.

Lucas waits another twenty minutes to check my temp again. It hasn't changed.

"You said if medication doesn't help then you go to the doctor."

"Yeah, but you need to be sick for more than a few hours." I slowly push myself up, needing to use the bathroom. I'm all wobbly on my feet and every second out of bed is too long.

"Are you hungry?" I ask Lucas, getting back into bed.

"I am not taking anything from you tonight, my love." Lucas pulls the blankets back up over me. "You need it more than I do."

"I can spare a little."

"No." He tucks my hair behind my ear and puts his lips to my neck. "Your heart is beating faster than usual."

"Lucas, I'm fine," I press and bring my hand up, cupping it around his chin. His skin is cool in my palm. "I'm human and humans get sick every now and then. We rest, take meds, and get better."

"I hope you're right."

I close my eyes. I hope I'm right too.

CHAPTER 28

"How is she?" Eliza sits at the foot of the bed.

"She's not getting any better," Lucas tells her. "I don't understand what's going on." He gently runs his hand over my hair. He thinks I'm still asleep, and I don't have the energy to open my eyes and tell him otherwise. "I've read everything I can about human colds and even the flu. Her symptoms don't match either."

Eliza moves up and feels my cheek. "She's burning up."

The sheets rustle and Lucas sits up, getting the thermometer. He doesn't say what the temperature is out loud, but it can't be good.

"It's been hours and it hasn't gone down at all?" Eliza sounds concerned. "I'll be right back."

Binx, who's been on my pillow, nuzzles his head against me. He's worried too, able to sense that my fever just won't go the fuck away.

"Uncover her a bit and it will help her cool off," Eliza tells Lucas, coming back into the room. I force my eyes open.

"Callie," Lucas breathes. "How are you feeling?"

"Shitty," I croak out and then start coughing. Lucas sits me up and Eliza gives me a cool washcloth to put on my forehead. "What time is it?"

"Almost nine." Lucas readjusts the pillows again. "Are you hungry?"

"Not really."

"You should eat."

"So should you," I counter.

"I've already healed. You haven't."

My eyes fall shut and I grimace from the pain. My whole body hurts.

"I think it's time to call a doctor." Eliza looks me over with a mixture of worry and disgust on her face.

"I'm calling your sister." Lucas takes the washcloth from me and flips it over to the cool side.

"She might be at work," I say, teeth chattering. These fucking chills are awful. My body hurts enough as it is, and adding in the nonstop shivering makes everything hurt that much more. "I'll text her."

"Get her phone," Lucas tells Eliza.

My phone is still in my purse, and the feather is still hidden in there. "I'll get it."

"No." Lucas puts one hand on my shoulder, keeping me from getting up. "You're not going anywhere, Callie."

I try to give him a pointed look but end up coughing and choking on my own mucus. I don't realize Eliza left the room until she returns with my phone. I send Abby a text, asking if she's at work today, and then lay back down. Just sitting up for a few minutes was exhausting.

"Can I do anything to help you feel better?" Lucas asks.

"My back hurts," I say, voice muffled from my face being smashed into my pillow. Lucas starts to massage my back right away, and if I weren't coughing so much, I'd fall asleep.

My phone dings with a text, and Lucas hands it to me. It's a text from Abby, and I have to squint my eyes to be able to read it. Everything is kind of fuzzy.

Abby: Yeah, I am. What's up?

Me: I think I'm sick.

Abby: What's wrong?

Lucas, looking at the phone, takes it from my hands and calls my sister. "She doesn't think she's sick, she knows she is," he tells Abby. "She's had a hundred-and-three fever all day and has a terrible cough." He pauses, listening to what Abby is saying. "I agree. Tell her that because your sister is as stubborn as she is incredible."

Lucas hands me the phone. "I'm fine, right?"

"A fever that high is dangerous, Cal. You need to come in right away so we can get it down. You're probably dehydrated too."

There's no use arguing. I feel awful and I know I'm not going to be able to beat this on my own. "Okay."

"We're pretty busy in here today, but I'll do my best to come to you as soon as I can. Text me when you're checked into the ER."

"I will. I'll see you in a little bit."

"Love you, Callie."

"Love you, too." I end the call and need Lucas's help to get up, go to the bathroom, and put on leggings and a t-shirt. He carries me into his car, and Binx shadows in with me, shifting into a black cat and settling on my lap. He's warm when he's in cat-form, and his body heat feels wonderful.

"Correct me if I'm wrong, but you can't take cats into hospitals." Lucas pulls out of the parking space.

"I'll say he's my emotional support cat." I grit my teeth before swallowing, knowing it's going to hurt my throat.

"Don't you need paperwork to prove that?"

"He can go unnoticed, trust me."

Lucas grips the steering wheel tight with one hand and keeps his other on my thigh. My eyes flutter shut, and my body continues to shake the whole way to the hospital. Lucas parks and gets out, zooming around to my side.

"I can walk," I protest when he picks me up.

"You look like you're going to pass out."

"I feel like it too." I let my head fall against him. "Don't go too fast," I say and hate the words coming out of my mouth. I don't want anyone giving Lucas shit for being a vampire. Not now when I need him most.

Because I feel awful and I'm still terrified of hospitals.

Lucas sets me down near registration, and I text Abby once I fill out all the paperwork. Lucas offers to take it to the desk for me, and I put my head in my hands, coughing hard again.

"You'll be better soon," he tells me, taking a seat next to me. I shift my weight in the uncomfortable chair and take his hand.

"Thanks for coming with me."

"You don't have to thank me, Callie. You're mine, and we go through shit together."

A door opens and a nurse calls my name. That was fast. Too fast.

"Did you—?" I start but get cut off from all the coughing. Lucas wraps his arm around me and doesn't answer, which alone is a dead giveaway he held the people at the registration desk spellbound to make them get me in right away.

The nurse eyes Lucas and her cheeks flush. He has that effect on women without even trying. He's incredibly good-looking, but the ancientness surrounding him is alluring. Even if you don't know he's a vampire, you feel its pull, making you want to find out more, ignoring the little voice in the back of your head telling you he's dangerous and you should stay away.

Which makes him even more appealing.

The nurse takes my vitals and writes down my symptoms, and then leaves, saying the doctor will be in shortly. Binx shadows in as soon as the nurse leaves, settling on the hard foam bed. He curls up in my arms, purring. Lucas paces back and forth in the little room.

"I'm going to be fine," I tell him. The pacing is getting annoying. "Sit down with me?"

He comes to the side of the exam bed. "You will be fine. You have to be."

"People get sick. It's not a big deal."

"It feels like it to me." He crouches down and takes my hand. "I can fight demons with you. Kill vampires who try to hurt you. But this...I'm helpless and it's making me realize how precarious things are. If I lose you..." He trails off, eyes heavy with emotion. "I can't. And I won't."

"You won't," I promise him. "I'm not going anywhere."

He kisses my fingers and stands, rubbing my back until Abby comes in.

"You brought Binx?" She closes the door behind her and goes over to the computer.

"He brought himself."

She looks over my chart and then gets up. "You still have a really high fever, Cal. Can you sit up?"

"I think so," I say with a cough, feeling like my body is about to give out. She puts her stethoscope in her ears and listens to my chest on both sides.

"Normally, I'd order an x-ray to confirm, but you have pneumonia, Callie. Your lungs are full of crackles, and here..." She puts the stethoscope over my lower ribs and tells me to deeply inhale, which hurts like a bitch. "I'm hearing rubbing."

"What does that mean?" Lucas asks, pacing again. He's so tall that it only takes a few strides to cross the room.

"Pleurisy."

"Is it serious?"

"Not usually. With treatment it typically clears up pretty fast." She listens to my lungs again and goes back to the computer.

"Are you sure I have pneumonia?" I lean back against the bed.

"Yeah. You sound awful. I want to admit you and get you started on IV meds."

"But I was fine yesterday. Like, completely fine. People don't just wake up with pneumonia, do they?"

"No, not typically." Abby looks up from whatever she's typing.

"You were probably sick and didn't realize it. It happens sometimes or we're just so used to functioning worn out we don't even notice we have a cold."

"I don't get colds very often," I say between coughs. "I'd notice if I had one. I wasn't sick, right, Lucas?"

"She was perfectly healthy. Sick people have more white blood cells and it gives the blood a different taste. Callie's blood tasted perfectly delicious yesterday."

Abby is really trying, but that might be too much for her. "You never got sick when we were kids." She looks back at the computer and quickly types something. "I'm going to order you some blood work and will start you off on with an IV. That fever is my main concern right now. You've taken Advil and it did nothing?"

"It didn't even lessen my headache." I bring my arms in around my body, shivering. Abby opens a cabinet above the desk and pulls out a thin white sheet.

"It's not much, but you can't be bundling up with a fever that high." She drapes it over me. "Do you have any allergies to antibiotics?"

"I've never taken them."

"Never?" Abby asks skeptically. "Do you have witch-medicine you need instead?"

"Witches are human," I remind her, turning my head away to cough. "And for as long as I remember, I've never taken them."

"Are you okay with getting blood drawn today?"

I'm not, but I feel so awful I don't argue. I just nod and wrap the thin sheet tighter around my shoulders. I never knew being sick felt this bad. Abby starts saying something else about the nurse coming in and doing my IV, but her voice is lost in a sea of echoes. Binx stands and meows, and Lucas zooms over, saying my name over and over. I want to answer him, really, I do.

But I can't.

Darkness surrounds me, pulling me down and pinning me against the cold, hard ground. A fire burns behind me, crackling and smoking, burning something that leaves the most awful smell in the air. A baby's cry rings out, blood-curdling and full of pain. His endless cries fill the night. Suddenly, there's silence, followed by a woman's scream. I can feel her pain as if the loss were my own.

Wind blows embers onto my face, and the sky above me is red.

He's been here before, and he'll be here again, as soon as they find someone worthy of calling him forth. He'll walk amongst the living and spread his—

Something sharp pierces my arm and my eyes slit open. Lucas is standing at the bedside, fear in his dark blue eyes. I go to jerk my arm back, moving away from whatever sharp thing is after me.

"Hold still, my love," Lucas urges, stepping closer and holding my arm still.

"Can you hear me, Callie?" It's Abby, and she moves around the bed, giving instructions to the person who's stabbing me. I tip my head, looking for Lucas, and see the nurse instead. She's trying to put an IV line in me.

"Get ice packs," Abby tells another nurse. "As many as you can get. We need to get her fever down."

I flit in and out of consciousness, seeing flashes of a blood-tinged sky. The IV fluid is cold inside my veins, and Abby arranges ice packs against me as another nurse wraps a blood pressure cuff around my arm. In just a matter of minutes, I have an IV going and am hooked up to several monitors.

I start to feel alive again as my fever goes down. I'm exhausted, though, and still can barely open my eyes. Screams echo around me, and a deep feeling of satisfaction seeps through my bones. Horse hooves click and clack over a cobblestone path and dozens and dozens of rats scurry around the horse.

"Callie?" Lucas's deep voice pulls me away from the burning village. I'm getting really fucking sick of these cryptic visions. Premonition isn't one of my powers, though this wasn't like I was seeing the future. It's not even like the other visions I had before where the Blue-Eyed Man purposely showed me.

No, this is different, like I'm accessing memories from a part of my brain that was only recently unlocked. Not by me, but by someone—or something—else, that has a connection with me.

I force my eyes open and look at my wrist, where the demon scratched me yesterday. He didn't break the skin and left only a neat little welt. My hospital bracelet is on that wrist, the thick plastic band covers that little red welt.

Only, the red line isn't red anymore. It's black.

CHAPTER 29

"I don't understand," my sister says into a phone. "That's not possible. Run it again." She looks at me and then turns away, talking to whoever she's on the phone with. Lucas has my hand sandwiched between his, and hasn't left my side for even a second.

The IV was placed about twenty minutes ago, and that paired with the ice packs have lowered my fever, but not as much as Abby thought it would. She ordered blood work and is waiting on the results before prescribing an antibiotic. She's been in and out of the room a few times, and I thought she was giving me special attention because I'm her sister.

But it turns out I'm actually really fucking sick.

"What do you mean, it came up as inconclusive?" Abby lets out a frustrated sigh. "Okay. Send someone up, please."

"What's going on?" I ask, throat sore. Every word hurts.

"There was an issue with your blood work." Abby puts the portable phone in the front pocket of her lab coat. "It's probably a machine malfunction. It doesn't happen often, but I've seen the computer readings be way off for blood work a few times over my years in the medical field."

"What's the issue?" Lucas asks.

"It's not reading it correctly."

"What could make that happen?"

Abby shakes her head. "A computer error, I'd guess. They can try to run the report again, but in order to do a new test, they'll need to take more blood."

"It's fine," I say, knowing that my sister is worried about me. I'm handling being in the hospital better than I thought, though I'm honestly too weak to be freaked out. And after talking to Lucas about my time in a research lab, being treated like a zoo animal, I was able to let go of a lot of the repressed fear and emotion. "They can just take it from that little port thing, right?" I look at the IV line in my arm.

"Right. You won't get poked anymore." She types something into the computer and stands. "I don't want to wait any longer for antibiotics, though. We need to start fighting off the pneumonia. I just put in an order for IV antibiotics and some pain medicine for the headache."

"Thanks, Abby."

"Of course, Cal. I have to go see another patient, but the nurse will be in soon. Hang in there, and we'll get you better." She pats my shoulder and leaves. I close my eyes, turning my head and snuggling with Binx until the nurse knocks on the door. Binx shadows away, staying close but out of sight.

Lucas gets up, moving out of the way. I take a pain pill and then the nurse hooks the antibiotics up to my IV. She stays in the room for the next few minutes, taking my vitals and making sure I don't have a reaction to the medication. I'm starting to feel sleepy from the pain pill, and my mind is all fuzzy when a girl comes in for more blood to take to the lab.

The nurse checks on me again, and the constant poking and prodding is getting annoying. I just want to sleep. The blood pressure cuff on my arm automatically inflates every twenty minutes, so even when someone isn't in the room, I'm being bothered.

"You feel hot again." Lucas gently runs his hand up my arm.

237

"Your whole body is hot." He stands and touches my forehead. "The fever is back."

"It can't be," I mumble.

"It is." He smooths back my hair. "I'm getting your sister."

"There's no need for that." As soon as the words leave my mouth, I feel something take hold of me. It presses down on me, dark and heavy. My heart rate spikes, making an alarm on one of the monitors start going off. Sickness twists in my stomach, and it's a struggle to sit up. I make a feeble attempt to point to the trashcan, and end up puking all over the floor.

My hands start trembling uncontrollably, and the sick smell of death surrounds me. The sound of a horse trotting along cobblestone echoes through the room, and my body heaves again, pushing up the last bit of food left in my stomach.

Lucas calls for the nurse and holds my hair back. Everything starts to echo again, and I can't hear what he's saying. It's a fight to keep my eyes open, and the trembling in my hands plagues the rest of my body. I go limp in Lucas's arms, and he holds me upright, afraid I'll choke on my own vomit.

A team of nurses come running in, and the rapid beeping of the alarm grows louder and louder until it turns into children's cries. They're all together in one room, and two men wearing masks and robes walk in.

Lucas lays me back down against the mattress and the head of the bed is raised to keep me from choking. Everything happens in a blur, and I go back and forth between the ER room and the dark room with rows of cots, filled with sick children.

"Callie." Lucas's voice sounds so far away. He's holding my hand again, and he picks up my wrist, fingers sweeping over the welt from the demon scratch.

And then I pass out again.

Silence.

Everything is silent.

The sky. The air. Even the ocean.

I look at the line where the water meets the sky, not wanting to turn around and see the piles of bodies behind me. I bring my hand up to block out the sun, and I see it. The welt on my hand has darkened, and the veins around it are turning black.

"How's she doing?" a voice rings out, but I can't tell where it's coming from. I recognize that voice.

"They can't figure out what's wrong." Deft fingers run up and down my arm. Cool fingers. Lucas's fingers.

"She's strong and incredibly stubborn. If anyone can pull through this, it's her."

"She is strong," Lucas agrees, and I place the other voice. It's Eliza. I try to open my eyes but can't. They're too heavy and I'm too weak.

The sounds of the hospital slowly start to register, but I don't think I'm in the busy ER anymore. The blood pressure cuff tightens around my arm, and someone knocks on the door.

"Did you get the test results back?" Lucas asks someone.

"The results are still inconclusive," my sister answers. "Are you sure witch blood is the same as human blood?"

"Yes," Lucas tells her. "Biologically witches are human. There is nothing in their blood that's different than humans who don't possess magical powers."

"I don't understand what's happening then. The lab ran her blood twice and got the same results. I can't treat her if I don't know what I'm dealing with, and so far nothing is working to keep her fever down." She comes around the bed and picks up something that was resting against my head, replacing it with another.

Oh, it's more ice packs.

"People can't survive with fevers this high. I honestly don't know how she's alive and not having febrile seizures."

"But she'll be okay, right?" Eliza asks.

"Yeah," Abby says and even I don't believe her. "I'll...I'll figure something out. I was able to pull a favor from a friend who works in pathology in a private lab. She's analyzing her blood now and will call once she gets results. Until then…we'll keep her as comfortable and stable as we can."

Abby smooths my hair back and rearranges the ice packs. "I have to go back to the ER, but I'll come up when I can."

Back to the ER? I was right, I'm not there anymore, but where am I? Exhausting myself trying to open my eyes, I fall asleep again. For how long, I have no idea. I'm woken up when someone moves my feet, bending my knees a bit and putting a pillow under my legs. It's the nurse, and she repositions my weak body to keep it from getting any sores.

"There's something familiar about this," Lucas says once the nurse leaves. He leans in and puts his face to the IV port, smelling my blood. "And I think I might know what it is. Stay with her," he tells Eliza.

"Where are you going?"

"To find her sister," he says. "Because it all makes sense now."

"What does?" Eliza's heels click against the tiled floor.

"The rats and the demon and now Callie's symptoms. Remember the way that body smelled? So rancid you didn't think it was human?"

"I'll remember that smell forever."

"I smelled blood like that before, but not since the 1300s." He turns away. "Fuck! I didn't see it until now."

"What are you talking about, Lucas?"

"She has the plague, Eliza. The Black Plague."

"People still get that?"

"Not this strand." I can hear Lucas pacing around the room. "The hunter, Melinda, brought over police reports. All the bodies were found in a state of advanced decomposition but hadn't been missing for more than a week. And whatever is making Callie sick is burning right through her, faster than it should."

He comes over and wraps cool fingers around my wrist—the one that the demon scratched.

"Holy fuck," Eliza exclaims. "What is that?"

"The demon scratched her, but instead of trying to hurt her, it was infecting her."

"I'll stay here, go get her sister," Eliza tells Lucas. "They can treat her now that you know what she's sick with, right?"

"No," Lucas replies in a grave tone. "They can't help her because what's making her sick isn't biological. It's supernatural. I need her sister to sign her out of here. There's a demon virus coursing through her veins and if it's not vanquished, Callie will die."

CHAPTER 30

Binx nuzzles his head against me, and I blink my eyes open. Two people are arguing in hushed voices at the foot of the bed. My vision is hazy and I can't sit up even if I tried. I turn my head and realize I'm in the ICU instead of the ER. There's a small window in my room, and it's edging toward dawn. Lucas and Eliza won't be able to stay here much longer.

Binx meows, getting someone's attention.

"Callie." Lucas rushes to my bedside and takes my hand and laces his fingers between mine. "You're awake."

"I am." I try to push up and fail. Abby stands on the other side of the bed and raises the head of it up a little more. "What's... what's going on?"

"Lucas wants to check you out against medical advice," Abby spits out, which must be what they're arguing about. "You're way too sick to go anywhere."

Memories come back in flashes and I'm not sure what was real or not real. The piles of bodies ready to be burned? That didn't happen.

Black veins stemming from the demon-scratch? I don't know. I twist my wrist and look down.

That's real.

The rats. The demon. The way the bodies were covered in thick, dark veins, just like the ones on my wrist.

Lucas is right.

I'll die if I stay here.

"You should call Tabatha." Lucas paces around the little room again. "Other than you, she's the most powerful witch I know of, and we're going to need all the help we can get."

"I can't call her," I protest.

"I will for you." Lucas picks up my phone from a bag of personal items the ER sent up with me.

"No." I use my powers to take the phone from his hand and terrible pain ripples through me. It starts in the center of my chest and spreads, burning and stabbing and contracting all my muscles.

The monitors go crazy, beeping and blaring with warning. I cry out in pain and Abby and Lucas both come rushing over.

"What's happening?" Lucas asks.

"I...I don't know. It's like her body's going into shock!" Abby calls for the nurse but as suddenly as the pain came on, it goes away.

"It happened when she used magic," Eliza whispers before the nurse runs in.

Lucas turns my wrist over, watching as the black travels up my veins. He covers it with his hand.

"I'm...I'm okay," I pant, shaking from the pain. Tears well in my eyes and I rest my head back against the pillow. Abby tells the nurse to go get more ice packs just to get her out of the room.

"You can't call Tabatha," I breathe. "It's too risky."

"I don't care about the Grand Coven," Lucas counters. "And neither will she." Lucas moves his hand and looks down at my arm.

"What is that?" Abby leans in. "That wasn't there last time I saw you."

"It's the demon virus." Lucas straightens up and looks at Abby.

"It kills fast. If we don't act now..." He casts his eyes down. "I'm not losing you, Callie."

"You won't," I tell him, but I feel like I'm lying. I didn't know it was possible to feel your body shutting down, but that's exactly what's happening right now as the virus courses through me.

"I thought you killed the demon." Eliza crosses her arms tightly over her chest. Her hair is up in a fancy braid again, one so elaborate Daenerys Targaryen herself would be jealous. Her dress is pale pink with little flowers hand-stitched along the hem. She really is pretty.

"We did." Lucas takes my hand again. "Unlike the rats, the virus isn't linked with the demon."

"Rats?" Abby echoes. "You're talking about demon rats?"

"Don't worry, they're dead."

The lights shine down on Eliza, who's pacing back and forth now. Apple doesn't fall far from the tree, it seems. "You look like a fairy princess."

"Who are you talking about?" Lucas asks.

"Eliza. She's so pretty. Like a fairy."

Eliza stops pacing. "As much as I like compliments of any kind, that has to be the fever talking."

"The plague makes you delirious," Abby explains. "I can't believe I didn't think of it. I mean, we've seen modern cases. It's rare, but her symptoms do fit. It comes on suddenly too, not this sudden, but if it's paired with a demon virus...medical school did not prepare me for this."

"It prepared Sister Ross." I reach for Binx, wanting to feel his sleek fur. "Actually, she might...she..." I start coughing again. My chest hurts and the pain radiates through my body.

"Take your time, my love." Lucas smooths my hair back, taking the old ice packs off. "Who is Sister Ross? Could she help?"

Binx stands and jumps off the bed, shifting into shadow-form before he hits the floor. Abby has never seen him like that before, and I will say he's quite terrifying. He moves like black mist through the air, taking on a human shape with red eyes that glow like coals in the dark. Abby jumps back and screams, but Lucas is faster and covers her mouth before anyone can hear her.

"Sister Ross is a witch-doctor, so to speak." Binx's voice is deep and raspy at the same time. It fills every inch of the room while being impossible to tell where it's coming from.

"Where is she?" Lucas asks, letting Abby go.

"At the Academy." Binx shadows over to the bed, hovering above me.

"Can you go get her?"

"I will not leave my master." Binx turns into a cat again, right as the nurse walks in with more ice packs. She comes to a sudden halt, eyes wide. If only she'd come in a second sooner…

"Therapy cat," Abby blurts. "It's a therapy cat."

"Oh, how, uh, nice."

"I'll take those." Abby holds out her hand for the ice packs. "Thank you." She ushers the nurse out and closes the door. "That's what Binx really looks like?" Quickly shaking her head, she puts the ice packs around me. "Will she be able to help you?"

"She might," I say.

"It's worth a try then." Lucas gets my phone. "Do you have her number?"

I shake my head. "She won't be able to get a call if she's at the Academy. I can send Freya and Pandora." They stayed at the house in case anyone from the Grand Coven stopped by to make sure I was holding up my end of the deal. My familiars would let them in so they could have a look around and see that my windows weren't covered. A vampire couldn't be living with me.

"I'll call for them." I close my eyes but as soon as I try to put out a message to my familiars, I'm hit with a horrible pain, just like when I telekinetically took the phone out of Lucas's hand.

I scream, feeling like my entire body has been plunged into boiling hot water. Lucas grabs a hold of me, clutching me until the pain passes. Once I stop shaking, he inspects my wrist. The darkness has traveled farther up my arm.

"Every time you use magic it gets worse." He touches the dark vein. "It's as if the virus is feeding off your powers." He holds my phone up to my face to get it to unlock with the facial recognition. "I'm calling Kristy and having her get a hold of Tabatha."

"Lucas, I can't risk her."

"And I'm not going to sit here and watch you die." He gets up, stepping out of the room so I won't be able to try and stop him, and calls her. Abby takes a step back and sits on the register under the window. Her eyes flit from me to Binx.

"Told you he wasn't really a cat," I say, struggling to get each word out.

"I know, but I had no idea he looked like that. Do your others?"

I nod. "Pretty cool, huh?"

"That's one way to put it."

"Do you have to go back to the ER?"

"No," she says. "My shift ended."

"You can go home." Binx moves to my side, resting his head on my arm.

"No, I'm not leaving you. I just need to call Phil and let him know I'll be late."

"What are you going to tell him?" I curl my fingers through Binx's fur.

"The truth. Well, not that you're infected with a demon virus and we're trying to get a witch-doctor to cure you, but I'll tell him you're really sick."

"Thanks, Abby."

"You're my sister."

Lucas comes back into the room, brows furrowed with trepidation. "I spoke with Tabatha, and she's on her way. We need to take Callie back to my house."

"I really don't think that's a good idea," Abby argues. "She's weak."

"She is, and she will continue to get weaker."

"Can't they come here and treat her? I'll close the door."

"No. Tabatha told me that Evander has been researching this

demon since we first ran into it a few nights ago. He has a lead, but if it's true..." He sits on the edge of the bed, looking down at me with glossy eyes. "If it's true, we don't have much time."

"What is it, Lucas?" Eliza snaps, unable to hide the fear in her voice.

Lucas tears his eyes away from mine, looking pained. "Pestilence."

CHAPTER 31

"Pestilence?" Eliza echoes. "I...I don't understand."

"Like the Horseman?" Abby asks, voice shaking.

"Yes."

"Wait a minute." Abby is terrified and trying to hold it together. "One of the Four Horsemen of the Apocalypse has poisoned my sister?"

"Not the horseman directly, but a demon with connections who wants to bring them forth from Hell." Lucas turns back to me. "The demon said something to you...that you might be strong enough?"

"It said it'd been waiting for one that was worthy, and then it kept asking me what I am." Wincing, I sit up. "Demons say that kind of stuff all the time, though. They want you to feel special so you'll let them in." I close my eyes, thinking back. "It did say it didn't want to take me to Hell as its bride but do the opposite... whatever that means."

"It wants to break the seals."

"Great," I groan as another shudder of pain goes through me.

"I'm not following." Poor Abby sounds like she's going to cry.

"Break the seals, the Four can come out and start an apocalypse," Lucas explains quickly.

"Oh. That wouldn't be good." Now she looks like she might pass out.

"Don't worry," I tell her and push myself up even more. "We won't let that happen. I already killed that demon. And if any more try, I'll kill them too." I cough up mucus. "Well, once I'm better."

Abby takes in a deep breath and sits back on the register. "Why do you have to take Callie out of the hospital, though? She's sick, and at least here I can try to treat her symptoms."

"The virus is demonic. Witches have the power to vanquish and banish demons. The right spell might be enough to weaken the virus if not kill it completely."

"Holy shit." Abby puts her head in her hands. "She still needs supportive care. That fever is going to burn her up. And I still don't understand how the virus works...is she contagious?"

"I don't know," Lucas answers honestly. "She can't infect me, though, if she is."

"Right...you're a vampire." Abby closes her eyes and thinks. "Okay...you need supplies."

"Supplies?" I ask.

"IVs and medication. If the virus is killed but you still have the freaking bubonic plague, you're going to need a strong dose of antibiotics."

"Can you go get some?" Eliza asks.

"It's not as easy as it is in movies to steal medical supplies. Things are accounted for, especially the medication. When things go missing, someone will get the blame." Abby chews on her lips and then looks at Lucas. "You can do that hypnotism thing, right?"

"Yes," he answers.

"Come with me then. I have a plan."

$\sim$

"ARE YOU COMFORTABLE?" LUCAS SMOOTHS THE BLANKETS OVER my legs. I'm back at his house, tucked in bed.

"As much as I can be." I force a smile and my eyes fall shut. The little movement I did to get from the hospital to the house wore me out, and Lucas carried me most of the time. Abby puts on gloves and wipes the IV port on my arm with an alcohol wipe, disinfecting it before hooking another up.

"I need to hang it," she tells Lucas, holding the bag up. "I should have had you steal a pump."

"How high?" Lucas asks.

"About where I've got it."

"I'll find something." Lucas kisses my forehead and leaves the room.

"Thank you again, Abby." I turn on my side and bring my legs to my chest. Everything feels wrong inside my body. My stomach is full of acid. My muscles are deteriorating. There's fire inside my lungs, and my head might crack open from the pressure at any moment.

Dying is awful.

It took twenty or so minutes for Abby to get everything she needs to take care of me here, and then another twenty to get back to Lucas's house. Tabatha, Evander, and Kristy are all on their way, and should be here within a half hour. I want to sleep until then.

"Stop thanking me and I'll stop apologizing."

"Deal."

"How are things coming on your house?" she asks and I know it's to calm her nerves.

"I'm not sure. I haven't had a chance to look." The chills are back and I tighten the blanket around my shoulders. I don't remember how long it's been since we had dinner at Abby's house. Days? A week? It feels like so long ago. "Maybe I'll go home and find it's almost done."

"I don't think that'll happen," Abby laughs. "Unless you use magic. Can you use magic?"

"Not for a whole house reno like that. But I use magic to help me clean and cook."

Lucas returns and punches a long nail into the wall with his bare hands. Abby hangs the IV bag and then lays out the rest of the medication. She takes my vitals and records them in a notebook.

"You're a good doctor," I tell her, eyes feeling heavy.

"I try." She yawns and runs her hand over her face.

"You're welcome to any of the guest rooms," Lucas says. "And there are clean clothes in the closet. I don't think Callie would mind sharing."

"Thanks. I have a change of clothes in my bag. I don't like to wear my scrubs home. They're way too germy to have around Penny." She leaves to change and lay down until Tabatha and my friends get here.

"Lucas," I start.

"Shhh," he soothes. "Close your eyes and get some rest, my love." His lips press against mine and he combs his fingers through my long hair. I let my eyes fall shut and start to fall asleep, waking up to cough. I just know that I'm dying and it terrifies me.

"We're really going to need that vacation once you're better," Lucas says softly.

"Yeah," I agree. If I'm better...because right now I don't see how I'm going to get through this. The pain is getting worse and worse. I grit my teeth and squeeze my eyes shut.

"Do you want me to rub your back again?"

I weakly nod my head and Lucas helps me lie down in such a way that I'm still propped up on the pillows. Having him rub my sore muscles helps me relax a little, but not enough to fall asleep, which is all I want to do.

The chills turn into tremors, and I moan in pain. "Everything hurts," I cry, tears spilling from my eyes.

"Abby brought you pain medicine."

"I don't think it'll help."

"It won't hurt to try it. I'll get her."

"No. Don't leave me."

"I will never leave you," Lucas whispers, saying each word slowly. "Never, Callie. You are everything to me. I won't lose you, and I won't leave you." He lies down next to me, sliding one arm under my body. "I told you I wasn't going to let anyone take you away from me, not even the Horsemen of the Apocalypse."

My throat burns and I feel like I'm going to puke up stomach bile. The pain in my chest intensifies, burning both my lungs and my heart now. Humans can't live with temperatures this high for long, and I know my time is running out.

Will Lucas let me die?

Or will he turn me into a vampire?

I'll lose my powers. I'll lose the sun. My familiars. The coven.

But we'll be together.

It should be an easy choice: death or immortal life. Yet for me it's not, and if it does come down to it...I don't want to be a vampire.

CHAPTER 32

"You were right to call me." Tabatha sits on the bed and brushes my hair back. "My darling girl, we will get you well."

"She looks awful." Kristy sniffles. "She's never been sick, not even once, since we met."

"I don't remember her being sick when we were kids either," Abby says. "Is it a witch thing?"

"No," Kristy answers. "Witches get sick."

"We should get started. I fear we've already wasted time." Tabatha rests her hand on my cheek and gets up. I force my eyes open and see my friends moving about the room. The automatic blinds have been come down early, no doubt to keep anyone from seeing inside.

"What are you going to do?" Abby asks.

"We're going to start with a simple banishing spell." Evander lays sage smudge sticks on the dresser across from the bed. "We'll see how she fares and then move up from there. Kristy is making a vanquishing potion now."

"I've combined it with a health serum that should hopefully counteract the effects of having Callie consume the vanquishing potion."

253

"Is it going to hurt her?"

"Yes," Kristy answers after a moment of hesitation. "But if it saves her…"

"Then it's more than worth it," Lucas finishes.

"I'm going to get the potion started in the kitchen," Kristy says and pulls a little glass vial from her bag. "I need the final ingredient."

Lucas takes the vial and draws his fangs. He bites himself, sinking his fangs into the vein in his wrist and catches the drops of blood in the vial before he heals.

"Thanks." Kristy puts a cork on the vial and goes downstairs.

I start coughing, getting everyone's attention. Binx shadows behind me, helping me sit up. "Hey, guys."

"Oh, my sweet girl." Tabatha puts her heavy Book of Shadows down and comes around to my side of the bed. "Never hesitate to call me."

"This puts you in a bad situation."

"Not quite as bad as the one you're in," Evander says with a half-smile.

"I'll get out of it." I close my eyes again and hunch forward. "I've gotten out of every bad situation I've been in so far."

"Maybe you should stop getting into them? Ever think of that?" he teases.

"That's no fun." I groan, teeth chattering together. "Are you ready to do this?"

"Just about."

I have Lucas take me to the bathroom, and Abby checks my vitals once more. Nothing has improved. Head pounding, I get back into bed. The room is spinning and my insides are liquifying…or at least that's how it feels.

Lucas messes with the pillows, fluffing and rearranging them until he's convinced it's good enough. Evander lights a smudge stick and the smoke wafts around me. The smell is usually comforting, but right now it's making me feel sick.

Tabatha sets a white candle on either side of the nightstand

and ignites them with magic. She moves to the foot of the bed and holds out a quartz crystal wand. "Powers of North, South, East and West, I call on you with this request. Remove the evil in the space, and leave good fortune in its place."

As she speaks, a sharp pain starts in my wrist. When she holds up the crystal, my arm starts to tingle.

"Powers of North, South, East, and West," she repeats and it's like someone took a hot iron from the fire and shoved it inside my veins. I scream in pain, clutching my arm. The IV lines pull but the pain of that is nothing compared to my skin which feels like literal fire.

I look down, convinced I'll see charred and burned skin. My skin is fine, but the black lines travel up my arm. Lucas, who's next to me, sees it too.

"The spell," he rushes out. "It's making it worse. You have to stop."

"No," I grunt. "Keep going." I squeeze my eyes closed and take a tangle of the blankets in each hand, bracing myself.

Tabatha sets her face and points the crystal wand at me. "I call on you with this request." Her words bring more pain and I inhale sharply before screaming again. The black lines move up farther, poisoning more of my veins. "Remove the evil in the space, and leave good fortune in its place."

"Stop!" Lucas yells. "You're hurting her!" He wraps me in his arms, and I fall against him, heart pounding.

"Should we take a break?" Evander whispers and Tabatha shakes her head.

"Join me," Tabatha tells him and Evander holds out his hand, thumbs and forefingers together.

"Powers of North, South, East, and West," they chant and pain shoots through me. "I call on you with this request. Remove the evil in the space, and leave good fortune in its place."

My entire body stiffens and my head flops back. My vision blacks and I'm shaking uncontrollably again.

"Oh my God," Abby breathes and runs over. "Stop! Stop! It's

making it spread!" I go limp in Lucas's strong arms. My heart is racing and I can't catch my breath. The muscles in my legs are cramping like I just got done running a marathon. "It's to her shoulder now. If it spreads to her heart…"

"What's going on?" Kristy's voice comes from the hall as she runs into the room, followed by Eliza, who's doing her best to act uninterested but really is worried sick. "I heard screaming."

"The virus seems to feed on magic," Lucas answers. "When Callie used her powers she had the same reaction. And look." He turns my hand over. "It makes it spread."

"Does that mean magic isn't going to work?" Abby asks, though I think she already knows the answer.

I do.

"It means we can't fight it with magic," Tabatha replies, voice thin. "Which… means we have no way of stopping the virus from spreading."

"No." Lucas slips his arms around me. "No. She's not dying." His voice breaks and he brings his head down to mine. "I'm not losing her."

"Lucas," I mumble, mustering up all the strength I have to open my eyes and bring one hand to his face. "I love you."

"Stop it," he growls and tears fall from his eyes, landing on my cheeks. "Stop acting like this is goodbye." He holds me closer. "You're going to be okay."

"I…I'm not." My body shudders. "I can feel it…burning me from the inside out. It hurts."

"But you're strong, Callie. The strongest person I've ever met. You can fight through this."

"I…I can't use ma-agic." My words come out all jerky.

"Use the other magic." Lucas pulls me tighter into his arms. "You healed yourself before. I saw you do it. Do it now."

"It was the Blue-Eyed man," I breathe, so quiet only Lucas is able to hear me. "He did it."

"It was you. You did it, my love. Heal yourself now. *Please*," he cries. "I can't lose you." He kisses me once more and draws his fangs. "I won't lose you."

The pain starts to fade, and I'm so, so cold. "Lucas...I...I..." My head lolls back.

"Callie?" Lucas calls frantically. "Callie?"

"No!" Abby cries. I feel her weight sink down on the mattress. "Is she—?"

Before she can finish her question, bright golden light fills the room. I can't open my eyes, but yet I know who it is.

It's him.

He's finally here.

The Blue-Eyed Man.

CHAPTER 33

Everything moves in slow motion. The light is blinding, making it impossible to see. It warms my face and gives me strength. I open my eyes right as the light is fading, and I see the outline of great feathered wings behind the man for just a split second before they disappear.

Fangs bared, Lucas lays me down on the mattress and lunges for the man. I've told him about the man and who I think he is, but he's not convinced this man isn't a threat. The Blue-Eyed Man holds out his hand, forcing Lucas back down. He holds up his other hand and all the humans in the room slump down. He lowers both hands at the same time, and Lucas and Eliza fall to the ground, asleep, too.

Binx growls and the man turns to him. "I wouldn't try that." His voice is warm and familiar. Binx backs down, sitting at my side, flicking the tip of his tail back and forth. The man walks across the room, holding out his hand.

I push myself up, wincing with pain that shoots through me.

"Who…who are you?" I ask, voice thin and small.

The Blue-Eyed Man stops next to the bed and gazes upon my face. His lips curve into a smile, eyes warming. "You look just like your mother. You have her stubbornness, that's for sure."

"My mother?"

"I know you have questions, but now is not the time." He reaches out and lays his hand on my head. All the pain, all the sickness, everything that felt wrong disappears. I inhale with no pain, my headache is gone, and the black veins on my wrist fade away.

"Rest, my child." His eyes meet mine, and for a split second, everything is okay. My anxiety slips away, and I feel like I'm where I'm supposed to be. He steps back and I dive forward. No dizziness crashes down on me. I'm completely healthy again. He healed me.

Just like he did before. I knew it was him. But why? Why help me three times now only to leave?

"Wait!" Desperation speeds up my heart. "Who are you?"

"You already know the answer to that."

My eyes fill with tears and I suck in air. He's my father. The confirmation sends a chill through me, causing goosebumps to break out along my flesh.

I'm not a Martin. Abby isn't my sister. Scott was right when he said we weren't related.

I am not fully human.

I blink away the tears that burn the corners of my eyes. "What are you?" My throat tightens with emotion.

"You know the answer to that as well."

A tear rolls down my cheek. "You're an angel," I whisper.

"I am." He takes another step back and great, white wings spread out behind him, stretching across the room. His eyes begin to glow a brilliant bright blue. My mouth falls open and another chill works its way down his spine.

The Blue-Eyed Man is my father.

My father is an angel.

I'm *half angel*.

Everything I thought I knew my whole life has been a lie.

I'm not just a witch. My father is an angel and he said I look like my mother. But I look nothing like the mother I grew up with. My eyes shut in a long blink and the pain of my childhood hits me like a red-hot knife to the heart.

I grew up feeling like an outsider in my own home, picked on and ridiculed until I was cast out, sold like an animal to the highest bidder, studied and tortured. Tabatha rescued me and I made amazing friends at the Academy, but even then I felt alone. I was different from the others, and it didn't go unnoticed. There was an emptiness deep inside me that grew and festered, hurting me and making me feel so, so alone.

And all the while he was out there. Watching me. And doing nothing.

"Why did you leave me?" My brows furrow and anger takes over, making the lights flicker.

The peaceful look on the Blue-Eyed Man's face fades, twisting into one of regret and pain.

"I had to."

"No you didn't." Tears fall like rain and I shake my head. "You didn't have to leave me, and the people you left me with…did you know what they did to me? Did you just stand by and do nothing?" The chandelier over the bed rattles. "You…you abandoned me."

"There are things in play you don't understand."

"Then explain them to me!" I throw back the covers and get out of bed, planting my feet firmly on the floor. The Blue-Eyed Man—my father—stands a good half a foot taller than me. "If you had to leave me, then why did you come back? Why did you save me? Why even care?"

"I've always cared, Callie."

I jerk back. It feels wrong to hear him call me that. Is that even my name? My family's not my family and I'm not even human.

"Did you know?" I can't keep the emotion in my voice. "Did you know what they did to me?"

"Yes," he confesses, looking pained. Good. I hope it fucking hurts like hell.

"Why didn't you stop them?"

"I couldn't."

"Why are you here now?" I angrily wipe away tears. "And why were you there before?"

"You'd been discovered."

"By the demon?"

"Not just the one." He strides forward and holds out his hand. "We don't have much time."

I swallow the lump in my throat and let out a breath. "Why should I trust you?"

He gives me a half-smile. "I did just save your life. Though I like your skepticism."

"Are they okay?" I ask, looking at everyone on the floor.

"Yes, they're sleeping."

Against my better judgement, I take the Blue-Eyed Man's hand. The world spins again, but this time it's like I'm on a ride. When it stops, evening light spills down on me and sand covers my toes. Warm, salty air blows in from over gorgeous aquamarine-colored ocean water.

"What the hell?" I throw out my hands to steady myself.

"The dizziness will pass in a moment."

There are a few people on the beach, but none seem to have noticed our sudden appearance. "Where are we?"

"Western Australia. It's been one of my favorite places since creation. It's beautiful, isn't it?"

"Taking me here isn't going to distract me."

"That wasn't my intent. Everything is better when you're on one of the world's most beautiful beaches." He starts walking down the shore.

"Nancy Martin isn't my mother?"

"No, she's not."

I stop walking, head spinning. "But she was pregnant with me. I've seen the photos. She has my umbilical cord still and I've heard my own birth story."

"Nancy Martin was pregnant and did give birth to a baby girl the same day you were born." The Blue-Eyed Man stops walking and turns around. "The baby she carried was stillborn."

"What?" I ask, feeling a little sick.

The Blue-Eyed Man sits down on the sand and motions for me to sit next to him. Heart in my throat, I lower myself onto the warm sand. "Relationships between angels and humans are strictly forbidden. But the heart wants what the heart wants, and it seems you're not so different from your parents after all."

I stare at him, eyes wide and unblinking.

"I fell in love with your mother, as she did with me. I don't need to explain to you how you came about. Most humans cannot survive carrying a divine child, but your mother was no ordinary human."

"She was a witch." My throat constricts with emotion and more tears fall from my eyes.

"Yes, she was a strong and brilliant witch."

"Was?"

His own eyes get a little misty. "Yes, was. We knew how risky it would be bringing you into this world, but we loved each other and loved you. Being able to carry you to term...some would say it was a miracle. She wanted to raise you, and oh, did she love you, Callie."

I wipe my nose with the back of my hand, sniffling.

"It was her idea to hide you in plain sight if anything were to happen to her."

"What did happen?"

"Surviving a divine pregnancy is one thing, but giving birth to a divine child is another. You came into the world at the exact second Nancy Martin left."

"You swapped us."

"Yes. The Martins weren't ideal, but the timing had to be exact. It was our only option, and it worked. You were a Martin, part of a conservative family in the public eye, and the last place anyone would think to look for a Nephilim baby. I bound your angelic powers as best I could that day."

I cover my mouth with my hand, not quite able to process this information yet. "Did you know what my fath—William Martin did to me? That he sold me?"

"Yes."

"Why didn't you save me?"

"I couldn't. It's not just demons you have to worry about, Callie. Nephilim are ordered to death amongst angels. If I intervened, it would have drawn attention to you and I couldn't risk that. My brothers would have killed you without question. I did send help by directing the spirit Oberyth to you."

"You...you sent me Binx?"

"Directed. He still chose you, but I knew he would. Only the most badass familiar would do for my daughter."

I look out at the ocean. Is this really happening? Did I pass out again and this is some weird, illness-induced dream?

"But you're here now."

"There are some who never believed the divine child died. They spent years searching, and then Varrador was able to narrow it down. You'd been compromised."

"If he knew then others know."

"Yes, and once word gets out that you've been alive all these years, a war will rage for you."

"So you're saying both angels and demons want me dead?"

"Yes."

I stare out at the ocean again. I'm sitting on the dry shore but feel like I'm drowning. "And I thought vampires hunting me was bad enough." I look at my father, my *real* father. "Why don't angels want Nephilim to live?"

"You are half human, and they fear you could be easily swayed to the dark. It's happened before and caused much damage. You possess great power, my child. Being part angel, you have the power to hurt us."

"You said you bound my angel powers."

"I did, in hopes of keeping unwanted attention away. But after the demons found out you were still alive, I knew you'd need it.

I've been slowly unlocking it since that day in the woods. Turning the key and letting it all out at once would have been overwhelming for your human half."

I don't know if I should laugh or cry. Maybe do both? I'm going to need a big glass of wine when I get back to my house.

"I thought angels were supposed to be all pretty and kind and wear flowing white dresses."

"We are warriors. Rest assured there are others who disagree. They think you should be allowed to live and know you can be of great service to the divine."

"Really? How many?"

"Two. Including myself."

"So there's only one other person out of all the angels who doesn't want me dead. Great. I love those odds." I rub my temples. I was healed, but a headache is quickly coming back. "The demon that made me sick. Is it gone?"

"Yes, but the threat is more real now than ever. The demons have been looking for one who is worthy of breaking the seals for over a century now. Who is more worthy than one who can answer both the call of light and the call of night?"

"Let me recap: demons currently want to use me as a key to start the apocalypse and every angel besides you and one other will kill me on sight."

"Yep. That about sums it up."

"What do I do?

"Keep living your life the way you were. I'll continue to keep the angels off your trail and...here." He holds his hand over my heart and yellow light glows around his palm. "I unlocked more of the angelic grace you have inside you."

I take a deep breath, feeling like I just chugged two coffees.

"I am proud of you, Callie. And I know your mother would have been too."

"What was her name?" My voice is all shaky with emotion again.

"Callista." He smiles. "For some reason Nancy Martin knew you didn't look like an Ashley the moment she laid eyes on you."

"I always thought Callista was too exotic of a name for her to have picked."

The Blue-Eyed Man looks at the sky and then rises to his feet. "It's been long enough. I need to get you home."

"Will you tell me your name?"

He takes my hand and the world starts to spin, wrapped in a bright, golden glow.

"Michael."

CHAPTER 34

I'm back in the master bedroom, blinking rapidly to get them to adjust to the dim light. Michael is gone, and I'm standing in the same spot he did when he first appeared. Slowly, the others start to wake up.

"Please tell me you saw that." I'm still not sure I did.

Lucas rushes over and takes me in his arms. "You're alive."

"And well."

He looks me up and down, running his hands all over my body checking for black veins. Once he sees I'm fine, he kisses me, tongue plunging into my mouth. He wraps me tight in his embrace, kissing me until I have to stop for air.

"Who the hell was that?" Eliza fusses with her braids, which got messed up when she passed out on the floor. My gaze travels from everyone in the room, stopping on Abby.

"You saw him, right?" I need to be sure.

"I did," Kristy says and the others nod. "He had blue eyes. Like the man you've been talking about. Was that him?"

"Can we talk downstairs? And maybe order a pizza or something. I'm starving."

"You're completely better?" Kristy peels me out of Lucas's arms.

"Yes. He healed me. And then took me to a really pretty beach in Australia." Everyone exchanges confused looks, and I lead the way downstairs. "My phone is dead," I say as I get two bottles of wine from the fridge. "Does anyone else have the Papa John's app already downloaded?"

"I do." Lucas zooms away to get his phone.

"Why do you have a pizza app?" Kristy asks when he gets back, sitting at the large island counter.

"I order pizza for my employees at least once a week."

"Oh, that's really nice of you."

I open a cabinet and get out five wine glasses. Using magic, I pull out the cork and then hold out my hand, telekinetically pouring the wine into each glass.

"Wow, Cal," Evander gasps. "That's a new trick."

"Michael gave me a power boost. Well, not really a boost. Just helped me tap into what was already there." I look over my shoulder at Lucas. "Can you order two pepperoni pizzas please?"

"It's dawn, Callie. They're not open yet."

"Dammit."

"I'll find something that's open for you."

"Thank you."

I sit between Kristy and Abby and use magic to bring everyone their glasses. This kind of power is going to make me fat and lazy. No one says a word and I can feel their gazes on me, waiting for me to speak.

"That man…his name was Michael?" Tabatha asks slowly.

I swallow a mouthful of sweet rosé. It's going to hit me fast since I haven't had anything to eat in a day. Taking a breath, I push my shoulders back and remember the way I felt, for just a brief moment, when I was with him. He made me feel safe and loved, like everything was going to be all right. It's the same feeling I get when I hold the feather, just…more.

Maybe all angels make you feel like that. They are divine, after all. Or maybe that's how fathers are supposed to make you feel. Like they'll protect you, care for you. Love you for who you are.

"The Blue-Eyed Man...he's the one that helped me escape the hellfire. And he confirmed something today, something I've had a feeling about even though it didn't make sense, though it did make sense at the same time, but really it didn't because I was basing things off of feelings and the notion that maybe somewhere in the great wide world I fit in, like really fit in."

"You're rambling," Kristy says gently. "And totally losing me."

"I've never fit in with my family," I start. "Obviously. They're normal assholes—other than you, Abby—and nowhere in the Martin family history have there ever been witches. None on Nancy's side either. But it happens that a witch or wizard is born to nonmagical parents."

I take another sip of wine. "Even at school, I was different and I knew it. But you guys accepted me and I felt like I was where I was supposed to be. Most the of the time, at least. And I was supposed to be there, since half of me is a witch."

"Half of you?" Evander repeats. "What are you getting at?"

"Witches can't command hellfire. They can't break through wardings and they don't have more than one familiar."

"What does this have to do with that man?" Kristy presses. Gulping down another mouthful of wine, I look up at Tabatha. Like the others, she's waiting for me to go on, but unlike Kristy, Evander, and Abby, she looks like she already knows.

"The Blue-Eyed Man is my father." I spit out the words and there's no taking them back now.

"You were right all along." Lucas rests his elbows on the counter. "I knew never to doubt you."

"What?" Abby's face is pulled down with horror. "What do you mean?" She picks up her wine but doesn't take a drink. "How can he be your father?"

How am I supposed to tell her that her real sister died before she was even born and I took her place? It sounds so creepy and fucked up even to me. I'll have to tell her the whole story, and that's even more to take in. I don't want to break my sister.

Lucas sits up, tipping his head. "You spoke another language, one I hadn't heard before and one you didn't know. It was Enochian, wasn't it?"

"Enochian?" Evander's face lights up with amusement. "Nobody speaks Enochian. It's the language of—bloody hell." He turns to me. "You're saying...that he...he was..."

"Yes. My father is an angel." A chill makes its way down my spine again. "I know it sounds crazy, but it makes sense."

"It does."

"Wait." Kristy holds up her hand. "His name is Michael. Is he the archangel Michael?"

"He didn't say and I didn't think to ask. If I see him again, I'm bringing a list of questions."

Abby sucks down a mouthful of her wine and then starts laughing. "Sorry, I'm sorry." She puts the glass down and doubles over with laughter. "It's just...you were dying quite literally and then some guy—who might be the archangel Michael—shows up, tells you he's your father, and now you're better. It's...it's...I don't even know."

"It's a lot," Evander supplies, taking a drink of wine.

I meet Tabatha's eye. "Did you know?"

"I knew you weren't related to the Martins," Tabatha admits, and the confession lifts an invisible weight off her shoulders. "As did the man you thought was your father. Once he realized you were not his true daughter, he sold you like a pig to slaughter. But as to knowing that you weren't a full witch..." She reaches over and puts her hand on mine.

"I had my suspicions. I destroyed your file the day I took you from that awful laboratory, but not before I saw inside. Your blood showed qualities that weren't human. Witches have human blood and the only way anomalies could show up like that was if you were half witch and half something else. Witches and shifters have half-magical babies with diminished powers and pathetic shifting abilities, but as soon as you got to the Academy, I knew there was nothing *half* about your magic. And it didn't matter," she presses. "You were my student and my daughter. It didn't matter to me what you were, as it doesn't today either. It's who you are, and you are an incredible young woman."

And now I'm back to blinking away tears. Silence falls over everyone and I want things to go back to normal. A weird feeling sinks to the bottom of my stomach, and I don't want to admit it to myself just yet, but I know: things will never be normal again.

Abby finishes her wine, still visibly shaken. "You're really okay?"

"I am. Even my bite marks from a few days ago are gone."

"I didn't see any on you." Her eyes go to my neck.

"I prefer the inside of her thigh more than her neck," Lucas says, not looking up from his phone as he orders my food. "Right above her—"

"Lucas," I scold and he just shrugs.

"That is a good place to bite," Eliza agrees with a smile. "Very tender and always close to fun."

"I'm still so confused." Abby's voice is high and strained. "How can he be your father? Does that mean Mom had an affair?"

"No. I have a different mother too. She was a witch." I put my hand on hers, eyes filling with tears again. "But you're still my sister."

A tear falls from her face and she nods. "Then Penny has no chance of having magical powers."

"It's probably a safe bet to assume no, even though you do see it every now and then."

"Half-witch, half-angel," Evander muses, studying me. "I didn't know Nephilim existed. I've heard the lore but thought it was just that. Lore. Even still...an angel and a witch. In all the books I've never once come across that."

"Michael said most humans aren't able to carry a...a... Nephilim to term and they end up dying, both baby and mother. Because my mother was a witch, she was able to handle being pregnant with me but didn't survive the birth."

Silence falls over us again as we all let this sink in.

"How did you end up with the Martins?" Kristy asks a moment later.

"Michael told me it was my mother's idea to hide me in plain sight if she were to die. Nephilim are the result of a forbidden relationship and demons would do anything to get their hands on a half-angel baby so they can taint them with evil and use their powers for their own good. By putting me with a nonmagical family, no one suspected anything, not even when I started showing signs of witch powers. And it worked. I didn't suspect anything under Varra—that demon figured out the Nephilim that had been born twenty-five years ago was still alive."

Everyone is staring at me and it makes me feel weird. "Do you think I'm a freak now?"

"I've always thought you were a freak, sister." Evander doesn't miss a beat. Abby gets up abruptly and leaves the room. Hearing Evander call me "sister" and knowing that Tabatha was more like a mother to me than our mother ever was upsets her. And now I'm telling her we're not really related...

"I should go after her." I hurry out of the kitchen. Abby is in the living room, sitting on the couch with her head in her hands. "Abby?"

She looks up, wiping away tears.

"Are you okay?"

"Yeah. It's a lot to take in and I went from thinking my sister was going to die to learning that you're not really my sister at all."

"Not by blood."

"Who was your mother?"

"A witch named Callista. I'm named after her."

"How did Mom know to name you that?"

"She didn't. Michael somehow suggested it or something."

"How do you do this? How do you find out this information and keep it together?" Abby lets out a breath. "It's so overwhelming and it's not even me."

"I've developed some really unhealthy coping mechanisms

271

over the years, and if repressing upsetting emotions and memories was a contest, I'd win first place."

Abby turns, bottom lip quivering. "Being related was the only thing we had."

"No, no it wasn't. We're sisters."

"But we're not."

"We're not related by blood. But I grew up with you, and spending time with you again has been really, really nice. You are my sister and I love you."

Abby sniffles. "I guess it's not any different than if you were adopted. You'd still be my sister then."

"Exactly. Besides, you know way too much about me to just part ways now. It's a stay-with-me-as-my-sister or I'll have to kill you kind of deal."

She laughs and uses her sleeve to mop up more tears. "How did you end up with us? Mom was pregnant with you, I remember. I was in the room when you were born."

"Mom really was pregnant with a baby girl. You were in the room when she was born, but Michael must have altered your memories because that baby...she was born sleeping. Your biological sister died the same exact time I was born. I don't really get the significance of it, but Michael made it seem like if the timing didn't match, the cover wouldn't work. So he...he switched us and Mom got a living baby."

"I need more wine." Abby stands only to whirl around and face me. "I know this might sound really shitty since you were sold like cattle, but I'm glad you're my sister."

"I'm glad you're mine too." I pull her into a hug. "Given my line of work, having a sister who's also an ER doctor really comes in handy." Abby laughs and wraps her arms around me. "Come on, let's finish that second bottle."

"Everything okay?" Lucas asks when we go back into the kitchen. He stands and takes me in his arms.

"Yes, we're good." I take solace in the way his body feels against mine, resting my head on his chest and closing my eyes. I stay like that for a brief moment and then turn to face everyone else again. "I'm still me, you know that, right? Nothing has changed and I don't want you to treat me differently. Even Michael said I should go back to how things were before but be prepared for more demons to attack."

"That is normal for you," Evander says seriously and we laugh. Some of the tension leaves the room.

"And thank you for coming here to help save me."

"I figured I owed you after you exorcised a demon from me," Evader jokes. "Now we're even."

Kristy smiles. "And I only hired seasonal help. You need to come back to work eventually."

"We all love you," Tabatha says, eyes misty.

"I tolerate you," Eliza deadpans. "Though I have to admit you're growing on me."

After almost dying by the hands of demonic rats to almost dying from a demonic virus, this little moment with my friends is needed. My body has been healed, but my mind is a mashed-up, bloody mess.

Things aren't the same, as much as I want to believe they are.

CHAPTER 35

"I can say it now." Lucas licks blood off my thigh and looks up. His head is between my legs, and my blood is smeared across his lips.

"Say what?" I ask, voice all breathy. We just got done having sex, and it was as primal and passionate as ever. It's funny how almost dying brings you together.

"That I've been *touched by an angel*." Lucas moves up and takes me in his arms.

"Seriously?" I say with a snort of laughter.

"Oh, yeah. I've been touched by one and I've touched one myself. Many times."

"I'm only half angel."

"I'm still saying it." He licks the rest of my blood off his lips and nuzzles his head against my breasts. "I love you, Callie."

"I love you, too."

"I thought I lost you—again." He rolls us over so I'm lying on top of him. We resituate so we're both comfortable. "I don't want to go a single day of my afterlife without you."

"You will...someday."

"Will I, though?" He combs his fingers through my hair.

"You're half an immortal being. Angels don't age. I don't even know if they can die."

"I have so many questions for Michael."

Lucas pulls the sheets over us and kisses the top of my head. "Do you think you'll see him again?"

"With how close I come to dying on a weekly basis, probably. Though...Lucas...there is something I didn't tell you all. Something Michael warned me about." I swallow hard, and the good feelings start to fade. I haven't allowed myself time to really think about this because it scares me.

"What is it?"

"There was another reason I was hidden with the Martins." I take in a steadying breath. "He had to switch me with a baby who'd died at the same time I was born to be able to convince the other angels that I was the one who'd perished during birth. Nephilim aren't allowed to be. If the other angels find out about me, they'll kill me."

"And now demons are finding out about you. It's only a matter of time before the angels do too."

"Right. He said he'd try to keep them off my trail, but...I...I don't know how to fight angels."

"Stay calm, my love." Lucas softly strokes his fingers over the curve of my hip. "You've lived twenty-five years on this earth and haven't been tainted with evil. You won't be now. Doesn't that eliminate your threat?"

"I suppose so." I splay my fingers over Lucas's muscular chest. "I wish I knew how to talk to him."

"Go play in traffic. Maybe he'll show up."

"Hilarious," I retort dryly and an unsettled feeling washes over me. "I almost wish I didn't know."

"And before, all you wanted was to know the truth."

"It changes everything I thought I knew. Not only am I not really a Martin, but I'm not fully human. Angels aren't the pretty, ethereal beings you can pray to and have them grant miracles.

They're fierce warriors who kill each other's babies." I feel like I've been tipped upside down and I'm dangling from the ceiling.

"You were right when you said you're still you. Nothing has changed that. You're still Callie. Badass witch and incredible lover. You have the same kind heart, you still show mercy for those who don't deserve it, and you're still the woman I love."

His words turn me back around, and things start to feel better.

"You have an indiscernible amount of power inside of you, power that could have been swayed to the light or the dark. You've never once come close to choosing the dark side, even when you were treated terribly."

My eyes are all misty again and I push up, putting my lips to Lucas's. I taste my own blood on his mouth, and he flips me over, pinning me against the mattress. My heart swells in my chest, and I just want to feel. Bucking my hips, I rub myself against him and his cock hardens. We kiss as he pushes into me, fucking me hard and fast as our love for each other physically manifests between us.

We come at the same time, and then fall back onto the mattress, tangled in each other's arms. It's mid-morning, and Lucas hasn't slept in over a day. I should be tired, but when Michael healed me, it reset everything and I feel full of energy. I stroke Lucas's hair until he's asleep, and then I slip away to use the bathroom and get something to eat.

I take my food onto the rooftop patio, enjoying the warm sun along with Binx as we share the leftover breakfast food Lucas had delivered earlier this morning. Binx doesn't see me any differently. He wouldn't if he found out I was half demon either. We've bonded and no matter what I do, Binx will be on my side.

We hang out in the sun for an hour and then I'm too hot to stay out any longer. Lucas is up and in his office when we go back inside.

"That's all the sleep you need?" I ask, finding him incredibly sexy. He's shirtless, wearing those damn gray sweatpants that drive me crazy, and sitting behind his desk.

"Your blood...it tastes the same but feels different. It's more filling than before."

"Michael said he was slowly unlocking my angel grace, whatever that means." I shrug. "I think that's why my powers have been a bit wonky lately. They're stronger than before because I'm tapping into a different part of me."

"I'll tap into a different part of—"

"No butt stuff."

"You'll enjoy it with me."

"Nope." I cross my arms and laugh. "Like I said, I wouldn't be able to sit for a week with you."

Lucas closes his laptop and gets up, speeding over and taking me in his arms. "Do you want to go out on a date tonight? We keep talking about it but it hasn't happened."

"Yeah, I do...but can we go back to Thorne Hill? I want something low-key."

"If that is what you want, then yes."

"It is."

He puts his lips to mine. "Good, because I have business there."

"In Thorne Hill?" I raise my eyebrows.

He nods. "Some real estate has come up for sale that would be a good investment opportunity for us."

"I'll leave that to you. And I want to see our house."

"There's a good chance it's safe enough to fuck you in it now." He pulls my hips to his, and even though his cock isn't hard, feeling it against me makes warmth spread through me. We just marathoned sex this morning yet he's turning me on again. "And if not, the porch is always a good option."

"Is it now?" I stand on my toes and kiss him. His phone rings, and he goes to answer it, getting back to business. I go into the theatre room and make popcorn, trying to keep my mind busy.

Normally, after I defeat a big-bad demon, a sense of peace comes over me knowing I have a few days at least until something else tries to kill me. But now…now I can't stop thinking about what I am.

Half witch.

Half angel.

I just want to feel like me again.

It feels good to be home.

Freya and Pandora bombard me as soon as I'm through the door. Relenting, I sink down onto the floor and let them rub against my face, purring loudly.

"I missed you guys too," I tell them. It's about an hour after sunset, and the moment we drove into Thorne Hill, I felt like I was home. Lucas carries my bags in and puts them upstairs for me. We get settled inside, and I look through my pantry for something to eat.

"Let's go out," Lucas suggests. "We can stop by our house on the way."

"Okay. I'll change really fast," I tell him. Freya and Pandora follow me up the stairs, rubbing all over me again. "I promise I'll take you with next time." I give Pandora a look. "I know, you're right. I could have used your help."

I change into a sleeveless black dress. Using magic, I curl my hair, and I quickly put on the minimal amount of makeup I need to look put together.

"You are beautiful, my love," Lucas tells me when I come back down the stairs. He's wearing dark jeans and a gray t-shirt. Always effortless in appearance, it's unfair how good Lucas looks without trying.

We get into my Jeep, and turn down the road, driving only a few miles until we get to our house. There's a distinct path in the grass now that's been used as a driveway. Two large dumpsters sit in the yard, and part of the roof is covered with big blue tarps right now. Most of the windows have been removed and are temporarily covered as well, and it looks like the trash and ruined furniture that was left behind has been cleared out and moved into the dumpster.

"Oh wow," I say when we get out. "I didn't know what to expect, but they've gotten a lot done already."

"Wait until we go inside." Lucas takes my hand and leads me up the stairs. The front doors are locked, but all it takes is a quick wave of my hand over it to unlock them. I conjure an energy ball so I can see, and this one is bigger and brighter than usual.

"Tapping into your angel side, I see." Lucas looks at the magic with awe on his face, not caring that if he gets too close it will burn him.

"I need to be careful I don't blow shit up."

"Right. Not in the house at least."

I laugh and gently toss the energy ball up, lighting the foyer, and look around. The door and any remaining fixtures have been removed so they can be restored and put back if possible. We pick our way through the house to see what else has been done.

The awful kitchen is in the process of being gutted, and the linoleum has been removed, revealing severe water damage to the floorboards beneath it. It smells like mold and rat droppings, but at least these rats aren't demonic.

Nothing has been done upstairs, so we go back onto the front porch. Lucas closes the doors and I magically lock them.

"It's coming along nicely," I say and rest my hands on the porch railing, looking out at the woods that surrounds the house. There's something about the woods at night that's always drawn me to it, and I remember Michael's words about feeling the call of night from my mother's side.

Knowing I'm half angel is a big pill to swallow, but knowing my mother was a witch…it changes everything even more.

"It is." Lucas steps behind me and puts his arms around my waist. "It will be perfect for us once it's done."

I spin in his arms and hook mine over his shoulders. "It really will." Excitement floods through me and a big smile breaks out on my face. "I can't wait. Being able to wake up with you next to me, to have all our stuff in one place…it'll be perfect."

"Only one thing will make it better."

"And what's that?" I ask, expecting him to come back with some sort of comment about a sex swing or adding a sex room in the basement.

"We move in together as husband and wife."

"What?" I heard what he said, but—what?

"I love you, Callie. More than I've ever loved anyone. For nearly two-thousand years I have lived in darkness. I let it consume me, fill me, until I swore that's all I could have…all I could be. And then I met you…I have lived more in the last few months that we have been together than all my time on this earth combined. My heart may not be beating, but with you, I'm alive. Marry me." He steps back and drops down to one knee, pulling a ring from his back pocket. "Be my wife."

My hands fly to my open mouth and tears pool in my eyes, blurring my vision. My jaw quivers and I can't get anything intelligible out. Moonlight shines down on the ring, glinting before me.

I nod, happy tears marring my cheeks. "Yes, Lucas," I finally say and he takes my hand. He slides the ring on my finger, and it fits perfectly. The center stone is a large oval, sandwiched between two circle cut diamonds. The entire band is encrusted with smaller diamonds and it's so damn sparkly and beautiful. My friends were right about Lucas going all out with an engagement ring.

"I love you so fucking much," he growls, standing and taking me in his arms.

"I love you too."

We stand there for a minute, wrapped in each other's

embrace. The bad shit in the world doesn't disappear, but seems manageable. Because with Lucas, I can get through anything.

"Vampire-human marriage is legal in Michigan," he tells me, caressing my face with his large hand. He turns my chin up and kisses me. "We'll have to file paperwork there but as far as the wedding ceremony…we will do whatever you want. Traditional. Vegas. I don't care as long as I'm with you."

I pull my hand away and look at the ring again. "I'm engaged," I say with shock. Happy shock. "And now I get to plan a wedding —and our honeymoon!"

Lucas laughs and pulls me to him again. We kiss once more, and I'm so happy nothing can ruin this moment.

I really need to learn to take my own advice about jinxes.

Lucas snaps his head up, fangs bared, and looks out into the woods with a growl.

"Stay here," he tells me and zooms forward, jumping over the porch railing and disappearing into the woods. I'm left standing there, still holding my hand in the air to look at my ring.

Heart in my throat, I run down the porch steps. Magic burns around my fingers. "Lucas!" I call. Eyes wide, I start into the woods only to have someone crash into me. It's Lucas, and he picks me up and carries me onto the porch.

"Unlock the door," he demands and I wave my hand over it. He slams it shut as soon as we're in.

"How do you ward off angels?"

"I have no idea." I shake my head back and forth. "Why?"

Lucas holds out his hand, showing me something I can't see in the dark. I conjure a string of blue magic and my heart skips a beat. Tossing the energy ball into the air, I take the feather from Lucas's hand. It's slightly darker than the last one I found, but has the same feeling.

Divinity.

My stomach bottoms out and it's like I stepped through thin ice and I'm trapped below the surface.

"Michael warned me that other angels will kill me if they find me."

Lucas takes the feather back and holds it up to the light. "They found you."

Still of Night, book four in the Thorne Hill Series, is available now!

THANK YOU

Thank you so much for taking time out of your busy life to read Call of Night! I hope loved the continuation of Callie and Lucas's love story! :-) I appreciate so much the time you took to read this book and and would love if you would consider leaving a review. I LOVE connecting with readers and the best place to do so is my fan page. I'd love to have you!

www.facebook.com/groups/emilygoodwinbooks

ABOUT THE AUTHOR

Emily Goodwin is the New York Times and USA Today Best-selling author of over a dozen of romantic titles. Emily writes the kind of books she likes to read, and is a sucker for a swoonworthy bad boy and happily ever afters.

She lives in the midwest with her husband and two daughters. When she's not writing, you can find her riding her horses, hiking, reading, or drinking wine with friends.

Emily is represented by Julie Gwinn of the Seymour Agency.

Stalk me:
www.emilygoodwinbooks.com
emily@emilygoodwinbooks.com

ALSO BY EMILY GOODWIN

First Comes Love

Then Come Marriage

Outside the Lines

Never Say Never

One Call Away

Free Fall

Stay

All I Need

Hot Mess (Luke & Lexi Book 1)

Twice Burned (Luke & Lexi Book 2)

Bad Things (Cole & Ana Book 1)

Battle Scars (Cole & Ana Book 2)

Cheat Codes (The Dawson Family Series Book 1)

End Game (The Dawson Family Series Book 2)

Side Hustle (The Dawson Family Series Book 3)

Cheap Trick (The Dawson Family Series Book 4)

Fight Dirty (The Dawson Family Series Book 5)

Dead of Night (Thorne Hill Series Book 1)

Dark of Night (Thorne Hill Series Book 2)

Call of Night (Thorne Hill Series Book 3)